Praise for the first Halloween Bookshop mystery
CHAOS AT THE LAZY BONES BOOKSHOP!

"An exciting mystery whose answers lie deep in the past of the complex characters."
—*Kirkus Reviews*

"Details of running a bookstore and literary festival and the whimsical, small-town, Halloween-themed setting frame this satisfying series starter, narrated by Bailey and peopled by a well-delineated cast including Bailey's Great Pyrenees dog, Jack Skeleton."
—*Booklist*

"Fans looking for a lighthearted cozy to get them in the Halloween spirit won't be disappointed with *Chaos at the Lazy Bones Bookshop*."
—*BookPage*

"For fans of cozy mysteries, bookshops, and a Halloween-themed town setting."
—*BookRiot*

Books by Emmeline Duncan

Ground Rules Mysteries
FRESH BREWED MURDER
DOUBLE SHOT DEATH
FLAT WHITE FATALITY
DEATH UNFILTERED
FATAL BROUHAHA

Halloween Bookshop Mysteries
CHAOS AT THE LAZY BONES BOOKSHOP
MAYHEM AT A HALLOWEEN WEDDING

Published by Kensington Publishing Corp.

Mayhem at a Halloween Wedding

EMMELINE DUNCAN

Kensington Publishing Corp.
kensingtonbooks.com

KENSINGTON BOOKS are published by

Kensington Publishing Corp.
900 Third Avenue
New York, NY 10022

Copyright © 2025 by Kelly Garrett

All rights reserved. No part of this book may be reproduced in any form or by any means without the prior written consent of the Publisher, excepting brief quotes used in reviews.

Without limiting the author's and publisher's exclusive rights, any unauthorized use of this publication to train generative artificial intelligence (AI) technologies is expressly prohibited.

All Kensington titles, imprints, and distributed lines are available at special quantity discounts for bulk purchases for sales promotion, premiums, fund-raising, educational, or institutional use.

This book is a work of fiction. Names, characters, businesses, organizations, places, events, and incidents either are the product of the author's imagination or are used fictitiously. Any resemblance to actual persons, living or dead, events, or locales is entirely coincidental.

To the extent that the image or images on the cover of this book depict a person or persons, such person or persons are merely models, and are not intended to portray any character or characters featured in the book.

Special book excerpts or customized printings can also be created to fit specific needs. For details, write or phone the office of the Kensington Sales Manager: Kensington Publishing Corp., 900 Third Avenue, New York, NY 10022. Attn. Sales Department. Phone: 1-800-221-2647.

The K and Teapot logo is a trademark of Kensington Publishing Corp.

ISBN: 978-1-4967-4617-7 (ebook)
ISBN: 978-1-4967-4616-0

First Kensington Trade Paperback Printing: August 2025

10 9 8 7 6 5 4 3 2 1

Printed in the United States of America

The authorized representative in the EU for product safety and compliance is eucomply OU, Parnu mnt 139b-14, Apt 123
Tallinn, Berlin 11317, hello@eucompliancepartner.com

Dedicated to everyone who counts down the days
until they decorate for Halloween

Chapter 1

Everyone hears "dream big." Growing up, I'd always gotten the message that dreaming big is great, but creating a plan to bring that dream to fruition is the first step to success. Having the mental fortitude to persevere when the plan goes off track is where dreams become reality.

When I started the Spooky Season Lit Fest, I knew it was a risk. What if no one came? What if people did show up, but the talks didn't go well, or we didn't have enough chairs? Or it just failed in some unimaginable way? I didn't know, during the first year, I should've asked myself, "What if someone dies?"

Thankfully, the second year of the festival went off without a hitch. The authors I'd brought in were charming and, more importantly, showed up on time to the events they were scheduled to do. They were warm with readers, and in return, the readers were respectful if they caught sight of the authors wandering around town.

Those same readers had dropped by Lazy Bones Bookshop, the store I'd inherited from my grandparents, and bought books by the armful for the authors to sign. I'd sold out of my shop's T-shirts and tote bags and had to pay for a rush order to restock for the rest of the Halloween season. People had traveled in from all of the country, and two had even flown in from Canada, promising to come again once they'd soaked in the charm of Elyan Hollow, Oregon.

Halloween is always the best time of year in Elyan Hollow. At one point, we'd been the filming site of an iconic Halloween movie. Some towns would've said, "Oh, that was fun," and left it as a distant memory.

But not Elyan Hollow. We'd rolled with our newfound reputation as a Halloween destination. Fans had come into town to see filming sites, and someone saw the untapped opportunity.

After a contentious town vote, we became Halloween-themed year-round, at least in downtown. The mills on the other side of town were exempt. We get Halloween fans throughout the year, regardless of season, and have fun during the Christmas season. St. Patrick's Day is also a highlight.

But our time to shine has always been our extended festival from late September to the big day itself: Halloween. Elyan Hollow is magical in October.

Now that the lit festival was over, I had a new project to juggle while running my shop during our busiest time of the year: a wedding.

Not my own, thankfully, but my old college roommate had decided to fulfill her lifelong dream of a Halloween wedding.

After growing up in town followed by running a business, I knew most of the vendors Raven should contact. I could give feedback on the venues. Be her person on the ground in Elyan Hollow since she worked about a thousand miles away.

Little did I know secrets from the past would show up and haunt her big day.

When I adopted my dog, I didn't realize how much time he'd spend following me around, his eyes intently focused on what I was eating, nor how much time I'd spend following him, yelping, "Jack! What are you eating?"

But Jack is always good company, even if he was chowing down on a handful of peanut butter candy that was supposed to be part of my friend Raven's wedding favors. It wasn't his fault that the candy had been dropped on the floor. He was just helping us clean up.

At least it wasn't his fault the candy was on the ground this time. Jack's tall and not opposed to helping banana bread and other delicious treats fall to the floor, where he will do his best to help by cleaning them up.

Food theft aside, he's a good boy. And at least the candy wasn't chocolate. Although at almost one hundred pounds, a small amount of chocolate was unlikely to harm Jack the way the same amount could harm a Chihuahua. Not that I planned to test the theory.

Raven stuck her head under the table and looked at Jack, who pointedly ignored her as he crunched. "Thank you for cleaning up the candy I dropped, my fuzzy ring bear."

"He's always happy to help," Colby, my BFF, said. She'd finished folding the one hundred gothic black boxes shaped like coffins with "Til Death Do Us Part" printed on the side. I added "Night of the Living Wed" buttons with a matching small pumpkin and sage candle in a coffin tin to the boxes before passing it along to Raven, who was supposed to add a small black mesh bag of artisanal peanut butter candy.

"You should've bought M&Ms instead of these weird peanut butter candies," Raven's sister, Harmony, said. So far tonight, Harmony hadn't been happy with anything. She didn't like her sister's Halloween wedding theme. She thought her sister should give out small potted succulents instead of the favors. Harmony was supposed to seal the boxes with a custom sticker of two skeletons staring longingly into the eye sockets of each other's skulls with the text "Emmett & Raven" beneath, and then store them in the bin next to her, but she'd been fiddling with her phone, so Raven was taking care of the final step.

"Emmett is allergic to chocolate," Raven reminded Harmony.

"Causing the groom to go into anaphylactic shock would make the wedding memorable, but not in the way Raven intends," I said.

"Don't even joke about that. It would be a nightmare, and not the good kind," Raven said.

Jack moved out from under the table, sat beside me, and leaned down to put his chin on my thigh. He looked at me with clear brown eyes that said he was hungry, and that he hadn't been pet before in his life, ever.

"Watch yourself, Jack Skeleton, and chill on the candy," I said. I used his full name so he'd know I meant business.

"I can't believe you're using that dog as your ring bearer," Harmony said.

"Ring bear," Raven corrected her. "I debated flower boy, but he's almost like a polar bear. So he's our ring bear."

Raven looked at Jack, and he gazed soulfully back.

"It's annoyingly dead in here," Harmony said. Her eyes darted around the taproom.

The Elyan Mortuary & Deli Bottle Shop, owned and operated by my friend Ash, only serves beer, along with a handful of canned nonalcoholic drinks, plus a hard cider and wine option. No sandwiches.

No dead bodies in a mortuary, thankfully.

Harmony was somewhat right. The taproom was quiet for a Wednesday evening during the spooky season. The only other customers were a guy sitting at the bar, wearing a T-shirt with a goat on the front and reading a cozy mystery, and a woman reading a graphic novel in the corner. But there was a good chance a local running club or another group would descend soon, bringing chatter and chaos. It was only 6:00 p.m.

Harmony glanced at my drink with a scornful look. "Are you enjoying the why-bother mocktail?" Her words were singsongy and instantly made every nerve in my body tense up.

"Chill out, Harmony," Raven said.

"The zero-proof cocktails are excellent," I said. Ash had added a line of zero-proof canned cocktails to the drinks cooler in her taproom over the winter to appeal to fans of the "sober curious" movement and people looking for nonalcoholic but interesting options to drink when out with friends. So far, they'd been a hit. The mojito I was drinking wasn't bad, although I might've preferred a lemonade instead of the artisanal NA drink.

Harmony was on her third glass of wine, while Raven was

drinking a locally made pale ale at a sedate pace. Colby had opted for sparkling water as she also helped compile the favors.

"I just don't see the point of zero proof," Harmony said.

There were several answers I could've offered up. It was a work night, and I had an early start tomorrow since I was planning on meeting Colby for a long run before opening the bookshop. I've never been a heavy drinker, even during my wildest days as an undergraduate, which hadn't been particularly wild.

And when I'd met my biological father last year, I'd found out that my paternal grandfather had battled alcoholism. Calling Rex Abbot my dad still felt odd, but I understood why he drank sparingly. I'd followed along, although I still grab a drink occasionally on the weekends. I'd been glad when Ash had started introducing more zero-proof drinks, and supposedly, she was about to offer a fantastic nonalcoholic beer on draft from a local brewery, which she was launching with a tap takeover. Plus, both of my grandmothers had died of cancer, one from ovarian and one from breast cancer. I didn't want to spoil the mood by telling Harmony about how alcohol can increase the risk of breast cancer.

"You don't have to understand other people, Harmony, you just need to respect them," Raven said.

Harmony made a "wah-wah" sound like the teacher in the Charlie Brown TV specials.

Colby looked at me and then at the bar, where Ash was flipping through a magazine. "Ash! Have you considered scheduling a showing of *It's the Great Pumpkin, Charlie Brown*?"

"Good idea!" Ash said. She left her spot behind the counter and sauntered up to our table. Ash's hair is an ever-changing variety of colors, and now her pixie cut was purple at the roots and silver at the ends. I'd admired it earlier tonight and wanted to study it closer. Which might be weird, so I kept my eyes on my part of the wedding favor project.

"Do you need any help?" Ash asked. "I'm happy to help when I have time."

"You can seal the boxes with stickers." Raven showed Ash what to do.

"These are lovely," Ash said.

"Bailey drew them for me," Raven said.

Ash flashed a smile my way. "Of course she did. Which reminds me, Bailey, that I have a project I want to talk to you about. But it can wait until next month when all of the festivities are over."

"The town's obsession with Halloween is just weird," Harmony muttered.

"But my obsession with Charlie Brown is totally, one-hundred-percent normal," Colby said.

We chatted about creating a Charlie Brown night as we worked while Harmony scrolled on her phone.

"Just think of the photos if we convinced people to dress up as the Peanuts gang. Jack can be an extra-large Snoopy," Colby said.

"And you could get a Charlie Brown–inspired Christmas tree and keep the theme going through the holidays," I added.

As Olivia, the co-owner of Boorito, carried our dinner order in from the food cart out back, a loud voice from the taproom's entrance caught our attention.

"Now that the maid of honor is here, this party can start!"

Ivy Monroe, aka Raven's maid of honor, had arrived, followed by a guy with a fancy-looking DSLR camera hanging around his neck, and a long narrow bag hooked over one shoulder. They sloped our way. Ivy's baby doll dress had nineties flare, as did her vintage leather jacket.

"Is Ivy traveling with her very own paparazzi?" Harmony asked as the duo walked up.

Olivia stared wide-eyed at Ivy momentarily, then dropped our food off and fled. I scrunched my eyebrows as she hustled away, her Doc Martens practically causing sparks against the polished concrete floors of the former fire station turned taproom.

"This is your burrito, I think," Colby said. She handed over a plate and took the torta in front of me. Raven snagged the tacos in front of her sister and swapped it for a salad topped with pollo asado and avocado. Aka two of my favorite food groups, although I prefer them in burrito form.

The photographer pulled two chairs over to our table, and Ivy plopped into one without thanking him.

"This is way too sedate. Who's up for causing some trouble? We only have a few more days until Raven chains herself to Emmett," Ivy said. "How long is the Uber to the nearest club or bar that's not dead?"

Colby immediately glared at Ivy, as did Harmony. Even though Harmony had already complained about the taproom being too quiet for her.

"It's a Wednesday night. Some of us work tomorrow," I said.

"Suckers. All the more reason to celebrate being alive instead of being all responsible and buttoned up," Ivy said. "Although I know that's your life, Bailey. All work and boring play."

Colby and I both glared at Ivy, but I dropped my gaze down to my work. The sooner I was done, the sooner I could ditch Ivy. We'd never been exactly friends, but I would've hoped that she'd start out civil considering we hadn't seen each other for several years. But I wouldn't give Ivy the satisfaction of arguing with her; she wasn't worth the aggravation, and all I wanted was for Raven to have a wonderfully spooky wedding.

"Like you know the meaning of the word 'responsible,'" Harmony said. She looked at Ivy, then moved her gaze away, as if the maid of honor wasn't worth looking at.

"Everyone who hasn't met him, this is Nate, our wedding photographer," Raven said. "All of you should remember Ivy."

"You were in my year, right?" Colby said, and Nate nodded.

"Imagine my surprise when I licensed photos for an ad campaign at work and found out Nate was not just a phenomenal photographer but also a former college classmate," Raven said, referring to her day job at an ad agency. "I've used his work in some of my favorite campaigns."

"Hopefully, I get some good Halloween shots this week, in addition to your wedding," Nate said. "Fall in Oregon is always gorgeous. I'm glad to be back for a week."

"Will you try to sell the Halloween photos?" Colby asked.

"Ideally I'll license the best of them, and maybe use one or two in a show if they're right."

I remembered Nate from my student days, although it was more like a static image than a living breathing memory. He'd barely changed, still dressed in baggy jeans and band T-shirts, although he'd added a hoodie as a nod to the autumn weather. I remembered that he'd worn the same burgundy-and-gray-striped sweater virtually every day one winter when we were students. I'd seen him around the art building, and I vaguely remembered seeing some of his photos in the Senior Spotlight at the end of the year.

"You did a senior thesis with photographs," I said.

Nate's eyebrows rose in surprise. "Found objects."

"The centerpiece was a rusted Chevy." The photograph was coming into view in my mind's eye. The grass around it had been lush, a bit wild, with a blooming rosebush entangled around one side mirror. The truck was rusty, but I'd felt like it could've told us stories if it could talk.

"A 1955 Chevy Cameo Carrier truck. It would've been beautiful if it had been taken care of," Nate said. "I'm surprised you remember."

"I was impressed."

"Bailey's senior thesis was all illustrations, and she blew everyone away. People thought she must be a professional coming back to take classes, or one of the faculty members," Colby said.

Ivy yawned loudly, then smirked. Which earned her additional glares from Colby and Harmony.

The comic I'd drawn for my senior project was close to my heart, as it'd been a response to my grandmother being diagnosed with ovarian cancer. I used my grandmother as the model for the librarian in my haunted library comic, and her face stared out of the pages of the comic, including in the graphics I'd blown up to display for the senior show. I later realized that the evil spirits she'd tamed on the page had been lurking death, who weren't evil, per se, but trickster figures that everyone faces someday, unless we as a society somehow figure out how to turn immortal. I hadn't put all of the comic pages on display, and both of my grandparents had ended up with tears in their eyes when they dropped by the show.

Two more couples walked into the taproom, and Raven waved to them.

"We're going to check in, then join you!" one of them called out. They pulled rolling suitcases toward the bar, and Ash hustled over to meet them.

"Those are the people staying upstairs with us?" Harmony asked.

"Yes." Raven's response was clipped. A few years ago, Colby and I helped Ash decorate the upper level of the building, which she rented out as a handful of hotel rooms and one hostel-size room with bunk beds, with all the rooms sharing a small communal living room and kitchenette. Raven had rented all the rooms for her wedding.

"So, who is sharing the hostel room?" I asked. I pictured Harmony and Ivy sharing a bunk bed and held in a snort.

"A group of Emmett's friends volunteered. They said it'd be like summer camp," Raven said.

Summer camp. I'd read books about summer camps as a kid, and wondered what it would be like to have gone to one.

"We could've stayed at the B&B where Emmett's parents are. It looks way nicer," Harmony said.

"You're welcome to get your own hotel room." Raven sounded like she was gritting her teeth. Raven's and Emmett's parents and assorted family members were booked into various B&Bs in town, including the Sleepy Hollow Inn, which was owned by one of my family friends.

Ivy laughed. "But then what would Harmony complain about if she wasn't mooching a room off of you?"

"You're one to talk. Raven's paying for your room." Harmony glared at Ivy.

"At least I can pay my rent by myself, princess," Ivy said.

"Like you've never borrowed money before."

"I pay back my debts," Ivy said. She grinned spitefully. "Eventually."

"You're such a—"

"Will you two just cut it out before someone makes you?" Colby's voice filled the room. When we made eye contact, Ash raised her eyebrows at me, and I shrugged. Next to me, Jack sat up straight on alert, ready to step between me and any threats.

Harmony jumped to her feet, and her hip knocked into the table. Raven grabbed her pint glass before it fell over, but Harmony's salad fell to the floor in a sad loss of perfectly seasoned chicken.

"You're a plague on humanity, Ivy," Harmony said. Her words were a tad slurred from the wine she'd practically chugged.

"A plague? Big words from a shopgirl," Ivy said in a singsong voice. She'd clearly been working on her Harmony imitation, as she'd sounded exactly like Raven's sister.

As Ivy waved her hand at Harmony, dismissing her, I noted that Ivy's pupils were blown, making her eyes look like black pools.

Harmony slurred again when she said, "You're going to regret this."

Ivy's only response was to toss her hair over her shoulder.

Ash marched up with her hands in fists. "Knock it off because I will kick you both out," she said.

"Whatever. I'm done with this place." Harmony marched off, although she couldn't keep a straight path.

Raven watched her sister go, then closed her eyes.

Ivy stood up and strutted across the room toward the seasonal artwork on display. This year, Ash was showcasing a mixed-media artist with a Halloween theme and a photographer who'd taken dramatic black-and-white photos of Elyan Hollow. Ivy approached one of the photos of the bridge in Goblin Gate Park, stopping inches away.

"Did you seriously take photos of their argument?" Colby asked Nate.

Nate lowered his camera to his chest and smiled. "It's instinct. Professionally these days, I'm a documentary-style photographer. Action shots are my specialty."

"He does a lot of bands in concert photos," Raven said.

"I can't resist photographing drama," Nate said. He smiled as he scrolled through the photos on his camera's small screen.

"Please do not include those in our virtual wedding albums," Raven said. Her cheeks had flushed, and I wondered who was going to annoy her the most this weekend: Harmony, Ivy, or Nate.

"Thanks for your help, Jack," Ash said.

I looked down to see that Jack had systematically pulled the chicken and avocado out of Harmony's discarded salad, but he'd left behind everything else. He stopped to spit out an olive before gobbling down the last bite of chicken.

As Ash swept up the salad, Colby glanced at me.

"This wedding is going to be fun," Colby muttered. From the look Jack gave her, he agreed.

Or maybe he was just hoping for more chicken.

Fireworks aside, we would be an interesting bridal party, at least visually, as long as we didn't brawl in the aisle during the processional. And if Harmony and Ivy kept up the sniping, Colby could pull on her Youth Services Librarian persona and break it up. Even the most over-confident teen boy quails when Colby gives her patented "quiet down and don't mess with me" look.

Plus, Colby is taller than both Harmony and Ivy, with a muscular, sturdy build, and if needed she could loom with the best. Add in naturally tan skin and thick, silky black hair, and she's unforgettable. Harmony was on the petite side, about five foot two, with a plump, busty figure and gorgeous brown hair that falls in perfect ringlets. I'm nondescript in comparison, five foot five with an athletic build, hazel eyes, and wavy chestnut hair that I'd grown out from a chin-length bob to almost shoulder length. Ivy is about my height, but heroin-chic thin, with bleached-blond hair that tends to be lank and startling green eyes. When I'd met Ivy in college, she'd been slender but not as skinny as now. On principle, I never tell someone they should or shouldn't eat. But the sight of Ivy's arms, which look like bone with no muscle, concerned me, and I was tempted to offer to order a burrito for her.

Raven was almost as tall as Colby, with an hourglass figure that would make a 1940s pinup girl proud. I'd seen her light brown natural hair color once, when we were still teens at our college orientation before she'd started dying it a deep black. It used to be long, cascading down her back to her hips, but she'd chopped it into an edgy but cool asymmetric bob with spiky bangs last year. She was promoted to art director at the advertising agency for which she worked. When she'd video-chatted me to show off her new hair, she'd said she wanted a change to match her new job title.

Although Jack would outshine all of us as the official "ring bear" of the wedding. He was even getting groomed the day before Raven exchanged her vows, so he'd be as white and fluffy as possible.

After she cleaned up the salad, Ash stopped by Raven. "Keep your sister and friend under control. You're a friend of Bailey and Colby, so I don't want to kick you out, but this is a no-drama establishment."

"Sadly, Harmony lives for drama," Raven said. "I'm sorry, and if I have to, I'll send one of them away. Or both, if they keep up their obnoxious acts."

"Remember, this is a drug-free establishment, including upstairs," Ash said. Her gaze pointedly moved to Ivy, who was still staring at the photograph.

Raven closed her eyes, then opened them and looked at Ash. "Noted. The only thing I saw in her suitcase was prescribed meds. I'll talk to her."

Ash left to return to the bar, and Raven turned to me. "I don't have time to deal with this during my wedding week. But it's my fault for bowing to pressure and having Harmony as a bridesmaid. I should've kept her as a guest. But my grandmother really wanted me to include her."

"Family loyalty?" I said.

"My grandmother thinks it's important for Harmony to feel included."

Ivy wandered back to our table, and Nate stood up.

"Let's go get dinner," Nate said, and Ivy nodded.

As Nate escorted Ivy toward the taproom's door, Jet, a local artist, started to walk in. But then she turned and quickly walked away.

"And then three were three, and one fluffy dog. Let's get these favors finished," Raven said.

As we finished the final few coffin boxes, a crowd of Raven and Emmett's friends slowly formed in the taproom, although the groom had yet to appear. While she'd gone to college in Portland, Raven had eventually ended up taking a job in LA. At the same time, Emmett came from somewhere on the other side of the Continental Divide. They met, presumably with a background of fireworks, leading to this moment in time.

"I can't believe this place is Halloween year-round," one of Emmett's friends said. Something about the relative formality of his dark denim and tailored button-down shirt made me think he was one of the group that had flown in from the East Coast. It was subtle, but his casual attire didn't have the PNW flair I'm used to.

Versus the flannel and baggy jean–wearing woman I vaguely remembered from my college days, accompanied by a guy in pristine Carhartt, who was chatting up a storm with Colby. Both practically had signs with "PNW natives" stamped on their heads.

"I still say we should've stayed in Portland and just drove out here for the wedding," the guy added. He glanced around the taproom and, based on the way he scrunched his nose, he wasn't impressed.

But the woman he was with patted his arm. "Oh, you. This place is so charming. And the boutiques in town look charming, and the winery has won a Decanter World Wine Award, or maybe a recognition? Something impressive, anyway."

I glanced at Raven. "I need to head out. Early day tomorrow."

"Can you drop by the Sleepy Hollow and see what's taking Emmett so long? He's not responding to my texts."

"Sure." The Sleepy Hollow Inn was out of our way, but the journey would serve as Jack's evening walk. After an evening in the taproom, we both needed to stretch our legs.

After a round of goodbyes, Jack and I started to leave. . . . But my steps faltered when a familiar face walked into the taproom. Jack immediately stepped forward and pushed his snout under the man's hand.

Rex Abbot. Best-selling author. Usually straight-faced, with wry humor. And my biological father. I'd only met him last year.

"You're back a few weeks early," I said. Right after the Spooky Season Lit Festival ended in late September, Rex had left to teach a workshop and was supposed to spend a few weeks traveling afterward. I'd agreed to drop by his house and accept, and unload, his grocery delivery the evening before he arrived.

"Hey, kid. I realized I just wanted to be in my own house, so I changed my plans," Rex said. "I take it you're heading out?"

I nodded. "I have to drop by the Sleepy Hollow, and then I'm going home for the night."

"I'll walk with you."

Rex walked with us in the direction of the Inn. He'd stayed there last year when I'd brought him in for the inaugural lit festival, which was only the second time he'd returned to town after graduating from Elyan Hollow High School. The second festival earlier this year had thankfully gone much smoother, with no dead bodies and long lines of readers eager to get signed books or chat with their favorite authors.

As we crossed the street next to the taproom, I asked, "Did you hear about the pie vending machine?"

"Pie like fruit pies? In a vending machine?"

I nodded at the newly opened Museum of Peculiar Oddities gift shop. "They have one in their foyer, which is open twenty-four hours. The slice of marionberry I tried was pretty good, too." I didn't tell him that the shop owner, Finn, felt oddly familiar. But he had introduced himself to me like we didn't know each other.

"Hmm. I can't say I've ever thought pies were a natural fit for a vending machine. But I was extremely excited to come across a donut vending machine in an airport while traveling."

We chatted until we'd reached the edge of downtown, with just the riverfront in front of us and the Sleepy Hollow a half block to the right. Rex paused, like he'd come to the end of the line. "I'm going to find food, but we should get dinner soon."

"For sure."

Jack gently bumped his snout into Rex's hand again, reminding my father that he still needed attention.

We waved goodbye, and Rex headed back up the street to downtown, and I turned toward the Sleepy Hollow.

It was time to check on the groom.

Owned by Marion, a longtime family friend, the Sleepy Hollow Inn was almost like a second home to me. I'd worked for Marion occasionally as a teen and still helped on the odd day if she was in a jam. She'd also hosted the opening reception for my literary festival with style and housed several authors when she could've charged her top rack rate for rooms instead of giving me the friends and family discount.

The Sleepy Hollow Inn has been a popular destination during the spooky season ever since it was used in the iconic movie, *The Haunted Hounds of Hamlet Bay* that had been filmed in town. It's one of the more, if not the most, expensive lodgings in Elyan Hollow, but it's worth the premium, given the gourmet breakfasts and upscale rooms. It's across from the waterfront park with a view of the Columbia River, in a Victorian large enough to have nine en suite rooms and a carriage house in the back.

Raven had managed to reserve rooms for the groom's parents and grandparents. But she'd booked her parents and grandmother into the kitschier Haunted House B&B along with a few other family members from both sides. She'd wanted to reserve both B&Bs in their entirety, but they had other reservations they, rightfully, had refused to cancel.

I watched several tourists snap selfies in front of the inn's wrought-iron front fence and sign. I texted Marion that I was dropping by to find the groom, and then Jack and I walked up the stairs, past the Victorian "gas lamps" lining the walkway which are powered by solar instead of coal, to the covered front porch and straight into the inn. I shut the door softly behind me.

Only to hear a clearly annoyed voice say, "Darling, are you serious? This whole wedding is a joke."

A measured voice responded. "This wedding might not be your style, but it's perfect for me. For us." I recognized the voice. Emmett, aka the groom.

A male voice spoke. "If you cancel the wedding, we can pay for everything you need for graduate school. You always talked about earning a PhD. We would pay for everything: your rent, the program, books, spending money."

"As long as I don't get married to the woman I love." Emmett's voice dripped with sarcasm, but I could hear the current of controlled anger layered underneath.

"Your life could be so much better."

"Can't you just act happy for me for once?"

I reopened the front door and shut it harder. Jack and I walked forward.

When I stepped into the living room doorway, Emmett was standing with his arms crossed over his chest. A man and a woman, presumably his parents, sat stiffly on the sofa designed to look like a Victorian camelback but was a reproduction in gray and white stripes. Marion had redecorated last winter, and I'd helped her pick the paint shades, although her eye for colors is as good as mine, if not better. The room was now decorated in a tasteful mix of pumpkin, white, and modern gray that were a nod to the Halloween season while matching the home's period charm. She added a handful of tasteful Halloween knickknacks to the room for the season, like a handblown pumpkin she'd bought from my shop, carefully arranging everything to keep the room from looking cluttered.

Jack paused beside me, and I wondered how he assessed this situation.

I spoke, amping up the tension in the room. "Hi, Emmett. Some of your friends have arrived in town. They're with Raven at the taproom."

Emmett darted a glance my way, and I got the sense he was hesitant to look away from his parents like they were snakes who'd strike if he didn't maintain eye contact.

Or maybe I was imagining things.

I'd only met Emmett a few times, but I knew he did something with analytics at the same ad agency Raven worked for. Emmett was tall and lean, with sandy blond hair cut in a messy quiff. He wore a *Nightmare Before Halloween* shirt and faded blue jeans. His mother's clothing reminded me of Emily from *Gilmore Girls*. I bet her baby blue sweater was cashmere, and her trousers were classic-cut wool that existed in the timeless space beyond trends. His dad's chinos and navy oxford looked perfectly tailored. Emmett didn't look like either parent, but I could see elements of both reflected in his face.

Marion bustled in, looking organized as usual, and she immediately zeroed in on Jack.

"How's my angel dog?" she asked. Jack pushed his head against her hand. She looked at me. "Good to see you as always, sweetheart."

"Likewise."

A man, maybe in his sixties, walked down the stairs and eyed Jack as he passed us. As he reached the front door, it opened, and he stood aside as two early-thirty-somethings walked in, pulling wheeled suitcases behind them. She wore a purse shaped like a pumpkin over one arm, while he had a Nate-like camera around his neck. The older man looked slightly annoyed as he stepped around them and left the inn.

"I can't believe we're finally here!" the thirty-something woman squealed. "Oh look, this dog could be a haunted hound!"

The couple cooed over Jack, who accepted the attention like it was his due. It wasn't the first time he'd heard he could be a ghost dog from *The Haunted Hounds of Hamlet Bay*.

Emmett's parents stood up from their spots on the couch.

"Think of what we talked about," his father said, his gaze serious as he stared at his son. They left and walked upstairs.

"Are you the Jenkinses?" Marion asked the couple.

"Yes!" The woman was vibrating in place again.

"The Rip Van Winkle suite is all ready for you. I just need to see a photo ID and have you sign a form."

The husband followed Marion to the desk in the hallway while the wife stayed with Jack.

"You need to tell me all the places I should visit to get the best Hamlet Bay experience," the woman told Jack.

Beside me, Emmett smiled. "You might get a better answer from Jack's staff," he said.

The woman looked up and scrunched her eyebrows. "Staff?"

"That dog's name is Jack, and this is Bailey. In addition to catering to Jack's every need, Bailey runs the bookshop in town. I heard she has a guidebook for the filming sites. My fiancée bought several to give to our out-of-town wedding guests."

The woman's hands had stilled, so Jack nudged her with his nose.

"I love bookstores! And I must drop by to purchase a guide and check out the bookstore because I love to read," the woman gushed. Her eyes returned to Jack. "So you're a bookstore dog? Do you help people pick out books? What should I read next?"

Jack gazed steadily back, and she realized she'd been slacking and resumed scratching behind his ears.

"Honey, we should check out our room," the male half of the Jenkins couple said, and the woman petting Jack stopped.

"I'm sorry, ghost doggo, but hopefully, I'll see you in town!"

She bounced away and followed her companion as Marion led them up the stairs. He carried both suitcases.

"So, Bailey, did you stop by for a reason?" Emmett asked.

"Raven sent me to find you. She's been trying to contact you but couldn't get through."

"I put my phone on silent while finishing a work project. I can just focus on the wedding now that it's done," Emmett said. He pulled his phone out. "Oops, don't ask how many texts I've received."

Emmett and I walked out of the inn together.

"Thanks for coming to get me," Emmett said.

"It's not a problem. I was on my way home, and Jack and I enjoyed the detour." Being able to catch up with Rex had been an unexpected bonus.

"You're not heading back to join everyone?" he asked.

I shook my head. "I need an early night. I have work tomorrow, and I'm getting up early for a long run."

"Really? Tell me about the run."

I gave him a brief breakdown, and he asked if he could join us.

"You sure?" I asked.

"I've been training for a half-marathon and would love to have someone to run with. Especially since I don't know the area. I've been playing around with routes in Google Maps but it's hard to tell if it'll be a good running route."

I told him where we planned to meet and then said, "Text me if you're late; otherwise, we'll leave without you."

"I'd expect nothing less." Emmett nodded at me, accepting a morning run was a serious business. "So, back at the inn . . . how much did you hear?"

"Hear about?" I didn't want to answer.

"My parents."

"Well, hypothetically, my ears took in more than I wanted, but I'm planning to forget I overheard anything. It's not my business." I didn't need to promise anything for Jack because even though I anthropomorphize him, he's a dog. He has to keep everyone's secrets.

"My parents have never understood me. I'm not like my older brother, who followed the path they expected, which was supposed to end in either an MBA or a law degree and most likely followed by taking a job at the family business," Emmett said. "They've never understood my hobbies. My interests."

We walked up the hill to downtown. "I'm sorry," I said.

"Your parents must be proud that you're running the family bookstore," Emmett said.

Talk about a loaded question. "I was proud to take over the bookshop from my grandparents," I said. "It's their legacy, and it's essential to the heart of the town. Equally important, I love the store. I want to keep it vibrant." It is part of the heart of the community; a place where everyone is welcome, as long as they show respect to the world around them.

"What would you do if you had to change jobs?" Emmett asked.

"That sounds like a nightmare," I said. "Maybe I'd enroll in a master's in library science program or something involving literacy outreach. Everyone deserves access to books."

"Books, plus art, and music," Emmett said. "And everything weird. My parents don't understand the concept. If you asked them, they'd say they like art—but they like going to museums. They'd never enjoy spending a day trawling through the artist alley at a comic con, looking for something that speaks to them."

"Everyone has their own path, and their own taste. There's no such thing as right or wrong when it comes to art," I said. The words sounded bland to my ears.

"I wish my parents respected that I chose a different route than they planned."

After a goodbye, we separated.

I was lucky; my grandparents, who'd raised me, would have supported almost any direction I could've chosen. That I, unlike their children, had taken over the bookshop was a bonus, not something anyone had forced me to do.

Chapter 2

Thursdays are always one of my usual morning run days with Colby, and no matter how chaotic life gets, sticking to my workout schedule keeps me feeling balanced. Thankfully, Emmett was a few minutes early to our meeting spot. He was dressed appropriately and trudged along with us without whining that we were going too fast or too slow or any other unwelcome comment.

But when we stopped, I realized Emmett's breath was coming out in huffs. Maybe he hadn't talked because he was barely keeping up and couldn't say anything.

"That went better than I thought," Colby said after Emmett had returned to his lodging above the taproom while I was about to jog the few blocks home.

Colby had a point; neither of us had interacted much with Emmett other than the handful of times he'd visited with Raven for long weekends in Portland. We'd gotten dinner and hung out last year when they'd come up for the Rose City Comic Con. But most of their focus that weekend had been on the event and their matching fantasy medieval costumes with real leather armor. During that visit, Raven told us about her dream: to get married in Elyan Hollow because of its year-round Halloween vibes, which led to me promising I'd help her organize the wedding of her dreams. I'd flown to see Raven earlier this year, but Emmett had been out of town, making the trip a fun girls' weekend. She took me out for acai bowls, sushi, and pizza, and we'd visited the Getty and several other art museums and the Griffith Observatory. We'd walked along several boardwalks, and I'd convinced her to go paddleboarding on the Venice canals. Even though I enjoyed the trip, I knew SoCal wasn't for me.

After our run, I dropped by the house I share with my grandfather, also known as my childhood home, to shower, eat breakfast, and wake up Jack, who was still sleeping in his dog bed in my room. He picked out an orange bandana from his basket in the living room, and we headed downtown, pausing a few times to sniff very important bushes. I'd thought about adopting a dog who'd enjoy a long run, but Jack's lower-key approach to life was a better fit for a bookshop dog.

Opening the store followed the usual pattern. I was happy to see that several orders for signed and personalized Rex Abbot novels, along with another subscription to our mystery box, had come in overnight. Luckily, I still had a few October boxes available, and Rex was now in town to personalize the books.

Stanley, the shop skeleton, was on hand in his chair by the front register, keeping an eye on the store. I'd tied one of Jack's Halloween bandanas around his neck, like a jaunty skeleton scarf, so he could celebrate the season in style. Stanley had been broken once, but he was back, as good as ever. Maybe better, since he'd faced adversity and come through it with a happy viewpoint, given the smile on his face.

In some ways, the shop feels like it always had, back when my grandparents had run it. The sections of the store are in the same spots they've been in my entire life, but filled with the ever-evolving selection of books that reflect the tastes of the market and what publishers are producing, and hopefully those two are perfect matches for readers who walk into Lazy Bones. While our focus is on books, I have a few shelves of Halloween-related products by local artists and companies. I'm always on the hunt for new offerings that feel like they'll be popular with our clientele. But the shop has changed subtly over the years. I refurbished all the heavy wood bookshelves in a Herculean effort last February during the slow season, emptying them and moving them one at a time into the workroom to sand them down and repainted them a crisp white.

I checked the refurbished old cigarette machine turned into a toy dispenser in the children's area and took a moment to refill it with stickers and small toys I buy in bulk that our young readers love. Anything that glows in the dark or sticks to people when you throw it is always popular with the kids. My closer last night had wiped down the bean bag chairs and carefully vacuumed beneath them, one of the must-do daily tasks else the children's area turns sticky.

About five minutes after I'd flipped the shop's sign to OPEN, the door jangled. Rex backed inside, carrying an extra-large box.

"Usually people leave here with boxes," I joked. Which, given the size of our book deliveries, wasn't exactly true.

Rex put the box down on the counter with an "oof."

"It's not heavy, just awkward," he said. Once it was on the counter, it was taller than Rex.

"Good timing, since I have some orders for you to sign." I tapped a happy beat on the edge of the counter.

"Any chance we can take this into your workroom to open it?" Rex asked.

"Sure, but know if that's a refrigerator, we have one."

"This is way better. And lighter than a fridge."

"And the mystery deepens." I led Rex to the back. I generally try to stay in the customer side of the shop while working solo. But we have security cameras in the shop that are connected to screens visible from the front register, and also in the workroom. In some ways it's creepy, but it's part of doing business in the current world. And it'd allowed me to catch a few shoplifters. I can't exactly blame anyone for stealing food. But we have a great library in town so there's never a need to steal books.

Rex put the box down on our workbench, then paused. He moved the box to the floor. "I found this last week, and I thought of your shop."

I stood back. Rex motioned to the box. "C'mon, open it."

The top flap was taped down, so I cut it with the multi-tool I always carry around in my pocket when I'm at work. The top was full of foam popcorn, and Rex helped me to scoop it out into a paper bag so we could reuse it, as it can't be recycled.

Eventually, something black peeked out, and a moment later, I realized it was the turret of a dollhouse shaped like a Victorian, similar to the Sleepy Hollow Inn.

But unlike the Sleepy Hollow, the dollhouse was painted black and orange. But the paint was chipped. The rooms inside had once been wallpapered, but it was peeling off in a few rooms, and stained in others.

Someone had loved this dollhouse, once, but it hadn't been taken care of properly for years.

"I thought a haunted dollhouse could be a fun addition to the children's area," Rex said. "But I won't be offended if you don't like the idea."

"It's amazing," I said.

"It needs a bit of work, but you're creative, and I bet you could fix it up to add a ton of Halloween vibes. Maybe a ghost in the window, and a library of mini books." Rex picked up the dollhouse and put it on the worktable.

The general air of neglect already made it look slightly haunted. I pictured it with fresh paint to clean it up, but then carefully aged to look weathered. New wallpaper inside, with each room themed to reflect something I love about Elyan Hollow. Maybe a hutch inside filled with tiny potion bottles. Small gothic picture frames with mini portraits. Maybe a coffin in one bedroom, instead of a bed. A white Great Pyrenees like Jack to guard the house. One of the rooms needed to be a haunted library, filled with miniature versions of the shop's bestsellers.

Fans of *The Haunted Hounds of Hamlet Bay* were going to love the dollhouse. Maybe I'd name it the Ravenwood Mansion in honor of the movie and add a mini graveyard to the display around it.

For Christmas, I could add a wreath and spooky Christmas tree to the front room, and a wreath on the door.

"If I do all of that work, I'm not sure if I'm going to want to let the kids touch it," I joked. My hands were itching to start fixing up the dollhouse, although I knew I didn't have time to pick up supplies from the hobby shop until after Halloween.

"Do you like it?"

"I love it. I only wish I'd thought of adding a haunted dollhouse to the shop earlier," I said. "How much do I owe you?"

"Owe me? It's a gift," Rex said. "I'm still making up for a lifetime of missed holidays and birthdays."

That wasn't exactly true, but the lump forming in my throat didn't let me contradict him.

Rex pulled a smaller box out of the larger one. "I picked up some dollhouse furniture on my travels home. The woman working in the craft store was so eager to help me when she heard I was buying it for my daughter that I couldn't tell her you're old enough to own a bookstore."

We looked at each other and laughed, then made dollhouse refurbishment plans.

The day flew by, with a steady stream of visitors in town for the festival. October is our busiest sales quarter, and a successful season makes or breaks our year, with Christmas providing a welcome buffer. But a good Christmas season can't overcome a poor Halloween.

Tara, the shop's longtime assistant manager, came in around lunchtime and we worked together seamlessly. In the midafternoon, I left the shop in Tara's hands when one of our newest sales associates, Atticus, came by for the closing sales associate shift.

After dropping Jack off at home (and feeling guilty when he looked at me with sad eyes), I walked back downtown for another bridal party commitment.

I couldn't claim that Raven had bridezilla tendencies regarding the bridesmaid dresses. She'd worked with the fairly new to Elyan

Hollow vintage, vintage-inspired, and resale shop, HalloQueen, to acquire prom dresses from the 1980s and '90s. Raven was footing the bill for the dresses, plus the makeup artist and hairstylist she'd hired for the wedding.

HalloQueen has an upscale vibe. Today, the mannequins in one of the windows were dressed in a 1920s *Great Gatsby* theme, while the other side had 1950s-style dresses in Halloween prints. When I walked inside, I strolled past racks of vintage and vintage-inspired dresses that would be too fussy for me, but gorgeous on the right people. I beelined toward the burnt orange velvet love seat and matching chair outside the dressing rooms, where Raven sat with a binder in her lap. Although my gaze strayed toward the designer jeans racks in the back corner. I'd nosed through those racks before and ended up with a pair of pristine jeans from an upscale brand carried by Nordstrom, but at one-fourth the price.

"Oh good, Bailey, you're the first one here," Raven said. She closed her binder and tucked it into an Edgar Allan Poe–themed tote bag. A bag I recognized, as I'd not only sold it in the shop last year, but I'd sent one to Raven for Christmas.

Marnie, the owner of HalloQueen, came out from the back. Her black shirtwaist had orange pumpkins printed on the hem, and she wore a matching belt with a pumpkin buckle. "Are you ready to get started?" she asked.

"Yes, please bring the dresses out," Raven said. She turned to me. "Thank you for being the drama-free friend of this bridal party."

I was tempted to say Colby was also low-key, but she'd lose her temper faster than I would with either Ivy or Harmony. Or both. I settled for "I hope Emmett enjoyed our run this morning."

"He did! Thank you so much for letting him tag along. He gets antsy when he doesn't get exercise, like a Labrador retriever."

As we talked, I took in the shop's ambiance. The store is elegant, with a more "carefully curated resale" vibe than a "who knows what you'll find" thrift shop. So when Marnie rolled a rack of '80s prom dresses out of the back room, my eyebrows rose. The dresses were flashier than the rest of the shop, with tons of bows, lace, and feather trim. The colors ranged from gold to silver, with multiple shades of pink, blue, and green. It was like the '80s threw up in the dressing room corner of the shop.

"You're still going with a red gown, right?" I asked. Last I'd heard, Raven planned to wear a red gown inspired by Lydia in *Beetlejuice*, while her husband-to-be's suit was black-and-white striped. So far, I'd managed to keep myself from pointing out the almost-wedding scene between Beetlejuice and Lydia was creepy, versus romantic. And whenever I thought of the dress, the rhyme "marry in red wish yourself dead" echoed through my mind. So, I reminded myself the sentiment is counter to some traditions found elsewhere in the world. Brides in India, China, and multiple other countries tend to wear red; white is sometimes a funeral color.

Raven's face lit up, and she looked happier than I'd seen her since she arrived in town. "Yes, and it's gorgeous. It's not as poofy as the film's version and a bit sultrier. And so fab. Now I need to make sure the bridal party fits my theme."

My eyes strayed toward the fluffy pink monstrosities on the prom dress rack. Hopefully, none of them would fit.

"I have my eye on a specific dress for you," Raven said. She pulled a shiny purple dress off the rack.

"I like the color," I said. Mostly, anyway. Metallics aren't really my style.

I took the dress and headed into the dressing room. After carefully piling my clothes on the stool, with my favorite worn sneakers on the floor underneath, I pulled the dress on. The fitted bodice hugged my midsection, and I just managed to zip it all the way up. I took an experimental breath; it was snug enough to fit but not so big that it'd fall off and not so tight it would split, and I'd flash the wedding guests if I breathed wrong.

The floaty skirt had a staggered hem, but the feather trim really made the dress '80s-perfect.

Outside, I heard Colby arrive.

"I'm going to have to ask my mother if one of her prom styles looked like this," Colby said.

"I think this gold dress might have your name on it," Raven said.

"Just as long as it's not pink."

As I stepped out of the dressing room, my body felt awkward. My hands fidgeted in spite of my brain telling me to stand up straight. Raven and Colby turned to study me. The front door jingled shut as Harmony, Ivy, and Nate, the photographer, walked in.

"Not bad, Bailey. You just need fishnet tights and sky-high bangs," Colby said.

"Plus a few zombie touches, which our makeup artist will take care of," Raven added. Her goal was to make all of us look like we'd fit into the afterlife waiting room from *Beetlejuice*. Prom goers who'd met some sort of sticky end and were now in the process of moving on. Which hadn't been in the movie, but I understood her theory: the idea fits the scene, at least conceptually.

Marnie fluttered around me. "I agree; this fits Bailey well. We won't need to tailor it."

"You're still going with the prom theme?" Harmony asked. Her petulant tone sounded like she couldn't believe Raven was using an idea Harmony clearly disliked.

Raven looked annoyed, but she kept her voice moderate. "As I've told you eighty million times, yes."

"But there weren't any prom goers in the waiting room in that gross movie," Harmony said. "Just a football team."

"It's an inspiration, not an exact copy," Raven said.

"It's like wedding fanfic," Colby muttered in my ear. I held in a snort as my friend headed into the dressing room with a poofy gold dress. The front door of the shop jangled again.

"And you've left the dresses really late. They should've been decided on ages ago," Harmony said. She added in her singsong voice, "Proper tailoring takes time, as I've told you."

"This was the first chance to get all of you to try them on in person, and it won't matter if they're not perfect." Raven clenched her jaw.

"Whatever. Which dresses do you want me to try on? Dibs on

pink." Harmony continued to talk in her singsong tone. My back muscles tense up. Maybe she should've done that when I wore the purple dress so I could make sure I could flex without it ripping.

"Can you just chill out, Harmony? You're giving me a headache." Raven closed her eyes like she was counting to ten.

"You know this would've been easier if you'd let me handle the dresses," Harmony said. "I had a great designer we could have used, and it would've looked so classy—"

Ivy spoke. "Just try on your stupid pink dress, Harmony, and try shutting up for five minutes. Yes, we know you don't like the prom dresses or Halloween, or I'm starting to think your sister—"

"How dare you!" Harmony put her hands on her hips as she turned to glare at Ivy.

"So just shut your mouth." Ivy pushed lank blond hair away from her eyes.

"I just want my sister to have the wedding she deserves—"

"Enough!" Colby yelled as she walked out of the dressing room, dressed to the nines in a shiny gold dress. "This is Raven's wedding, so just get with the program. At the very least, quit whining."

"Who are you to tell me what to do?" Harmony said.

"You don't want to make me angry," Colby said. "You won't like the end result."

Raven spoke in a quiet voice. "Harmony, you can step down if you really hate the dresses. Ivy, I think the emerald-green dress would be perfect for you if you'd like to try it on."

Ivy grabbed a green dress and headed to the dressing room next to Colby's while Harmony stared at her sister.

"You'd kick me out of your wedding?" Harmony said in a shocked voice.

"No, I'm giving you the option to step down if you're unhappy. It's your choice."

As Colby inspected herself in the mirror, I heard a click.

Nate the photographer. Colby narrowed her eyes at him.

Raven turned to Nate. "Please leave the dress fitting," she said. "We don't need to memorialize today."

"You sure?" Nate said with a smile.

"Yes, Nate. But thanks for your diligence." Raven's sarcastic tone amused me, and given the way a crooked smile spread across Nate's face, he found it humorous.

"Text me if you change your mind." Nate turned and walked out.

"He's weird," Colby said. She halfway twirled, causing her gold dress to flare out. "Sort of like this dress."

"And like him, it's sort of awesome. Weirdly awesome," Raven said. "I'm glad I didn't have to explain to him why photographing women in the fitting rooms of a boutique is creepy, even if he respected the closed curtains."

I had to agree with Raven about the dress, but I wasn't sold on her photographer. Despite the poofy flounces, Colby looked surprisingly sleek in the one-shoulder, fit-and-flare dress, which had a bow at the top of the shoulder, and the fitted bodice was covered in gold sequins that matched the fabric below. The chiffon skirt seemed to be made of several fabrics, including a tulle layer.

"Oh, good!" Marnie said. "I snagged that dress because, when I examined it, I thought it'd fit Colby's measurements, and the color is perfect."

"She might outsparkle the bride," Harmony said.

"Not possible," Raven said.

Ivy walked out of her dressing room in an emerald-green dress. The spaghetti straps looked thin against her bony shoulders, and the dress was baggy around her narrow waist.

"Hmm," Marnie said. "I might be able to take this in quickly, but let's try the other green first. Or maybe the royal blue."

It took several visits to the dressing room with various poofy options, but Harmony agreed the metallic pink dress with a black tulle underskirt looked the best on her.

"It has Madonna vibes," I told her, which made Harmony brighten.

"I can work with that," she said.

Ivy ended up with a green dress that was velvet on top and satin on the bottom. Marnie put our four dresses aside, and I knew they'd show up, like magic, when we met up to get ready for the wedding in the cabin on Bardsey Island.

"How did you find all of these dresses, anyway?" Harmony asked. Her tone was respectful for once. Almost happy.

"Trade secret," Marnie said with a smile. She turned to write something down, and Harmony pulled a face behind her.

"It's been real, Raven, but I really need to get home," Colby said. "If I don't see you tomorrow, I'll see you at the bachelorette party on Saturday."

Raven said, "Wait! Don't forget your gift bags! You'll need this for the wedding."

Raven handed Colby a bag first, and my friend took off. She handed the rest to Harmony, Ivy, and me. I paused to examine its contents.

Inside, I found a pair of black Converse sneakers in my size, chunky rhinestone jewelry, fishnet tights, and a small wrapped box with a tag that said, "For Bailey. Thank you for standing up with me on my big day. Hopefully, this gift will adequately show my thanks (and please save it until after the wedding!)."

"Converse?" Harmony said. Her voice dripped with contempt.

"We're spending the day on Bardsey Island, and it's natural ground," Raven said. "I don't want any of you destroying your ankles trying to walk in high heels out there."

"I love it," I said. "The shoes are perfect." And I'd wear them again, which is always a bonus.

"I'll wear whatever you want," Ivy said. "What's going on in town tonight? Please tell me there's something we can do instead of staring at the walls of the taproom again."

"Emmett and I have a few wedding tasks, and we're going to grab dinner at the cocktail bar with some of his friends from out of town at eight. You're welcome to join us."

"Hang out with those snobs?" Harmony grumbled.

"Who said you were invited?" Ivy asked.

Harmony lurched away without saying goodbye. From the glimpse I caught of her face, she looked hurt.

"Good riddance." Ivy waved at Harmony's retreating back.

"Emmett's friends are not snobs," Raven said. "Harmony just doesn't click with them."

"Does your sister click with anyone?" Ivy asked.

And with that comment, I was done. "Text me if you need anything, Raven," I said, and started to walk away.

"Will do!" Raven said.

I started to turn back, but Ivy said, "Raven, look at this." My friend turned away to see the polka shirtwaist dress Ivy was holding up. So, I continued on my way.

I was beelining for the door, but Marnie called out "Hey, Bailey!" and waved me over, so I detoured her way.

"I found something that might have your name on it," Marnie told me. She pulled out a vintage Pendleton '49er jacket with red-and-gray plaid.

"It's amazing," I said. And maybe impractical for my usual life, which involved walking around town with Jack regardless of the weather. Although maybe it'd layer well under my raincoat. And it'd work on crisp autumn days, like today.

Hmm, it was almost blazer-like, and I could wear it in the shop, or when I wanted to look slightly dressed up but still comfortable. Maybe I could wear it to the next Pacific Northwest Booksellers Association conference, if it was cold enough for wool.

"When I saw it, I thought of you," Marnie said. "If you'd like, I can put it in the back for a few days so you can think about it."

"Please." Marnie was right; the jacket was calling to me, but I try not to impulse buy clothing, mainly because of my book habit.

Marnie and I chatted for a moment, then I left for home. I had a few details to confirm for Raven's bachelorette party, and a few tasks for the bookshop that I knew I should handle before the Halloween chaos descended.

Chapter 3

On my way through town to the bookshop on Saturday morning, my uncle Hunter stepped out of Morning Broo carrying an extra-large coffee, and his steps barely paused when he saw me. He acted like I was invisible, which he'd started doing last Christmas and hadn't stopped all these months later.

He'd get over his anger eventually. Maybe. Hopefully.

I had other things to worry about. Today would be a long day, as both the town's annual Halloween parade and Raven's all-night bachelorette party were tonight.

But this is also the most important time of year for Lazy Bones, so I pushed away thoughts of the upcoming evening and focused on what I needed to do. Checking our stock of seasonal bestsellers is an obsession of mine since I want to ensure we have plenty of books on hand. Reordering the novels that the horde of festivalgoers descending on town devour is streamlined and usually quick, as long as books are in stock at the distributor. But the guide to *Haunted Hounds of Hamlet Bay* filming sites is published by one of the local historical societies, thankfully the one that's easier to deal with, and reordering copies can also be a slow process if I miscalculate and don't order enough in June as part of my festival lead-up. Thankfully, we still had plenty on the shelves for our busiest weekend of the year.

Once everything in the shop was up and running, and Tara,

Milo, and Atticus showed up for their midday shifts, Jack and I used my lunch hour to check in on our Halloween parade float. Which I'd left in Danby Snow's hands, aka Colby's younger sister and former intern turned part-time employee. She'd transferred to the same four-year university in North Portland that Colby and I had attended after finishing community college. She'd convinced one of her professors to let managing the shop's parade float count as one of her school projects. I'd helped with the grunt work to build the float, but I wasn't going to be on board as it paraded through downtown later tonight. Which made me feel slightly sad, as I love being part of the parade. But it would be nice to only be a spectator for once.

Danby was sitting in a camp chair by the float with a book in her hand. She jumped to attention when she saw me. "What do you think?" she asked. She motioned to the finished float.

"It looks fantastic." Breathtaking, even.

We'd built two velvet thrones with silver stars on a small platform on the float. Sprinkled at their feet were a handful of stools that looked like stacks of books, which we'd painted with the names of my favorite horror titles.

My grandfather would sit on the throne, dressed in a skeleton costume with a pumpkin head. He'd read a series of picture books to a group of listening goblins, aka a handful of kids who were store regulars, alongside a couple of their parents, also in costume. Marion of the Sleepy Hollow Inn would play queen to my grandfather's king and preside on the other throne. We'd wound fairy lights from the exaggerated tops of the thrones to a light pole on the bridge on the back end of the float. One of the parents was scheduled to stand on the bridge, holding a flickering lantern in a costume that made him look headless.

Last but not least, my dog, Jack, would lie on a dog bed at my grandfather's feet while wearing a bandana that matched the vibe of the throne, probably assuming he was the true pumpkin king of the tableau. This would be his third Halloween parade float.

The sides of the float said, SPOOKY STORY TIME BY THE LAZY BONES BOOKSHOP AND THE SLEEPY HOLLOW INN.

Jack pushed his snout under Danby's hand, insisting on attention, while I jumped up on the float and double-checked that everything felt solid. The last thing we wanted was for a chair to break and for a mini goblin to fall off the float.

"The lights work, but feel free to double-check," Danby said. Both of her hands were scratching Jack, who had a blissful look on his face, like he'd never been petted before, ever.

I trusted Danby but still double-checked the battery-operated lights, which lit up in shades of purple and orange.

"It's beautiful, and it's really going to come to life once we've added the kids," I said. Hopefully, they'd all show up as promised.

"And once this big man is on it," Danby said. She was still scratching Jack, who showed no signs of moving again, ever.

We chatted logistics for a few minutes, then I returned to work, with Jack reluctantly walking alongside me.

"Bailey!"

Orson, the owner of the Popcorn Palace, waved me down. "Are we all good to go for tonight?" he asked.

"We should be set to go. Nothing has changed since we last spoke, and I dropped the supplies off."

"I heard you've invited local business owners who don't know the bride?" he said.

"Yeah, the more the merrier."

"Did you remember to invite Clarity?" he asked, referring to Clarity Blooms, the owner of the local apothecary, Eye of Newt.

My brain froze. "I honestly can't remember."

"Make sure you do, or else you'll hurt her feelings."

Orson walked on, and Jack waited alongside me as I shot Clarity a text and, for the heck of it, added several locals who I knew were coming to the event. **Just a reminder that you're invited to the all-night party at the Popcorn Palace starting after the parade. Pizza, snacks, movies, games . . . And you don't have to stay the whole night if you don't want to! It'd be lovely to see you for at least a while.**

★ ★ ★

Once Milo returned from his late lunch break, I left the bustling bookshop in my staff's capable hands. Jack and I walked home, where he would spend the rest of the day with my grandfather, including on the bookshop's float in the Halloween parade.

And with Marion, it turned out. She was sitting on the back porch of the house with my grandfather. She had her oil paints out and was working on a street scene of downtown Elyan Hollow that reminded me of French Impressionism while my grandfather read. It'd be nice to be in a relationship like that one day. To be able to quietly do something I'm passionate about alongside someone I love.

My grandfather and grandmother had felt like the perfect couple, and he'd been a bit adrift emotionally after she'd passed away, although he'd put on a strong enough façade to fool Hunter, but not me. A few years after her death, he'd slowly started dating Marion, who'd been widowed about a decade before. They'd moved so slowly it'd taken me a while to realize they were dating. I can't begrudge either of them the companionship they bring to each other, even if it initially felt odd that my grandfather was dating one of his deceased wife's best friends. But I've always loved Marion, and they seem good for each other.

It didn't take me long to get ready for the bachelorette party. I've heard stories of brides having intense requirements for their bachelorette party, with multiple fancy wardrobe changes, but Raven's desires were low-key. We were supposed to watch the parade in proper Halloween style, so I pulled on my trusty Ghostbuster costume. I'd found a tan jumpsuit at a garage sale a few years ago. After sewing a "no ghost" patch and custom name tag to it, and adding on a few tubes and gray elbow pads, black gloves, and a DIY proton pack, plus the black boots in my closet, I had a serviceable costume that was perfect for late October evenings, as I could add as many warm layers as needed underneath.

In my Ghostbuster costume, I headed back downtown after saying goodbye to my grandfather, Marion, and Jack. As my black Doc Martens thudded on the sidewalk, I wondered how many times I was destined to walk this route.

If—or rather when—my grandfather decided to sell his house, my commute would change since his home is more than I can afford if he charged me a market price. Since the bookshop, along with the building it's in, had already been formally signed over to me, bypassing his children and other grandchildren, I expected him to sell the house on the open market out of fairness.

Although given the Briggs family explosion last Christmas, I wouldn't be surprised by anything my grandfather chose to do.

But I put that out of my mind. Today's wedding activity should be fun, at least in theory: the bachelorette party. We were kicking off festivities by heading to Wine Ghouls for snacks, followed by watching the annual Halloween parade, which is always one of my favorite evenings of the Halloween festival.

The bachelorette party would finish the evening at the Popcorn Palace, where I'd already dropped off the "Boo Crew" T-shirts I'd designed and had printed on Raven's behalf at the movie theater, along with a small overnight bag with a pair of flannel pajama pants and toiletries since we all planned on changing out of our costumes when we watched the movies and played games, accompanied by two of the most important food groups: pizza and popcorn.

But a night of Harmony and Ivy bickering made me think I needed to bring the patience I've developed when working with challenging customers.

And I could follow the advice of the text I'd sent local friends and duck out of the all-night party early. Which I'd do if needed to keep my temper intact.

Thankfully, I should be able to create a human buffer between Harmony and me. Raven invited several of our college friends who still lived in the region, plus her friends traveling from all over the country. She had invited a few of my friends in town she'd met over the past week, like Lark and Ash, to join us, along with Evelyn, the attorney who rents the office space above the bookshop, for the movie theater portion of the evening. And I should tell Raven, I'd added Clarity of Eye of Newt to the guest list.

As I opened the door to Wine Ghouls, the seasonally named

tasting room of the award-winning Elyan Hollow Wines, I smiled, even though it felt fake. I could do this.

This could be a fun evening, even if I had doubts.

And, of course, I was the first to arrive.

"Oh, Bailey!" Celia, one of the co-owners of the shop and winery, waved when she saw me.

Given the ghostly bride decor on a handful of wine barrels turned into tables in the corner of the room, away from the front door but close to the windows, I guessed that was the reserved space for Raven's bachelorette party.

I looked out the window and enjoyed watching people in costumes walk by. Not everyone was dressed up—Kristobel from the Bad to the Bone pet shop was in a simple T-shirt and jeans—over half of the people I saw were in full Halloween glory. A grim reaper, a witch, a vampire, someone in a silver onesie with fuchsia hair, Olivia, practically running up the street in her usual Boorito T-shirt and, today, a pair of orange cords, another grim reaper, a trio of witches, a pizza and a princess walking arm in arm. Yet another grim reaper.

"Can I get you anything, Bailey?" Celia asked.

"Just a water," I said, quickly adding, "for now."

Celia nodded. "Hey, do you know the vendor timeline for setting up Bardsey Island for the wedding? Do we need to be there for a boat at ten a.m.?"

"Umm . . . I'm not sure."

"I was talking to Ghostly Gouda, and they said they weren't sure—"

Colby's parents owned the Ghostly Gouda cheese shop, one of the businesses Raven had tapped to provide locally sourced food for the wedding.

"—but they said the main caterer was picking up the cheese trays early, before they head to the island for setup. We're running the wine bar during the reception."

"From what I remember, Elyan Catering is heading over at nine to start getting set up. They're using the kitchen on the island. I think they've arranged to use the manager's boat then to get across."

"And the wedding starts at two?"

"The ceremony does, yes." Hopefully, the company that manages the island would be able to herd all the wedding guests across to the island in time for the 2:00 p.m. start.

"We already sent the wine to the caterers, and they're doing the main part of the setup," Celia said. "They have bartenders and servers with Oregon liquor licenses and offered to handle everything, but we want to have a presence in case anyone has questions about the wine."

"If you're worried, you should check in with Raven. Or ask the caterers when they want you to arrive. But we should be good to go. The wedding is pretty low-key." Just heavily themed.

"I guess I could check the email Raven sent. But she sends so many weekly status emails, with so many details."

Relief flew through me as Colby walked in, wearing a long green tunic, brown knee boots, and a green hoodie-slash-cloak that she wore year-round, but it fit with the elf vibe of her costume. She'd finished the look off with a sword hilt in a brown sheath that peeked out from her hip. Elf ears peeked out of her long black hair.

"You look festive," Celia said.

We chitchatted, and when Raven walked in, dressed as Ursula from *The Little Mermaid* in what I'd bet was a custom-sewn costume, Celia perked up.

"Raven! I have a few questions!"

"Darn, I'd hoped my emails were clear enough," Raven said. She followed Celia up to the front register.

"I like Raven's trident," Colby said. "It's very peak Ursula when she thought her plan was coming to fruition."

As Raven and Celia talked, Raven tapped the end of her trident against the floor.

"My wedding seemed stress-free in comparison," Colby said.

"You were definitely on high alert in the days leading up to it, but your wedding was chill. It helps that Hayes's family was super mellow." I'd been the maid-of-honor, and Colby's wedding, with the ceremony held in the park next to the Columbia River and the reception in the local Grange Hall, right after they'd remodeled it, had been a fun day.

"Hayes' family is so easy," Colby agreed. "I take it Emmett's family hasn't impressed you?"

Opting for diplomatic felt like the right move. "His family is very different from Raven's, with a different sense of how the world should work. If you divide the world into two camps, one that loves the idea of the Halloween wedding and one that hates it, they fall into the opposite side of Raven and Emmett. While Raven's family are all for it. Well, her parents love the idea." Raven's parents both made a living as artists and in some ways, they were two of the least pretentious people I'd ever met. But they also thought everyone shouldn't care about labels, which was its own form of pressure, but to not conform.

Harmony flounced in, dressed in a pink princess costume with Disney vibes and a rhinestone tiara shiny enough to be seen from outer space.

"No carriage pulled by mice?" Colby asked her.

"I hate this town," Harmony said.

"Do you like anything?" Colby asked. Harmony glared at her.

Celia came over with a tray of wineglasses and a carafe of red wine, followed by Raven. Celia placed the tray on the table.

"What type of wine is this?" Harmony's tone was skeptical.

"Our award-winning Pinot Noir," Celia said, and was clearly ready to settle into her usual wine spiel.

"I'm starving," Raven said.

"Oh! I'll be back with your hors d'oeuvres!"

Celia bustled off.

Situation saved. Celia's love of wine is heartwarming, but I've already heard her sales pitch on what makes their Pinot Noir unique too many times.

In her defense, her wine is excellent.

A trio of Raven's out-of-town friends arrived next, all dressed as witches, and fell on the wine and just-delivered charcuterie trays like vultures.

Raven checked her phone.

"Everything okay?"

"I'm just worried about . . . Oh wait, there she is."

Ivy walked in, carrying a large tote bag that clashed with her unicorn onesie. "I brought unicorn costumes for everyone!"

"I . . . think we're good, thanks," I said.

"Too bad. If anyone needs a costume, they can be a unicorn." Ivy dumped her tote bag by my feet.

Nate showed up in the doorway with his camera and took photos of us until Raven waved him off. "What happens at the bachelorette party stays at the bachelorette party!"

He waved and left, and I realized he'd been wearing the same hoodie as he'd worn on Wednesday.

The guy must pack light.

A few more of Raven's friends came in, dressed as 1960s go-go dancers, followed by two women in oversized pumpkin sweatshirts and black leggings.

Harmony ended up squeezing between Raven and me. "I can't believe you didn't follow Emmett's lead and hold a real bachelorette party," Harmony said.

Emmett and his pals had booked a party bus to drive them into Portland. They planned to visit a handful of breweries and then hit up Ground Kontrol, the classic arcade and bar in Old Town.

I stepped away, ceding the space to Harmony and her whines, pun intended. Colby leaned over to talk in my ear.

"Harmony would be horrified to learn Emmett and his friends debated an all-night Dungeons and Dragons campaign before booking the party bus, which made a custom tour," Colby told me. "They're definitely hitting up TPK Brewing for a quick tabletop gaming session as part of their evening. I told the best man about

Wyrd Leatherworks and Meadery, and now he and Emmett are excited to drop by there. I think they reworked their entire itinerary to include it."

"So they switched their plan to Peak-Geek Portland."

"Too bad they didn't invite Harmony."

I laughed.

"Thank you everyone for coming!" Raven called out.

"Whoo!" one of the witches yelled.

"Have some snacks and wine, and get ready for an evening of Halloween fun, followed by movies!"

"Whoo! Party on, my witches!" one of the trio of witches yelled.

"They're so annoying."

Oh great. Harmony was back hovering next to me.

"Can you believe—"

"Oops." Ivy tripped over her tote bag on the floor, bumped off Colby, and spilled her glass of wine on Harmony's chest.

Harmony sputtered and looked at her pink dress, now dripping with red wine. "You! You did this on purpose!"

"I'm so sorry, Harmony," Ivy said. She raised her hand to her chin, like she was pondering the situation, but the squint in her eye and smug look warned me an explosion was building.

I stepped between them. "Harmony, let's see if we can salvage your costume." I looped my arm around hers and pulled her toward the back of the room, where a short hallway led to the restrooms.

"Ivy is such a snake."

Celia hustled over. "Oh no! I have some club soda; let's see if that will help."

Harmony pouted as Celia and I tried to save Harmony's costume. Colby carried over the bag of unicorn onesies while Ivy trailed behind her. "How about a unicorn onesie?"

"That's a good idea! If we soak this, we might be able to get the stain out," Celia said.

"Do stains come out of cheap polyester?" Ivy asked.

"It's one of the easiest fabrics to clean!" Celia said.

"The two of you are pathetic," Harmony said. Her gaze moved between Colby and Ivy. "You did this on purpose."

"It was an accident, princess," Ivy said.

"I was just standing there. I hope your costume wasn't ruined," Colby said.

"I doubt it was ruined. We can save this," Celia said. "Why, if I told you about all of the shirts I've thought were stained but—"

Harmony took a unicorn onesie and stalked off to the bathroom. Ivy laughed and walked away.

"Thank you for your help, Celia," I said.

"This wedding won't be over soon enough," Colby said.

After leaving Wine Ghouls, we staked out a spot on the annual route. The parade mustered at the local elementary school, then headed to Main Street, where it would run through the heart of downtown and end at the waterfront park. The floats would either park, or, like our float, drive the few blocks back to our waiting garage.

Thankfully, Ivy and Harmony stood at separate ends of the bachelorette party. That would keep me from knocking their heads together if they kept squabbling.

"We really couldn't bring wine with us?" one of the witches asked.

"There will be more food later," Raven said.

"And wine?"

"If you're good."

The witch laughed.

The tones of the local, all-welcome Elyan Hollow Marching Band caught my ear.

It was time!

The parade was on its way.

The local adult volunteer band was dressed, as usual, as bananas. They'd led our parade every year since its conception.

A man dressed as Jack from *The Nightmare Before Christmas* followed the band down the street, impressively steady on his high stilts.

"There's my parents!" Colby pointed out the Ghostly Gouda float, followed by an Alice in Wonderland–themed tableau from the new local tea shop.

"Want a lemonade?" Colby asked me. She jerked her head toward the Ghoul Aid, run by a club from Elyan Hollow High. All the students working the booth wore bright yellow sweatshirts with the words LEMON AIDES printed across the front, with yellow hats painted to resemble lemons. Their stand was set up in front of the Eye of Newt Apothecary. I glanced inside and didn't see Clarity, but her shop was dark. Maybe she'd staked out her own spot to watch the festivities.

"Might as well," I said. I hadn't drunk much of anything at Wine Ghouls, and I'd missed out on all but the dregs of the charcuterie as well.

We shifted away from the bachelorette party and walked to the stand as the high school band marched by.

"Are those the elf ears you told me about? The ones you had the design for?" a teen girl working the booth asked.

Colby smiled and touched her ear. "Yes, I made these in the maker lab."

I smiled as they chatted about the elf ears. One of Colby's projects as the Youth Services Librarian for the Elyan Hollow Library was developing a maker space primarily focused on teen users. She held workshops and drop-in times so teens could use the 3D printer, craft and laser cutters, craft supplies, sewing machines, and more. Some of her workshops were high-tech, but the lower-tech programs, including soap and candle making, had been equally popular. Colby frequently wheedled me into volunteering in her programs, but it was never a hard sell since I loved helping with hands-on projects.

"Excuse me, I'd like a lemonade," an annoyed voice broke in.

Harmony.

Of course. The unicorn onesie was mostly baggy on her, but

also managed to be snug across Harmony's chest. The horn on the hood pointed crookedly toward the sky. Her annoyed face beneath felt like the opposite of what a unicorn should be. Unless Harmony was taking her inspiration from *Unicorns Are Jerks*, a steady seller from the shop's adult coloring book shelf.

"Umm, sure, I'll get one for you after I help out Miss Colby and . . ." The girl looked at me. "I'm sorry, I can't remember your name. But I adore your Ghostbusters costume. I'm jealous. It's way better than being a lemon."

"I'm Bailey," I said.

"You know, I always see you with your dog. It's weird to see you without him," the girl said as she cut two lemons in half and put each half in a large cup of ice.

"The big white dog? I love him!" Her friend poured what I assumed was simple syrup and water over the lemon in the first cup, then moved to the second.

Colby used her phone to pay for our lemonades, and Harmony pushed past us.

"Finally," Harmony griped. The girls both looked at with her with big eyes, but I suspected they were mocking her.

We rejoined Raven, Ivy, the witches, and the rest of the party-goers as a *Wizard of Oz* float moved down the road, complete with a wicked witch suspended in midair, "flying" behind Dorothy.

"Is that your boss?" I asked. A grim reaper with a basset hound walked by us.

"Yep, the head of the library is playing the wicked witch," Colby said.

"Talk about playing against type," I said. Colby's boss was driven and organized but also hilarious and warm. While they sometimes butted heads because they both had strong opinions, they were also allies in the fight to maintain, if not expand, library access to the masses.

A group of kids, maybe twelve years old, marched behind the float. I couldn't tell who they were representing, but they smiled and waved to the crowd with spirit.

"There's Jack!" Colby said. The bookshop's float came into view, with Jack sitting up straight like he was the king of the tableau. The children, dressed as goblins, looked adorable on their pillows. My grandfather and Marion looked regal.

"I'm glad I trusted your sister to do the float," I said.

As the next float, a haunted butcher–inspired scene from local Ahead of the Carve, moved in front of us, a loud explosion wracked the air, and it felt like the earth jolted.

People screamed.

The crowd tried to flee but ran into each other.

Then, a second boom rocked the air.

Chapter 4

The floats in the parade all screeched to a halt.

I stepped behind a cement planter as people rushed past me, panicking. "Calm down!" I called out, but I was just yelling into the void.

But I couldn't see any flames or smell smoke. When I turned, I saw a little girl, maybe three, cowering beside a bench. She was crying. Her knee was scraped through her red tights.

I recognized her. Georgie. Her mother and older brother were on the bookshop's float. I'd offered to include Georgie, but her mother thought she was too young. If I remembered right, Georgie was supposed to be watching the parade with her BFF and her BFF's mom.

"I want my mommy," Georgie cried.

"Georgie, hey Georgie. It's Bailey from the bookshop," I said. "If you come with me, I'll help you find your mom."

An almost black nose poked at us.

Jack.

I stared at my dog, wondering where he'd come from.

Jack nudged Georgie, who threw her arms around him.

"Should we go find your mom? Jack will help us," I said. "I'll carry you."

Georgie let go of Jack and nodded. She let me pick her up and promptly buried her head against my shoulder. I carried her away from Main Street, where I saw Colby about half a block away. I realized she was telling the crowd to calm down as I approached.

Raven and two of the witches were on the sidewalk against a building next to Colby, while Lark and the third witch were helping an older woman with an injured ankle.

"Did you see what happened?" Raven asked.

Colby's eyes widened. "Is that Georgie?"

Georgie clung on tighter, and I gave Colby the facial equivalent of a shrug. My friend turned her gaze to the fuzzy companion at my side. "Aren't you supposed to be with the Pumpkin King?"

"Can you text my grandfather and let him know Jack is with us?" I asked. Given Georgie's stranglehold around my neck, I was pretty sure Colby realized I couldn't text.

"Consider it done." Colby pulled her phone out of her back pocket and sent a quick text.

The crowd fleeing from the parade route had slowed to a trickle of people. "Was the parade canceled?" one of them asked me.

"My guess is yes," I said. A murder last year and an explosion this year. Maybe Halloween in Elyan Hollow really was cursed.

Raven scanned our group. "Has anyone seen Ivy? Or Harmony?"

"They're probably fighting over who is having the worst evening," Colby muttered.

Raven's gazed turned upward like she was looking for strength.

Then I saw someone who made me feel relieved.

"Look, Georgie, it's your daddy," I said. "Detective Whitlock!"

Detective Andrew Whitlock, one of the few, if not the only, detectives on the Elyan Hollow Police force, turned my way. His eyebrows rose, then narrowed, as he assessed the situation. But he quickly walked my way.

"Daddy!"

Detective Whitlock took his daughter from me, and she promptly resumed her stranglehold, this time around his neck. "How'd you end up with Georgie?" he asked me.

"I found her by a bench and couldn't leave her alone," I said. "She has a skinned knee, but she seems otherwise fine, physically."

"Thank you, Bailey," he said. We'd come a long way from the time he'd thought I was a murder suspect.

"Do you know what happened?" I asked.

He shook his head. "I'm off duty but headed this way to help. I assume it'll be all-hands-on-deck, but I'm a father first at this moment in time."

His phone dinged, and he tried to look at it while Georgie didn't budge.

I walked alongside him back to the parade route.

"Your daughter was there." I pointed to a bench. I turned to where the bachelorette party had been watching. I noticed the edge of a unicorn horn behind a trash can.

Oh no. Dread tightened my stomach as I walked over to the fallen unicorn.

"Detective?" I said. "You need to see this, but I should take Georgie for a few minutes."

The detective looked for a short moment, then pried his daughter off. "Please wait with Miss Bailey for a moment."

Georgie felt less frantic as she held on to me, but she still rested her head on my shoulder, like she wanted to block out the scary world. Her father leaned down over the unicorn.

When he looked up, I knew one truth.

Ivy was dead.

Chapter 5

With the explosion followed by Ivy's death, the bachelorette party was over. But we still headed for the Popcorn Palace, but with police officer companions. Harmony joined us outside the movie theater.

"Why the long faces?" Harmony asked. "Not into Halloween anymore?"

No one answered her.

Orson met us at the door of his movie theater.

"Hello, bachelorette party . . ." Orson's voice trailed off when he saw the police officers accompanying us.

"Slight change of plans," I told him.

"Is everything okay? I heard there was drama at the parade, some sort of explosion, but I missed it. If there's excitement, I'm always in the other room." Orson raised his hands in an exasperated gesture.

"Excitement is one way of putting it," I said.

After a quick explanation, the bridal party walked into the lobby of the Popcorn Palace, escorted inside by the two uniformed police officers. One loomed near the door while the other followed the party to the benches along one side of the lobby.

But I still stood by the door. "Is it okay if Jack comes in?" I asked.

"For tonight, it's okay, but don't make it a habit." Orson smiled at Jack but didn't reach out to pet him.

MAYHEM AT A HALLOWEEN WEDDING   51

I joined the bachelorette party, accompanied by Jack, who hadn't moved from my side since finding me. He wasn't on a leash but didn't show any desire to wander. He must still be freaked out by explosions.

"Wait, Ivy died? No way." Harmony's voice rang across the room. Raven looked at her sister for a moment, then walked to the other side of the room. Harmony glanced at Colby, then found a spot along the wall, away from everyone else.

Thankfully, the padded benches were comfortable, although one of the witches kept squirming. "I want to go to my hotel room," she said.

Our costumes looked ridiculous, considering everything we'd been through. Maybe I could talk to Ivy if I were a real ghostbuster. Find out what happened to her. Had it been accident? Or had someone struck her down on purpose?

Or caught Ivy's ghost in my proton pack to be faithful to the source material. The thought made my stomach flip.

It was hard to believe Ivy was gone. She'd annoyed me from the moment she arrived in town, but her death was fundamentally unfair. She should be with us now, preparing to watch a classic horror movie with a bucket of buttery popcorn. Not lying on the ground by a garbage can.

A while later, which felt like an eternity, Detective Whitlock walked into the movie theater. He'd added his badge to his belt, positioning it above his hip, and, presumably, had left little Georgie with his wife.

The door to the Popcorn Palace opened. "I have a special delivery from Slice Eternal?" a voice said.

I popped up.

I hadn't thought to cancel the pizza.

When the new, tiny, to-go pizza window opened in downtown last summer, I was excited. Their pizza was excellent, and I'd averaged one a week. I danced a happy dance when they agreed to deliver pizza to the bachelorette party since they don't normally offer a delivery service but were willing to do it this one time for a special event. I considered their agreement a good omen, a sign the evening would be perfect.

I'd been so wrong.

Detective Whitlock eyed me. "That better not be a stripper," he said.

"It's pizza! I'll take care of it," I said. "Thankfully, we decided to forgo having a cop strippergram tonight because that would've been embarrassing."

"Wait, seriously?"

"No, it's not that kind of party." I shook my head at Detective Whitlock.

"Bad time?" The delivery person was probably a student, maybe eighteen or nineteen. He eyed the uniformed police officers but didn't look scared, just curious.

"Yeah, but I can take the pizza." We'd prepaid for the pizza, so I gave the kid a generous tip and hauled the boxes to the snack bar from the small lobby with my fuzzy guardian alongside. My stomach grumbled at the smell, which made me feel slightly guilty. I shouldn't be thinking about food at a time like this.

Another police officer strode up to the theater, and the pizza delivery kid held the door open for him.

"Is there a party going on in here?" the new police officer asked in an exaggerated voice. His loose-hip stride was exaggerated.

"Who are you? And why are you impersonating a police officer?" Detective Whitlock barked out. The other police officers on-site had already snapped to attention, and the newcomer blinked.

"Umm, I was hired to be here. Is this, like a, group act? No one told me. If they had, we could've coordinated a song."

Detective Whitlock held up his badge, and the new guy looked confused.

"Was I supposed to bring props?" the new guy asked.

One of the uniformed officers was staring at the new guy. "Are those tearaway pants?"

The second officer asked, "Do your handcuffs have pink fur?"

MAYHEM AT A HALLOWEEN WEDDING 53

"It looks like he did bring props," I muttered.

Detective Whitlock looked at me. "I thought this wasn't that sort of party?"

"It's not supposed to be," I said. I stepped closer to the real and faux police officers.

"Wait, is he going to take his clothes off?" one of the witches asked. Two of them stood by the pizza with slices in their hand.

"Interesting turn of events," the other witch said.

"You were supposed to be a fireman, not a police officer!" Harmony wailed. Everyone turned to stare at her.

Raven stood as she turned toward her sister and pounded the end of her trident on the floor. "What is wrong with you, Harmony? I told you no strippers. It was supposed to be movies, popcorn, and fun, not you whining at me relentlessly. If you're that miserable here, you can leave. I don't want you here enough to deal with your current attitude."

"You're always so mean to me!" Harmony yelled back.

"I can go," the stripper copper offered. "And please don't think my costume is intended to make fun of your profession. Some women just dig it, or at least the idea of it."

"Yeah, we know." One of the uniformed officers escorted the stripper outside.

"Make up your mind, Harmony. Be pleasant or get out of my wedding." Raven sat down, looking completely exhausted. She'd just lost one of her best friends, and probably wanted space to grieve.

"It's always about you." Harmony sounded petulant.

"Is now really the right time? Give it a rest," Colby butted in.

Both sisters turned away from each other and crossed their arms in unison.

"Were multiple attendees in unicorn costumes?" Detective Whitlock asked me. His eyes lingered on Harmony. The hood of her unicorn costume was pushed down, making it look like the horn was protruding from her shoulders.

"Ivy brought a whole bag of the unicorn costumes, but originally, it was just her wearing one. But then Harmony's princess costume had an unfortunate close encounter with a glass of wine, and she had to change."

"So there were two unicorns at your party tonight." The detective's eyes looked far away like he was deep in thought.

"Yes," I said. Wait a minute. Had someone meant to attack Harmony, but killed the wrong unicorn? Why? Harmony was annoying, but there's no way she developed a fatal enemy in the few days she'd been in town.

"You know, I think I saw your librarian friend arguing with someone in a unicorn costume."

"Umm . . . To be honest, everyone argued with both Ivy and Harmony. Both were in unicorn costumes. If it was by the lemonade stand, that was less an argument and more Harmony being grumpy." An icy feeling settled deep inside my chest. Jack leaning against my side wasn't enough to keep me from shivering.

"Hmm." Detective Whitlock jotted a note to himself, when clearly, he should've been agreeing with me.

"And you know, Harmony wasn't with the group when Georgie and I found them. She disappeared somewhere." I'd throw Harmony under the bus any day if it kept Colby out of trouble.

But from how Detective Whitlock eyed my friend, Colby was a suspect.

Could Harmony have fought with Ivy after everyone else had scurried away?

And why would someone have harmed Ivy? Why here? Why now?

Or had someone tried to ruin Raven's wedding by attacking her maid of honor?

After pulling all of us aside for an interview, the police left. We were free. But everyone looked tired.

"You can stay and watch movies like you planned," Orson offered.

Raven shook her head. "Thank you for the offer, but we're calling it a night. Maybe when I wake up, this will have been a nightmare."

A herd of thirty-something-year-old men rushed into the theater.

Well, "herd" might be stretching it, but there were five, with Emmett in the lead. Emmett rushed up to Raven and put his hand on her shoulder.

"Raven, are you okay?" Emmett asked.

Raven nodded as Emmett gazed into her eyes, and tears started to trickle down my friend's face. Emmett pulled Raven into his arms.

"And end scene," Colby muttered in my ear. "They're like a movie couple. This could be the penultimate scene of a rom-com."

"Or a moment right before the villain attacks in a horror movie," I said.

Two of the other men checked on the witches while the third witch grabbed the remaining pizza box.

"This is going home with me," the third witch said.

I wished I could muster up the energy to say a non-ironic "You go, girl," or something similar, but all I wanted was to go home and sleep for the next decade.

The final two men stood awkwardly.

"I'd offer you pizza, but this is all mine," the third witch told them. She licked the pizza box in a drunken show of dominance.

I glanced around the room, wondering if there was anything I should take care of before leaving. I noticed Harmony staring at her sister with a look full of thick, choking jealousy.

It would be nice to have someone worried like this for me, and I'm sure Colby wished her husband, Hayes, was in town. But I wasn't about to glare at my friend for having something I'd love to have in my life, but for whatever reason, it hadn't happened yet.

But something told me Harmony's jealousy ran deeper than just Emmett. Harmony's style was more mainstream than everyone else in her family, and maybe she felt like the odd person out. Her rather bohemian parents had chosen alternate paths through life, and they seemed blissfully happy with the decision. Raven had chosen a traditional career path, but she hadn't lost her artsy vibe, and she'd found a partner who not only appreciated the unique qualities that comprised Raven but also joined her in cosplay and dressing up.

Colby and I walked out together, and neither of us said anything. We separated to go our different directions after a few blocks.

"Text when you get home," I said.

"Ditto."

As Jack and I walked home, questions swirled in my mind.

What had happened to Ivy?

Was the explosion an accident?

Could Ivy's death and the explosion have been connected in some way? A way to distract everyone while Ivy was targeted?

Was it just chance that Harmony and Ivy were both in unicorn costumes?

Jack stopped to thoroughly sniff a planter on Main Street. The sidewalk was taped off with yellow crime scene tape about a block ahead of us.

After giving my dog a moment to thoroughly investigate using his olfactory senses, I checked for traffic, nudged him on the back, and escorted him across the street. He wasn't on a leash, so I was impressed that Jack stayed alongside me.

The floats were still in the spots they'd been during the explosions, before they'd been abandoned as everyone fled.

The sidewalks were covered in more garbage than normal. People had dropped food, hats, and random costume parts as they fled the parade without thinking about what they were doing. Without worrying that they'd knocked over a small child, or that a woman had been killed.

A mix of firefighters and police were grouped around an orange-and-black float pulled by a black pickup with an Elyan Hollow Explorers flag along the front. Both the float and truck were partially covered in foam.

Hmm.

Our high school had been the Explorers for decades before *The*

Haunted Hounds was filmed in town, but with a pirate-like mascot. There's been talk of changing the mascot to something dog or ghost related. One group had wanted to rename our high school mascot after Seaman, the Newfoundland who'd been part of the Lewis and Clark Expedition. When someone pointed out that some people consider "Newfie" a slur, and "Seaman" was a clear no-go around teenagers and those of us who refuse to grow up, that idea was discarded. So the compromise was to stay the Explorers but redraw the pirate with a ghostly appearance. And we'd stitched from blue and gold to black and orange. Although I'd always wished we'd changed the logo to be a hiker. Not all who wander are lost, after all.

The police activity around the float was interesting. Was this float ground zero for the bomb? The homecoming court usually has its own float in the parade. Although a few clubs usually pull together more creative entries. The homecoming court was usually simple, with the various princesses, queen, and king in formal dresses.

One of the police officers started staring at me with a look of suspicion growing across her face, so Jack and I moved on.

On the next block, the space where I'd found Ivy was also taped off, with a single police officer standing alongside it. Jack and I ignored it, and our steps quickened as we headed home. I texted Colby, **We arrived home**, and she responded back, **Same, talk tomorrow.**

When we walked inside the house, my grandfather was awake. As I untied Jack's bandana, I realized there was another question I should ask.

"I'm so glad you two are all right," my grandfather said. He was in his favorite chair with a book. He put it aside and took off his reading glasses.

"How did Jack escape the float?" Jack leaned against me. Again.

"I wish I knew the answer to that. Jack was in his usual halter when I hooked him up to his spot on the float, and I noticed it had slipped down during the parade. But he was calm and looked regal lying on his bed, so I didn't fix it."

"I thought I'd tightened the halter to keep that from happening."

Jack always wears a halter when we leave the house, versus attaching his leash to his collar. Sometimes, if he lies down, he somehow slips one skinny leg, if not both, through the loops of the halter.

"When the explosion happened, Jack bolted off the float, leaving the halter behind. Once we ushered the kids into Ash's taproom—"

My friend must've loved that. She always said she chose to open a drinking establishment, versus a restaurant, because state law meant she had to enforce a twenty-one-plus age limit.

"—and I knew we were safe, I was worried sick about Jack. I didn't know how I'd tell you that I'd lost him. Colby's text was a relief."

I sat on the couch, and Jack sat in front of me. My fuzzy sentry.

"Is there any word on what caused the explosion?" I asked. My body felt bone tired, and I debated how I was going to muster the energy to walk upstairs to my bedroom.

My grandfather shook his head. "There's a rumor that someone died."

I looked down, and Jack made eye contact with me. "In the explosion? Because someone did die, but it was separate."

"You heard this from someone reliable?"

One thing I learned early from my family: always cite your sources.

"I found the body."

Chapter 6

When I wake up, it's usually go time. Depending on the time of year, I might have a stand-up paddleboarding session planned, a long run, a bike ride, or a yoga class. Once in a while, Jack and I enjoy a leisurely Sunday morning and take a stroll for a morning pastry.

But I'd planned on spending all last night at the Popcorn Palace, and I assumed I'd be exhausted today, so I'd cleared my calendar and taken Sunday off. My main plan had been to join Raven and the crew for mani-pedis at the Spooky Town Spa in the afternoon and then drop by Ash's taproom for the special takeover that she had planned and insisted I needed to attend.

Instead of moving, I stayed in bed. But my mind was whirling, even if my body wanted to imitate a slug. So I reached for my phone, noting that Jack had forgone his memory foam dog bed and instead slept on the rug next to me.

It'd been a few days, maybe a week, since I'd logged onto Discord. When I opened the app, I saw I had been tagged a few times in the server one of my college friends had set up.

The first post I was tagged in was by a friend asking us to post photos of Raven's wedding. She wasn't going to be able to make it because she was due to have a baby at any minute and couldn't travel.

"I can't wait to see all of you dressed up for Raven's big day!"

she'd added. She'd included a photo of herself with a hand on top of her huge pregnant belly.

The first reply asked, "Did Ivy really die? Is Raven's wedding canceled?" And one of my friends tagged me.

I read the comments as I debated how to respond.

"Ivy died? Did she overdose?"

"No, she quit drugs, right?"

"Maybe she quit selling them?"

"C'mon, guys, you know Ivy's not a quitter."

"The quitting joke is not funny if Ivy actually died. Otherwise, it's hilarious."

"Ivy, if this is a false rumor, my apologies. Love you and your banana pants energy."

"Just don't steal my Xanax next time you visit."

"She does that to you, too? Because of that, my girlfriend won't let Ivy enter our house anymore. She's afraid Ivy will raid our medicine cabinet."

"Wait, are you saying you have the good stuff at your house?"

I took a deep breath and slowly typed, "Everyone, it's true. I can't give you full details yet, but Ivy died during the Halloween parade. I'll ask Raven about her wedding."

I hit send.

I scrolled through a few channels within the server, admiring photos of everyone's lives, from pictures of pets and kids to beautiful cups of coffee to hikes and journeys. I switched to a different, book club–oriented server that I lurk in. I love seeing readers talking about books, and I've found some sleeper hits for the store through this book club. Seeing their book talk made me feel calm. Life would go on, both in real life and on the page of the books I love. Even if things were going to be awkward in Elyan Hollow for a while.

But someone tagged me in my friend server, so I clicked back, anxiety once again rioting through me. "Bailey, we need details," a friend had posted.

I added a "sorry" emoji to his comment.

My phone dinged with a text, and I looked at the preview.

It's true? About Ivy? the text read.

Who is this? I responded.

Aaron Blanton.

It wasn't hard to guess why Aaron Blanton, a college friend I hadn't talked to in person for several years, was texting me now.

I typed back a simple **Yes.**

Then added **the news is true. I'm sorry.**

Aaron's question made sense to me, as the two had dated on and off for our junior year of college before they'd broken up very publicly. And loudly. Ivy had thrown a drink in his face in the middle of the main dining hall on campus before stomping off while yelling that Aaron was more boring than an earthworm.

He responded immediately. **What happened? Is everyone right? Did she OD?**

I carefully typed back, **When I know more, I'll text you. Right now, I have no idea.**

I started to go back to the Discord server but decided it was too much. My friends had questions I couldn't answer, so I put my phone facedown on my nightstand and geared myself up to face the day.

Lounging in bed wasn't going to solve anything.

But leaving technology behind was easier said than done.

Colby being suspected of murder didn't work in my life goals.

After a quick shower, I'd pulled on my favorite jeans and hooded sweater, as if they'd give me a small measure of comfort on what I assumed would be an annoying day.

Then I got to work.

We have a distribution list for downtown businesses, so I wrote an email asking for video footage from last night.

The worst that could happen is someone would say no.

No, scratch that, the worst thing to happen would be for someone to reply all and say no, and for others to argue about it.

Then, an image crossed my mind. Jude, from the Elyan Hollow Historical Society, had been downtown with a video camera, taping the crowd and the parade. Maybe he caught something.

I woke Jack up, who blinked at me sleepily before slowly standing up and stretching, and we headed to the backyard.

On my way downstairs, my phone beeped. **Heard what happened. What do you need?**

Sam Maki. We'd gone on a few dates, but any potential romantic relationship had fizzled into a friendship. On paper, he looked perfect for me. He did triathlons, including a few Ironmen. But he was more intense about it than I was and kept detailed data about his run times, nutritional needs, and gear. While I ran and biked because I loved the feeling of movement and how it made me feel balanced. After swimming competitively on the local team most of my childhood, including throughout high school, an occasional swimming workout was second nature. But I don't spend much time in the pool anymore unless I am training for something specific. I prefer fresh air to chlorine.

And I don't enjoy competing, while Sam thrived on events. He said they kept him focused.

Sam ran his own business as a white hat hacker with a PI license and worked with various companies to ensure their servers were secure. He also did some sort of work for his sister's law practice. Plus, he was handsome. And smart. Sam was, unironically, the total package.

But we operated on different frequencies, and they didn't quite mesh, at least romantically.

But Sam was now a regular in my fantasy book club and frequently stopped by when he visited his sister's law office above the shop. He'd encouraged Colby and me to join him for long bike rides and tried to get us to sign up for the same regional triathlon he planned to complete last summer. Colby signed up, and I didn't, but I'd been there when Sam won his age bracket, and Colby's race ended early due to a bicycle crash.

Sam and I regularly grabbed a drink at the taproom with the same group of locals. His sister Evelyn was a friend in addition to being a tenant, and I enjoyed hearing their banter when they're together.

And I trusted Sam was serious about helping me. He'd used his skills before to look up information for me, although he only used legal sources.

I also suspected Sam would've asked out Colby if she'd been single. But my best friend is not only married but head over heels for Hayes, her husband. Who had been scheduled to come home the day before Raven's wedding. Colby was keeping a stiff upper lip but I knew she missed him, and would prefer he found a job that kept him home more. But his current job allowed him to save for the home they hoped to buy.

As Jack completed his morning circuit of the backyard to check that the boundaries hadn't been invaded while we'd been asleep, I texted Sam back. **I'd love your help.**

Where should I start?

How about looking into Ivy Monroe? And Harmony Crawford?

I'm on it. Let me know if you want me to see what I can find on anyone else.

I paused. **How about Raven Crawford and Emmett Finch?**

Isn't that the bride and groom? Colby's talked about someone named Raven, anyway.

Yep. I felt like a traitor, but was it really a chance that Raven had invited Ivy to town, only for Ivy to be murdered?

I paused, then texted. **I'm pulling together security footage from downtown shops. Want me to send you a link once I have it all put together?**

Yes. Want me to see if I can pull together social media footage of the parade?

If you can do that, I'll owe you a beer. Maybe a keg.

That's a worthy incentive. Okay, book dealer. Anything else?

That's it. Thanks, Samu.

Sam's real first name is Samu, named by his deceased Finnish father. Complicated childhoods were also one of the things Sam and I had in common.

We headed back inside, and I filled the teakettle and set it to boil, then put Jack's breakfast down.

A few thuds caught my attention, followed by the front door being shut, and then footsteps came our way. My grandfather joined us in the kitchen. He handed over a small bakery box.

"Muffins," I said.

"Marion's special marionberry. She thought you would need one after the night you had."

"Last night was a nightmare," I admitted. The sniping at Wine Ghouls had been bad enough, but I could've dealt with obnoxious personalities. Ivy's death was going to cast a shadow on Raven's wedding. The parade, one of my favorite events of the Halloween festival, being ruined hurt me deep inside. The parade is magical, and how many small children were now terrified of it?

And that could deeply hurt the town. We need the festival to survive. The parade was a highlight, alongside the haunted house, and a few other attractions. If people started avoiding our events, the whole festival would wither.

"Is there any word on the explosion?" I asked.

"Supposedly, the police found some sort of bomb in the homecoming float. But that's just rumor. Marion heard it was the drama club's float that had the bombs. Someone else said it was that new tea shop's float."

"It wasn't the tea shop, as they were ahead of you, and the explosion happened behind you, I think." And given the police last night, the homecoming float had been the source of the explosion.

But why? The homecoming float is usually a tad boring, with the various homecoming princesses wearing fancy dresses while waving to the crowd. They could at least build something fun instead of just standing on top of a blank slate. But it's tradition.

The kettle clicked off, so I poured a small amount of water, maybe a tablespoon, into my waiting rounded mug. I added matcha powder and whisked it with the water, hoping I managed to get all the lumps out because if I didn't, I'd regret it when I accidentally chewed them. I added more hot water, along with honey and a splash of milk. The usual pattern of making matcha was comforting at a time when everything felt upended. I sat down with my drink.

Maybe it'd help me craft a plan.

Chapter 7

I'd just finished a neighborhood walk with Jack and was taking care of some never-ending household chores when my phone rang.

The head of the parade was calling.

"Any chance you can move your float in about thirty minutes? We finally have the all-clear."

"Of course."

I texted Danby and Alec, the local delivery driver who'd been our go-to and driven the float for years, and they both said they were on their way.

I left Jack behind, despite the big, sad eyes he gave me as he watched me lace up my shoes and grab my favorite jacket. It was sunny, so I was able to forgo my raincoat.

When I got downtown, I was heartened to see a crew of volunteers already out cleaning up the sidewalks. There were still two floats in front of us, but the one in the far front was getting ready to move.

Kristobel and Lark waved to me. Lark was lugging a box labeled "Lost and Found," while Kristobel had a black garbage bag. Kristobel stopped and picked up a red hoodie, which she tossed in Lark's box before using a grabber-reacher stick to add a coffee cup to the garbage bag.

This was the true Elyan Hollow spirit. Getting out here and taking care of business because it needed to happen.

"No Jack?" Danby asked as she walked up.

"He's napping at home since I didn't think he wanted to get back on the float." Although he clearly wanted to be my side, so maybe I should feel guilty about leaving him at home.

"I was so worried when I saw Jack fly off the float. Also impressed since I wasn't sure how he'd managed to escape. But I didn't want my furry buddy to get hurt. Some of the kids on the float wanted to follow Jack, but we kept them under control. Gosh, it was scary," Danby said.

"Could you see what happened?"

She shook her head. "We heard the explosions, and the floats in front of us all stopped, and everyone bailed. The kids ahead of us scattered, and some poor kid tripped over the curb and had the worst nosebleed. We did our best to herd them straight into the taproom and waited out the panic. The little kids wanted to huddle in the far corner. But Ash was great. She found a towel for the bloody nose kid, and even managed to make cocoa for everyone. I swear all of their parents were relieved to see their kids safely ensconced in the taproom."

"I didn't know Ash even had cocoa." It wasn't on the menu.

"It was for the kitchenette the upstairs hotel rooms use. I asked as we waited for everyone's parents to show up."

"That was nice of Ash." And typical.

"Colby told me about Ivy," Danby said.

"Did you ever meet her?"

Danby nodded. "Briefly yesterday. Colby and I picked up sandwiches from my parents' shop and headed to the Pumpkin Plaza to eat them, and Ivy was in the plaza with some guy. She beelined over to us when she saw Colby."

"Colby didn't mention it."

"Probably because she and Ivy got into a screaming fight. Colby doesn't like to lose control." Danby tsked.

"What'd they fight about?" Colby and Ivy had a public argument in Elyan Hollow's town square?

Not good at all.

"Ivy asked Colby what it felt like to be a pity bridesmaid. She said that Raven only picked Colby since she'd be in town and . . ." Danby's voice trailed off.

I could fill in part of the blank even if I didn't know the specifics. "Ivy said something about me?"

"Yeah." Danby looked away. "She said you'd do the grunt work for Raven like always, and Colby being on hand meant that Raven had two servants."

"Thanks, Ivy," I said.

"It seemed like BS to me," Danby said.

A few thoughts and memories clicked together in my mind. "I suspect Ivy was always threatened by my relationship with Raven. This was years ago, but Ivy was always jealous of Raven's time. If we were all together, she'd always want to prove she knew Raven better than I did. She'd tried to set up mini competitions and make Raven choose one of us."

"How did you react?"

"I ignored her, assuming that not engaging was the best path, which annoyed her, so I kept with it. I'd pretend I didn't understand what she was saying, or if she tried to get Raven to leave a hangout, I'd pretend it was a great idea, and we should all go. I tried to keep Raven from getting caught in the middle."

"Raven let Ivy treat you that way? That doesn't show Raven in a very good light. I wouldn't let someone treat one of my friends that way." Danby crossed her arms over her chest.

Maybe this was one of the reasons Colby was so willing to push back against Ivy's behavior. She was standing up for me since I couldn't be bothered to. I should tell Colby that Ivy had never managed to get under my skin. I'd found her obnoxious, but she'd never found the right weak spot to push to get inside my head.

Although Ivy had tried.

I nodded, which made a new wave of sorrow fill me. "When you say it that way, you have a point. Once we graduated, we all took different paths and ended up in different cities, so I avoided Ivy. I was mostly successful until this weekend, so I never thought about how Raven reacted to Ivy's comments."

"Still, Raven should've stuck up for you." Danby's tone told me she would never budge from this point of view. Which ignited a sliver of warmth deep inside. I'm not sure I deserved the Snow sisters or their parents, but my life was immensely more prosperous by having them in it.

"Raven and Ivy were weirdly enmeshed. I always thought it was like Colby and me. Some people are naturally closer, and Raven has been a good friend," I said. "And speaking of friends. Colby didn't take the high road in the Pumpkin Plaza, did she?"

"Colby told Ivy that it was ironic being called a servant by a parasitic infection. Amongst other things," Danby said. She raised her eyebrows. "You know what's weird? I think the guy Ivy had been with took photos of them yelling at each other."

"That must've been Nate, and yes, he seems to enjoy photographing people at their worst. Although I think he'd call it their most authentic." I wondered if he'd post a series of "angry people arguing" portraits.

I could see the value of having stock photos of people showing a gauntlet of emotions, as they'd be helpful as reference photos when I work on my current graphic novel in progress. But I couldn't imagine photographing drama as a hobby.

"Alec!" I said. Our float driver walked up and smiled brightly when he saw Danby and me. Alec has his commercial driver's license and a truck strong enough to pull our Halloween floats. He'd been coming into the bookshop with his kids, who'd been a few grades ahead of me for my entire life, and he'd started bringing in the next generation last year when his son's wife had twins.

"It's good to see our fearless leader made it through the battles unscathed," Alec said.

"It was a valiant fight," I said.

"Bailey even saved Georgie! Do you know her, Alec? The little three-year-old?"

"Can't say I do."

"She's a regular at the shop with her mom and brother. Bailey is going to be Georgie's hero from now on," Danby said. She clapped her hands, which were encased in green-and-white-striped hand warmers.

"Actually, Jack is her new hero," I said. "She hugged him first, and I had to coax her to let me pick her up."

It wasn't long before the road cleared in front of us, and we were able to move the float. The float being in motion again felt like a good omen, and when we passed a couple of children, I wished they could've seen the float in its full glory.

Chapter 8

The idea of continuing with the wedding prep despite Ivy's death felt awkward and unfeeling. But Raven texted us that our mani-pedi appointment wasn't refundable. She said that even if the wedding was called off, we should get our nails done, and she hoped to see us there.

Once the float was safely stored in the garage, I checked in with my grandfather and asked if he'd take Jake outside. He quickly responded with a photo of Jack napping in the grass in the backyard.

We'd dismantle the float next week, then start it all again next year, provided the parade, and the town, survived this year's tragedy.

I'd be a bit early, but I headed, once again, downtown. There's a reason why I only buy shoes or boots designed for walking for my everyday go-tos.

The Spooky Town Spa is about as far away from the river as you can get while staying in downtown Elyan Hollow. If I'd kept going a few blocks, I'd cross Highway 30, which runs from Portland to Astoria along the Columbia River.

At one point, the spa's building had been a gas and service station, as the retro design indicated. But instead of gas pumps, the covered front had a handful of picnic tables under a large awning, with the new Grindstone coffee and bagel cart parked to one side. I was early, so I ordered a drink from the cart's simple menu. Their logo looked like a tombstone, with a cup of coffee with steam rising from it like a ghost. I liked it, although the line work could be a little cleaner.

I'd been to the Spooky Town Spa before but didn't visit very often. My life was too active for nail polish, which I ended up chipping off whenever I tried to look fancy. Calling their work manicures or pedicures almost felt like a diss since they'd turned the process into an art form. But as I waited for my house special matcha latte, I turned and analyzed the colorful building.

I loved how they'd renovated the old gas station, bringing it back to life. The building had been repainted in orange and white stripes, but the front half was mainly made of ceiling-to-floor windows, which let in tons of natural light. The front half of the business, which was nails to the left and hair salon to the right, shared a central desk, which was a wavy half circle that screamed retro cool. The waxing, facial, and massage studios were in the back half of the building, in private rooms away from the windows.

"Your matcha is ready," the barista told me. The logo on his pumpkin-orange T-shirt matched the cart.

"Thanks."

"You work at the bookstore, right? I think I've seen you there," the barista said.

I nodded, although I didn't recognize him. But the shop can be busy and I haven't waited on every single customer that's graced our door.

"Do you know if the owner has ever considered adding a coffee shop?" The barista leaned forward.

"I'm the owner. While I'd love to add a tea or coffee shop, we don't have the space." Not that I hadn't dreamed of adding a café before, which I could name Potboiler. We could name the drinks after some of my favorite books. There are the obvious drink options, like a Sherlock Holmes–inspired London Fog Tea Latte. I'd yet to decide on the ingredients of an Alice in Wonderland–inspired option, which would need to be called Drink Me. And we could offer literary tea blends.

But it wasn't suitable for my bookshop, even if it was a fun dream.

"You could carve out a corner of the store and add one in," the barista said.

Yes, by eliminating books.

"That's not something we plan to do. It looks like you've got a great spot here," I said. I didn't tell him he was on the opposite side of downtown from the beloved Morning Broo with its fantastic outdoor patio, so this location seemed like a good business plan. And if he needed to move, his cart had wheels. "Thanks again."

I took a sip of the matcha, which was excellent. My taste buds quickly told me the "house special" part of the latte was mint, which balanced nicely against the matcha's earthy bite, and I was willing to bet he'd used vanilla syrup to sweeten the drink.

Hmm, with the right signage, Grindstone could find customers from people commuting down Highway 30, or driving out to the coast. We couldn't see the highway from here, but we were maybe a fourth of a mile away, with the train tracks between us. Heading in that direction and crossing the highway would take us to several factories that helped fund the town's economy, and the cart wouldn't be too far out of their way, and they'd miss the bustle of downtown.

But I didn't say anything, since something about the barista in the cart, whom I assumed was the owner, had annoyed me.

Raven walked up to my picnic table, followed by Harmony, who had a pouty look on her face.

We gave each other a hug. "How are things?" I asked.

"Awful." Raven's eyes were tinged with red, and her black T-shirt and leather jacket made her look more washed out than normal. "I talked with Ivy's mom this morning."

"That must've been awful."

"Ivy was her mom's only child. She's devastated, of course. She's going to see if she can make it here—"

Harmony snorted. "She's in jail."

"She thinks she might be able to get a compassionate leave," Raven snapped. She glanced at me. "Ivy's mother has always been troubled. I promised to take care of everything, since clearly, she's not in the position to handle Ivy's funeral arrangements."

"What about Ivy's dad?" I asked. Colby walked up, her hair pulled back into a messy bun. But she looked ready to do battle.

"The jerk left the country when Ivy was four and is now remarried with a new family. Ivy hadn't seen him for decades. I left a voicemail asking him to call me, but I haven't heard back." Raven sounded like she was holding back tears.

Compassion flew through me. Poor Ivy. She must've felt alone in the world, which might've been why she'd clung so hard to Raven.

"Aren't his new kids young enough to be Ivy's?" Harmony asked.

"Are you still trying to stir things up?" Colby asked. "A woman died. Does it matter if she had younger half-siblings?"

"It's just weird," Harmony said. "Imagine having siblings twenty years younger than you."

"It's not that strange," Colby said.

I realized Colby was trying to protect me. My oldest half-sibling is fifteen years younger than me, as my mother waited until she was in her early thirties to have her second child and had her final child two years later.

"It must explain why Ivy was such a train wreck. Honestly, you guys. She was a mess," Harmony said. Her tone was oddly gloating.

"Harmony, why don't you leave," Raven said. She'd half turned so her sister was in her sight, like if she didn't look at her sister, she wouldn't exist.

It's the same way Jack handles puppies when he runs out of patience.

"But I need to get a manicure." Harmony's tone had switched to her patented whine. Had this tone ever been successful? From what I've seen, it just annoyed everyone.

"I'll pay for you to come back tomorrow without me. But there's no way you're coming into the spa with me today." Raven's tone was serious, like she wasn't going to budge.

Harmony stared at her sister for a moment, then flounced off. Her curls bounced on her shoulder blades. I remembered Ramona

Quimby getting in trouble in *Ramona the Pest* for pulling her classmate Susan's ringlets and saying "boing-ing!"

I now understood Ramona's temptation.

And Harmony's curls really were lovely. I wondered if they were fully natural, and what exactly she did to maintain them. Maybe, if I decided that I needed to talk to her, that'd be my in.

"Between Harmony and Emmett's mom, I'm ready to punch someone. How do you think it would feel to actually do it?"

"Actually punch someone?" Colby asked.

"Yes. I've only dreamed about it."

"I'd imagine it would hurt your knuckles and not be worth it in the long run," I said.

"Says the practical one," Raven said.

"Other forms of revenge would be way more fun," I added. "And more creative than punching. I mean, almost anyone can learn to throw a punch. But a well-crafted revenge? Priceless."

Raven blinked. "C'mon, let's go inside. It'll just be the three of us. Emmett's mom drove by the spa not long after they got to town and immediately hated it, even though she didn't go inside. She decided to go into Portland for a tranquil, uplifting experience."

Given the snide tone at the end of her statement, Raven was quoting Emmett's mother.

"Spooky Town is definitely a peppier spa than some," I said. "But the massage rooms are lovely. Very tranquil. Lots of candles and mood music." I mean, yes, the one time I visited and used a gift certificate for a massage, the room was designed to look like a crypt. But it was dark, and the masseuses played soothing music, and it was an excellent massage. I'd almost fallen asleep.

"It's the bridal party!" one of the front desk workers said as we walked inside. As Raven talked to the front desk worker, I glanced at Colby.

"Are you okay? You seem tense."

"Hayes' project ran into a snag. He might not come home until mid-November, or even early December."

"I'm sorry." I was also looking forward to Hayes coming home, but I wasn't married to him. He was a good friend to me, but I knew Colby's life felt muted without him around.

We were escorted to three pedicure chairs on the wall. Raven sat in the middle, with both of us on either side.

"Is it terrible of me if I don't cancel the wedding?" Raven asked after we settled in.

One of the nail techs returned with glasses of grapefruit sparkling water for us.

"I don't know," I said. "When you look back, will you regret postponing?"

"Or not postponing?" Colby added. "And no one wants to think of the financial side of something like this, but could you afford to schedule this again? I'm assuming you'd be out everything you've paid for the wedding since it would be such a late cancel."

"Honestly, I feel guilty about this, but I was starting to wish I hadn't asked Ivy to be part of the wedding party. Dealing with her, Harmony, and Emmett's parents is making me wish we'd eloped." Raven shook her head slowly. "And part of me feels guilty because now I have one less problem person to deal with."

"I can't blame you for feeling that way. Ivy was a nightmare," Colby said.

I glanced at Colby, wondering why I assumed there was a second, unspoken part of Colby's statement: that Ivy always was a nightmare, so what had Raven expected?

"That's not fair," Raven said. But our techs started the pedicure, and we quieted down.

The Spooky Town Spa only offers dry manicures and pedicures. Seeing my feet in collagen socks made me giggle as the nail tech shaped my toenails and prepared to paint them with a magnetic nail polish.

Which wouldn't be visible under my Converse sneakers, but oh well. I'd know they were pretty.

Detective Whitlock walked into the building and headed in our direction.

"Hi, Detective. Are you here for a manicure?" I asked.

"He looks like a pedicure man to me," Colby said.

"Hmm, I bet anyone with a stressful job would appreciate the massages," I said.

"Let's be fair, people with not-so-stressful jobs also deserve a good massage." Colby looked at me and nodded, while Raven stared down at her feet. Like she didn't want to be near the police detective again.

The detective looked at Colby. "I'd like to ask you a few questions. It'd be best if you came to the station."

"If you want to question me, do it here," Colby said. She leaned back in her chair. "I haven't done anything wrong, and I'm not leaving."

Detective Whitlock studied Colby for a moment, then glanced at me before returning his gaze to my friend. Raven was still pretending to be invisible.

"Last night, you were seen carrying a sword," the detective said. "I would like to see the sword."

"You're partially right. I was carrying a sword handle," Colby said.

"There's a difference?" the detective asked.

"A sword has a full blade, while mine is just a handle I made in the library's 3D printer when I was showing a group of teens how to make their own. I had to lead by example. It's part of the job description," Colby said. She'd leaned back in her manicure chair like this wasn't a big deal, but she was more tense than she wanted to appear.

Recognition dawned. "Is it from your 'build your own sword day' at the library? I heard it was awesome," I said. I was telling the truth, as several teen readers had raved about the program and showed me the swords they'd made in the library's maker lab.

"It was. I meant to make the full sword but never got beyond the hilt. But once I put the hilt in a sheath on my belt and wore a cloak, it looked like I had a sword. But I didn't have to deal with one hitting my calves, so I never bothered finishing the project." Colby turned her head and looked at the detective. "But if you'd like, I can drop my sword handle by the police station. It's made of resin."

Detective Whitlock grunted and wrote something down. "Where were you when the explosions happened?"

"Bailey and I were standing together. Her bookshop's float had just cruised by, with a herd of kids following. I couldn't tell what group they were supposed to be with."

"How did you react to the explosion?" The detective eyed Colby and something told me he wouldn't miss much.

"I tried to get everyone to stop panicking. One of the witches in the bachelorette party—that's a woman dressed in a witch costume, not a wiccan or someone with magic—was frozen in fear, so I pulled everyone up the street, out of the surge of the crowd. Raven grabbed her other arm. The other witches followed us, along with the rest of Raven's entourage. I thought Bailey was right behind us. If I had thought about Ivy, and I don't think I did, I would've thought she was part of our group."

"I was behind you, but then I found Georgie, and then Jack found us," I said. "Detective? How's your daughter?"

"Unharmed, thanks to you, although she insisted her knee needed three *101 Dalmatians* bandages. She'll be fine," Detective Whitlock said. "She was clingy last night, but she was impressed that Jack came to her rescue. She wants her own giant dog now."

"Maybe she'll settle for being able to visit Jack at the bookshop. She's welcome anytime," I said. And not just because her mother was a regular.

The detective's gaze returned to Colby. "You've fought with Miss Monroe several times."

"Fought is a strong word. I interrupted a few times when she and Harmony were being knuckleheads."

"And you had a loud altercation downtown in the plaza. And that wasn't the only one, but it might have been the loudest, although I've heard the one in Morning Broo was a doozy. Although the acoustics in that place aren't the best."

Colby's expression didn't waver. "Ivy was being a knucklehead again. But it was just words."

"You told her to chill out, else she'd regret it. Or something to that effect."

"Hyperbole. I also told her to go step on Legos."

"Seriously?" Detective Whitlock had chilled out slightly, but I had to wonder if it was just an act, a way to lure Colby into complacency. Did he really think the local Youth Services Librarian was hiding murderous tendencies?

"You haven't stepped on Legos before? Let me tell you, it's a terrible idea to have pajama story hour right after a 'fun with Legos' session. I didn't make the mistake of going barefoot after a library Lego session ever again."

Colby let out a deep breath. "Listen, Detective, Ivy and I clearly didn't get along. But I'd rather she be here, hopefully stepping on Legos, than what happened. The only revenge I'd debated was sending her a glitter bomb."

"You debated making a bomb?"

I winced. Wrong choice of words, considering last night's excitement.

Colby shook her head while an exasperated look crossed her face. "It's not actually a bomb. It's just glitter in an envelope, usually."

"Someone would do this?" The detective sounded skeptical, but I suspected he was playing dumb. There's no way he'd never heard of a glitter bomb.

"Because glitter is the most annoying craft supply in the entire universe. To be frankly honest, despite plenty of temptation, I didn't do it because Ivy was staying in one of the rooms above the taproom, and I'm friends with Ash, who owns the place. And Ash doesn't deserve the aftereffects. It would end up in every nook and crevice of her hotel and haunt her with glittery doom for years." Colby leaned back and closed her eyes.

"Please don't glitter bomb my bridal party," Raven said. "Although I can text you Harmony's home address."

Colby laughed, but the sound quickly faded. This wasn't the right time, especially since the detective was staring at them.

"Miss Snow, please let me know if you leave the area," Detective Whitlock said gruffly, using that as his parting line.

Once he'd disappeared out the front door of the spa, Colby said, "Like I'd actually kill anyone."

"You should talk to Evelyn before speaking with the police again," I said.

"You think I need a lawyer? I'm innocent," Colby said.

"You argued with Ivy all over town. Evelyn would say it's a way to protect your interests. She didn't want me speaking with police last year. She said innocent people can talk themselves into trouble once the police suspect them," I said.

"This is ridiculous."

I glanced at the nail tech, who'd painted my toenails black and orange, a cat's eye that looked beautiful. Since it was a gel, I knew it'd be a pain to take off, but I'd enjoy the beauty while it lasted.

I told myself to enjoy this all too brief moment of peace since trouble was brewing around us.

Chapter 9

After our spa appointment, Colby headed to her parents' house, and I walked with Raven. We headed to Goblin Gate Park.

"I should do the corn maze when I'm here," Raven said. She nodded at the maze, which had a line of people waiting to enter. The high school booster's hot cider cart was doing a brisk business. Setting up next to the maze had been a smart idea, and I'm sure other groups would fight over the spot next year.

"The maze is always well done." I'd avoided it this year. Maybe I'd go through it again, but I wasn't sure. But the Halloween crowd were clearly still fans, despite the events of last year. So maybe the parade would be just as popular next year.

"I know you were never close to Ivy," Raven said.

"I didn't hate her. We just didn't vibe," I said. "It's normal for people to have multiple friend groups."

"Yeah, you were never into the EDM scene like Ivy and me," Raven said with a half smile. "Although Ivy was into it way more than me."

Raven was right; the electronic dance music scene was never my style. But Raven had loved it, presumably because she loved every chance to dress up like a unicorn, or fairy, or whatever had taken her fancy at the moment.

"Do you still go to raves?" I asked.

"Sometimes, but going makes me feel old. I miss it, but I miss how much fun I had when I was my early twenties," Raven said. "Ivy still went. She stopped for a while, or at least claimed she did, but I suspect it was a business opportunity for her."

"Business?"

"Ivy kept trying to go legit, or at least she said she was. Get a real job, meaning one that pays taxes and doesn't risk a prison sentence. When we were in school, she did a brisk business selling Molly and similar at raves, plus she hooked some of our classmates up. She kept trying to get out, but the money was too easy. She said she was trying to make a fresh start when she left Portland for Denver. But I suspect she started dealing again, given her Instagram posts." Raven looked straight ahead.

"I remember hearing rumors about Ivy dealing in college," I said. As I studied Raven's profile, she looked even more statuesque than normal.

"Ivy was the go-to person on campus. She didn't deal anything too hardcore. Lots of Adderall during finals. Mushrooms. She expanded her business a little off-campus, but only by referral. She did it for the money. She wasn't in deep with a gang, or anything. Or at least she said she wasn't." Raven picked at a thread in her black T-shirt.

"She couldn't find a regular job? Or work-study?" I'd picked up several work-study jobs as an undergrad, spending the last two years as the lab coordinator of a multimedia computer lab during the school year, and working at Lazy Bones over the holidays and summers, plus the occasional weekend when they needed someone. I'd appreciated the excuse to drive home and see my grandparents, use their laundry room, while being paid for hours worked in the store.

A thought struck me. Should we tell Detective Whitlock about Ivy's drug-dealing past? Could a supplier she'd angered sometime in the past have found her here in town? Or a rival?

"She tried to find a normal job. Ivy had a pretty tough life. Her mom went to jail when she was little, and her father ditched her not long after and moved out of the country. He's never come back, and refused to pay to fly Ivy out to visit him. Her grandmother raised her, but then she died when Ivy was a freshman in high school, and her father refused to take her in. Ivy didn't have any other family."

"That's rough," I said. I couldn't imagine needing to navigate life as a teenager without my grandparents. It would've been so easy for Ivy to make bad choices.

"Ivy's social worker thought she was a success story, a foster kid who got into a good school. And Ivy didn't want to let her down. And I think she wanted to succeed as a sort of eff-you to her dad for abandoning her. She started out with a part-time job, but she made more selling Ritalin to rich kids, as she used to say, for less effort than busting her butt waiting tables or washing dishes."

"I can't imagine Ivy working in food service," I said. She had always seemed languid, moving at her own pace regardless of the beat of the world around her. I couldn't picture her hustling around, taking orders from other people.

Raven laughed, but I could hear the grief inside. "She was fired from at least one restaurant."

Not a surprise, but I didn't say anything. Raven was clearly in enough pain already.

"Ivy was a bit of a lost soul, but I always loved her," Raven said. "I mean, you and Colby are great friends who have my back, and you have your lives together. Being around you makes me feel like I can make the world a better place. And our talks are epic. But Ivy . . . Well, she needed me. I wanted to help her. To fix her."

I wanted to ask Raven if her friendship with Ivy had been one-sided and if Ivy had given as much as she took.

Raven must've heard herself.

"And it's not like Ivy was just a taker. If I was having a terrible day or doubting myself, I'd video chat with Ivy, and she'd always prop me up. I could show her the worst sides of me, the side I don't want people to see, and she never made me feel bad or guilty." Raven looked at the ground. "I'm not claiming Ivy was a saint. But her good side made up for her flaws, at least to me. But it's now clear not everyone feels the same."

By everyone did she mean Harmony and Colby, or had other people weighed in about Ivy?

It'd be terrible to lose one of your best friends, only to find out that other people close to you hadn't valued her. Hadn't thought she was worthy of a spot in your life.

We left the park and walked downtown, which had mostly returned to its usual state, except for one float, a boat that I guessed was a zombie version of the Lewis and Clark journey. It was still on Main Street, causing a minor traffic jam, but two guys in crossing guard vests were directing traffic.

The crowds were back, with tourists buying candy apples from Wicked Treats and carrying bags from the local boutiques. The town may have survived last night's double tragedy.

Lazy Bones Bookshop might survive.

As Raven stopped at Haunted Artifacts to check out a squat milk glass vase in the window, I followed her inside, my thoughts whirling.

Had Ivy shown the worst sides of herself to Raven or just the best? Did Raven realize that what she thought was Ivy's worst sides were, in fact, fundamental parts of her personality? I was skeptical that Ivy even had a best side, which made me feel mean.

"I'm going to put little black eyes on this and turn it into a ghost," Raven said. She motioned to her Haunted Artifacts bag.

I left Raven at the front door of the Sleepy Hollow and headed to one of the benches along the river path. It was a beautiful day, with cool, crisp air. The trees on the other bank were a dramatic mix of green and orange as the seasons changed.

But instead of admiring the view, I pulled out my phone and looked up Ivy's Instagram account. The sight of my newly polished nails briefly distracted me. Those weren't the fingers I was used to.

Given my conversation with Raven, I wasn't surprised to see quite a few of Ivy's posts featured Ivy in club wear. She was prone to showing off her skinny abs in bra tops or tiny T-shirts, usually paired with short skirts or booty shorts, with colorful wigs finishing off the looks. To me, she looked too thin in the recent photos, while her photos from a year before she looked better. Still very lean, but healthier.

Ivy also had been fond of fairy costumes, with iridescent wings and glittery makeup. I read one of her posts: "Come join me in another realm! The journey is the best part." She mentioned a rave and that she'd be the fairy in pink and silver with fairy dust to share.

Was this how Ivy advertised she'd be around with illicit goods to sell? Raven had thought Ivy had slipped back into dealing based on her Instagram posts, after all.

And I wondered if Ivy had been using her own products a little too frequently, hence her sickly appearance.

I walked up the hill to downtown.

I had a mission.

Chapter 10

As I walked through downtown, my feet paused outside the Museum of Peculiar Oddities gift shop and waited for my brain to catch up.

Pie sounded like the perfect pick-me-up.

The Museum was across the side street from the Elyan Mortuary & Deli Bottle Shop, which was a good pairing of quirky small-town charm; the Museum was really a gift shop, despite the name, while the taproom was thankfully not a mortuary and didn't have a deli. Ash's taproom had been a firehouse at one point; the gift shop had been a hair salon for as long as I could remember. The owner had retired last year, and the unique brick building had quietly changed hands. Brown paper had quickly covered the windows as the new owner remodeled, keeping the business under wraps until he was ready to unveil it to the world. My uncle, Hunter, back while he was still talking to me, had been annoyed the building hadn't made it onto the open market, as he claimed he had buyers clamoring for downtown commercial real estate.

Presumably, these were the same buyers he had wanted to sell the building that housed Lazy Bones Bookshop and the law firm above to.

Elyan Hollow was prospering, but there are camps in town that see different paths the town should follow. Hunter was part of the group who saw the area as ripe for redevelopment. I fall into the side that wants to preserve as much historical charm as possible, especially downtown. I'm not opposed to intelligent changes that would make the town better for all of our residents. Like everywhere, we need to add more housing. But there's no need to tear down downtown in the process.

The door from the sidewalk opened into a light-filled lobby. One door led to the open Museum-slash–gift shop, and the other door, which should lead to another storefront, was covered with brown paper. I'd heard thuds inside when walking by, making me think some type of construction was underway. But there weren't any hints. No "Coming Soon" signs. No contractor names. But that was a mystery for another time.

Because my eyes immediately snapped onto what was quite possibly the best addition to town ever.

A pie machine. Rex might be skeptical, but I could promise this was something we'd needed without realizing it.

I could buy one or several treats with one swipe of a credit card. I clicked the button to rotate through the offerings: two whole marionberry pies, each topped with a crust shaped like mini ghosts; several marionberry hand pies shaped like mini pumpkins; several slices of pecan pie; and a pack of four salted honey pie cookies.

"People keep asking me for apple pie, but it's my least favorite flavor," a voice said.

I turned. Finn, aka the owner. I briefly met Finn a few weeks ago when he dropped by the bookshop to say he'd love to participate in the Spooky Season Lit Festival next year. He was about my age and several inches taller, maybe about five foot nine. Green eyes and short brown hair that had to be cut to be purposefully messy. But it was his voice that had caught my attention then, and again now. It was surprisingly low and deep but smooth. I wondered if he moonlighted as a bass singer.

And whenever I saw Finn, a flash of recognition ignited in the back of my brain. But I couldn't place him.

"Apple pie is anticlimactic. It looks good, and everyone raves about it, but it tastes like mushy sadness, which is a tragedy because fresh apples are the best," I said. "Do you bake the pies yourself, then?"

My eyes trailed to the pastry boxes Finn was carrying.

"My initial plan was to bake all of them, but then Elspie—do you know her?"

I nodded. Elspie ran the Bake It Spooky Pie Company out of her home, and her work was in demand during the winter holidays. Her cookies were as tasty as her mouth-watering pie.

"Elspie approached me about supplying pies, and now it's about fifty-fifty, which is easier on me," Finn said. He put the pastry box on a side table and opened the pie machine with a key. Cold air puffed out.

Finn handed me a marionberry hand pie before opening his box and adding slices of pie to the machine on paper plates wrapped in plastic wrap.

"Umm . . ." I said.

"Call the hand pie a gift," Finn said. "Unless you'd prefer the salted honey pie cookies? I'm going to rotate those out as well."

"No, this is fantastic." As I watched Finn add pie to the vending machine, I studied the side of his face. His nose was slightly wavy, which gave his face character, and his long, curved eyelashes were the type that women use cosmetics to mimic. I knew I'd met him somewhere, once. But I couldn't match his face to the Rolodex of images in my brain.

"Why'd you choose Elyan Hollow for your shop?" I asked. Maybe his answer would give me a clue. Had Finn been a classmate at the university I'd attended? But if he had been, I'm sure I would've remembered him. He hadn't gone to Elyan Hollow High. My classmates from there were seared into my brain.

Not being able to place him continued to rankle me.

"A town focused on quirky businesses and year-round Halloween spirit? Who could say no?" Finn said. His tone was amused, like he saw the punchline of a joke that was eluding me. "Can I help you with something, or did you just come in to salivate over the pies?"

"I was curious if I could get copies of your security footage from the parade."

"So, are you Velma? Or Daphne?" He crossed his arms over his gray-and-burgundy-striped sweater and leaned against the pie machine.

"What?"

"I guess you could see yourself as Scooby-Doo, but Velma is the brains of the group. Although you seem to have a twenty-twenty vision, unlike Velma, but perfect vision doesn't always mean people see clearly."

"I don't see myself as a *Scooby-Doo* character." I felt like Finn was talking about two different things at once, and it was making my brain tie into knots.

"Nancy Drew? Trixie Belden? Wait, Miss Marple?"

I smiled. "I'm not opposed to sitting in the corner and knitting." Under that rationale, I could also be Patricia Wentworth's Miss Silver, who emerged in book form two years before Agatha Christie's creation.

"Miss Marple is always the smartest person in the room, although not everyone realizes they could have gotten away with their dastardly deeds if it hadn't been for that pesky old lady." Finn straightened up.

"Is this your way of saying yes, you'll share your security footage with me?" I asked.

"I guess so. I can't block your burgeoning career as a detective, which I've heard gossip about, but don't do anything stupid. If someone really was murdered downtown, then I bet the killer won't hesitate to stop you if you get too close," Finn said. His head tilted slightly as he studied me.

"I just want to look at the footage from the parade," I said.

"Are you sure it's a murder?"

I shrugged. "All I know is that a member of my friend's bridal party is dead."

Finn motioned for me to follow him into the shop. We walked around the presumably life-sized Sasquatch, which wore a buffalo-check scarf similar to one of Jack's bandanas, around a few displays of locally made goods, and ended up in his office in the back, separated from the front register by a glass window with open blinds.

"What's your email address?" Finn asked.

"Bailey at lazy bones books dot com," I said.

As he clicked around on his desktop computer, I glanced back into his shop, which was being staffed by a high school student I vaguely recognized. Each section of the shop had unique flair. One corner was dedicated to retro video game memorabilia. A Pac-Man clock caught my eye, along with a giant Q*bert. Another corner had taxidermy. An entire stand had pun-named candles.

"I've emailed you a link to the video footage. I assumed that was better than clogging your email with multiple video files." Finn leaned back in his chair and laced his fingers over his flat stomach.

"Thanks, Finn. And thank you for the pie." As I walked out, I noticed a stack of invoices on a table near his office door. FinnRetroLLC.

Interesting.

A few stores hadn't responded to my email request for video footage, so I stopped at the next store I walked by.

HalloQueen.

Marnie was doing something at the front counter, and she smiled when she saw me. "How's it going, Bailey?"

"Good, considering everything."

"It must've been a rough weekend for you and your friends. I heard that someone from your friend's bachelorette party died. Is that true?"

"Sadly, yes."

"It's always hard to lose someone," Marnie said. "Are you here for a specific reason?"

"Did you see my email about collecting Saturday night security camera footage?"

Marnie blew out her lips. "Hmm, no, but let me see." She tapped around on her laptop. "Here's your email. I filter all the Chamber of Commerce messages to a folder I only deal with every few days. It stresses me out to read the messages daily."

"Wise decision." Some of my fellow business owners were wonderful, and others were way too intense over tiny details that ultimately didn't matter. Their petty grievances could flare out into anger that didn't feel minor, and I realized I had thoughts here to ponder later.

"And while I don't see how it will help, I'll send you a link to the video footage later tonight. The exterior cameras mainly cover the doors and windows, and the interior cameras won't be helpful at all." Marnie tapped around on her laptop.

"Thank you," I said. "Hey, you know that Pendleton jacket you put aside for me? I'll buy it."

A frown crossed Marnie's face. "I'm sorry to say that jacket has been sold."

A sad feeling filtered through me. I guess the jacket and I weren't meant to be, but I should've bought it when I had the chance. It was perfect, and vintage. A jacket like that wasn't going to cross my path every day.

Marnie laughed. "Cheer up. After you left after picking out your bridesmaid dress, your pal Raven bought it for you."

"Really?" She hadn't said anything about it.

"Yeah, Raven and that slender bottle blonde—the one who ended up with the velvet dress—tried on things for a while after you left. The friend told Raven that she should buy the jacket for you. That you had been doing a ton of things for the wedding, and it would make an appropriate gift."

"That was nice of Ivy." Suspiciously so.

"Then she made some stupid crack about thrift shop items being the perfect gifts for some people, but I ignored it since Raven bought sundresses for both of them and a couple outfits for herself. Plus your jacket, which I have for you. One second."

Had Ivy actually been disinterested when she recommended

Raven buy me the jacket? Or did she flash a kind, thoughtful side to keep Raven ensnared as a friend?

Marnie brought me the '49er jacket, which she wrapped in tissue and reverently put in a HalloQueen bag.

With the handles of the bag holding my new jacket over my arm, I headed to the next shop and squeaked in five minutes before it closed.

The Eye of Newt Apothecary has hosted events for the Spooky Season Lit Festival. It's not one of my usual haunts. The displays of crystals and other woo-woo products were beautiful, and their space was airy, and calm, so it'd worked well for ticketed events with tea and cookies, even if Clarity always wanted to read my tea leaves. I'd heard good things about the shop-made bath bombs, but I hadn't shopped much in the apothecary.

Bath bombs. Wrong choice of words again.

"Hi, Clarity," I said.

"Are you here for video footage?" Clarity asked. Her hair was pulled back into a headscarf, and I'm always jealous of anyone who can convince a scarf to stay on her head.

"Guilty as charged," I said.

Clarity handed over a thumb drive. "I hope you find what you're looking for, although I sense your journey won't lead you to your preferred destination."

"Thank you for this." I held up the thumb drive.

"You knew the woman who died?" Clarity asked. She fixed the collar of her flowy shawl neck cardigan.

When I nodded, she asked, "Can I see a photo of her?"

I pulled out my phone and pulled up a photo that Raven had texted, showing a group of us from our college days. I zoomed in on Ivy, then turned the screen toward Clarity. "This is older, but—"

"That's who I thought. She came in here," Clarity said.

"Oh?" I tilted my head slightly without thinking about it, then straightened it when I realized what I was doing.

"And she stole a necklace. It was one of a kind with pyrite that I was very fond of. Pyrite is supposed to promote peace, but stealing it was an excellent way to ensure she'd have the opposite." Clarity plucked a necklace from a nearby rack. "Pyrite looks like this. It's also known as fool's gold."

"I can't make any promises, but I can see about getting the necklace back for you." Clarity's intensity unnerved me, but I assumed her comment was about cosmic justice, not any actions she'd directly taken. If Raven was handling Ivy's funeral, she was most likely also responsible for her worldly possessions, or at least, taking care of the items Ivy had brought with her to the wedding. I knew Raven would keep an eye out for the necklace.

"I reported the theft to the police since I had video footage of the criminal in the act," Clarity said.

"When was this?" I decided to make a timeline of Ivy's time in Elyan Hollow. Which I suspected was filled with arguments and, evidentially, shoplifting.

"When she stole the necklace? Yesterday afternoon. I reported it to the police that evening. I was going to see if she was at the bachelorette party you'd invited me to. Your text invitation arrived exactly when I needed it as if the goddess was keeping an eye out for me. I'm glad I waited to share the screen capture of her, since our fellow business owners don't need to worry about her stealing anymore."

Clarity confronting Ivy for shoplifting would've been a train wreck. "If she was shoplifting from other stores, she might have angered quite a few local businesses."

"Or it was karma."

We chatted for a moment longer, then I hustled out so Clarity could close up for the day.

Chapter 11

All I wanted was to go home and read, hopefully, while eating snacks while a giant white dog snoozed nearby.

In real life, Jack would most likely interrupt my reading with frantic Pyr paws, meaning he'd slap me with one of his giant front paws, letting me know he'd never been pet before, ever, but I could dream.

Instead, my steps took me to the taproom and Ash's event.

The silver lining was that I could talk to Olivia. There was something hinky about her reaction to Ivy the other night.

And let's be honest, nothing is better than tacos after a long day. Especially if that day was mostly sad.

The taproom was about half full, but one of Ash's bartenders was hustling around, loading empty pint glasses in an almost packed dish bin, so I must've come in during a lull. I quickly noticed Emmett and his friends off to one side, so I mustered up a smile.

Ash spotted me first, and her smile was genuine. She called across the room, "Bailey! I have the perfect beer for you to sample."

As I headed her way, I realized Rex had been talking to Ash at the bar. He held a half-empty pint. Ash stood at the taps pouring a pint. She turned and looked over her shoulder. "Thank you for coming, Bailey."

"Of course." Considering how reluctant my feet had been to carry me toward the taproom, it felt disingenuous. "It looks like your pop-up is going well."

Ash handed me a pint of a golden beer. "As I said, this brewery is the biggest one to hit the scene for a while. People are coming from all over."

"It's nice that zero proof is becoming a thing. I used to order a beer and nurse it all night," Rex said.

"Bailey, do you have time to help me with something tomorrow?" Ash asked.

"That sounds ominous. But yes, depending upon the time." I took a sip. The initial flavor was good, but the final taste felt a tad flat compared to an alcoholic beer. But it was good.

"I'll text," Ash said. Her eyes were focused behind me, and I turned to see a large group streaming in. Ash and her bartenders sprung into action.

Olivia rushed by us with a tray full of food and dropped it off at a table before practically sprinting back to Boorito.

"Let's move out of the line of fire," Rex said. We headed to one of the standing tables along the wall crafted out of an old wine barrel. These are always my favorites, and I've thought about acquiring one for home. Maybe someday, when I have my own place.

"How was your trip? I should've asked when you came home."

"Busy since I was mostly teaching. But the retreat center was gorgeous."

We'd barely had time to talk before Emmett zeroed in on me. His friends had bellied up to the bar for another round, including the three witches from the ill-fated bachelorette party, and a few other women.

"Bailey, how are you recovering?" Emmett asked me. He leaned toward me with his hands in the pockets of his faded jeans.

"I'm okay." My words sounded hollow to my ears.

"Yesterday must've been so stressful for you. I can't imagine finding a body."

Rex's mouth fell open. "Body?"

We made eye contact. "You heard about the body at the parade, right?"

"After the explosion?"

"That's the one. It's a long story, but I found it."

"Bailey . . ." Rex reached out and awkwardly patted my shoulder.

Emmett eyed Rex, so I did the inevitable.

"Emmett, this is Rex. Rex, Emmett is marrying my friend Raven on Halloween."

Emmett's eyes brightened. "Hey, you're Bailey's father, right? Raven's told me about you two before."

Rex smiled and stood up straighter. "I am."

I wondered if this was a first for Rex, being recognized for his relation to me. If we'd grown up together, it'd be unmemorable.

"Ivy, the woman who died, was also in the bridal party," Emmett said.

"I'm sorry for your loss," Rex said.

"It wasn't really a loss for me, more for my bride-to-be. Ivy and I didn't see eye to eye much," Emmett said. "Raven sure had a blind spot when it came to Ivy. She put up with behaviors that she would've screamed at Harmony about."

"Oh?"

"I'm sad for her loved ones," Emmett said. His tone had gone more diplomatic. "But Ivy was always snarky to me when Raven wasn't in earshot. I told myself she was just jealous and afraid of losing Raven since our lives were changing in a different direction than Ivy's. We're not partying hard anymore, while Ivy was still going full force. And I suspect Ivy knew her tactics didn't work on me, and I wouldn't capitulate and do what she wanted the way Raven did. I hoped their friendship would wither after the wedding as Raven realized she could do better. Look at her other bridesmaids. You're all wonderful and easy to be around. And you've never hinted that I should send you money."

"You are always welcome to shop at my bookstore as a sign of support," I said.

Emmett laughed. "I already do. Raven and I order from you online at least monthly."

"Ah, yes, that explains a few of the science-related titles in Raven's orders." I'd always guessed those were gifts or for Emmett, since I'd doubted Raven was into popular science books, especially since when we talked about her reading, she always mentioned novels and comics.

"Where is Raven tonight?" I asked.

"She's getting dinner with her parents and grandparents, plus Harmony, so I'm sure they're having a blast," Emmett said.

Given the way Emmett had scowled when he said "Harmony," he wasn't on better terms with her than he'd been with Ivy. What did Raven think of Emmett's groomsmen? If they disliked fifty percent of each other's wedding parties, that had to be a bad omen. But as I'd told Raven, it's normal to have different friend groups. As long as Raven treated Emmett's friends with respect, and vice versa, I'm sure it'd be fine.

Emmett's crew came over with a round of beers.

"Did you know they have multiple nonalcoholic beers on tap for some reason? We got you a full-strength IPA instead." Someone handed Emmett a beer. "Be careful, it's like eight percent."

"It's your wedding!" one of the witches yelled, which led to a few whoops from Emmett's friends.

"Is the taco cart good?" one of the witches asked me.

"It's excellent."

"Good, 'cause we just put an order in, but it's not going to be ready for, like, an hour!"

"They must be slammed." Darn it. I hadn't put my food order in yet.

Olivia hustled past again, and it seemed like she was avoiding my eyes.

Or maybe she was just being run off her feet.

"You want another beer?" one of Emmett's friends asked.

"Nah, I'm good," I said. One was enough. I was tired enough that I didn't want to switch to anything with alcohol, because it'd been too easy to have a second to block out the pain of the weekend, only to regret it tomorrow when I woke up with a headache.

"How about you?" he asked Rex.

I'll say this for Emmett's friends: they were polite. Even if they liked to whoop a little too much.

"No, but thank you," Rex said. Rex glanced at me, then leaned over and spoke into my ear. "Any chance you'd like to grab dinner?"

"You know, I'd love that," I said.

We said goodbye to Emmett and his friends, settled up with Ash, and headed out onto the streets of Elyan Hollow.

Walking into Elyan Spirits, the posh cocktail bar on the other side of downtown from my usual haunt, aka Ash's taproom, almost felt like a betrayal. Even though I'd just been in her bar for the takeover.

But the small plates in Elyan Spirits were always fantastic, featuring seasonal ingredients almost exclusively locally sourced. And Rex clearly wanted to talk with me. Being with Rex was usually comforting, and while it wasn't reading at home with Jack level of mellow, it felt like the right choice for this sliver of time.

Growing up, my relationship with my mother was more like a sister, as my grandparents took on the primary parental roles in my life. My mother had left for college when I was a toddler, and started medical school across the country around the time I started first grade. By the time she'd been done with medical school and her subsequent residency, and moved back to Oregon with her husband, Spencer, to start new jobs, everyone said I was too settled into Elyan Hollow to change schools and move in with her. My roots in my grandparents' lives were too deep, too entrenched.

I hadn't even met Rex or known he was my father until a year ago when he came to town for my first Spooky Season Lit Festival. It turned out we'd met briefly as a toddler, which I didn't remember, but he'd agonized over it ever since. He hadn't known he'd had a daughter until he saw me, and it must've felt overwhelming as a nineteen- or twenty-year-old college student. He was still kicking himself for not stepping up then. He'd carried around a photo of me reading a book upside down in Lazy Bones for years. But he'd had a rough start to life, and I couldn't blame him, although I wondered what could've been. What would it be like to know him then versus now as an adult?

We were still defining our relationship. Friends? Distant uncle who came back to town after a lifetime abroad? We hadn't bridged the gap to a traditional parent-and-child relationship, and I doubted we ever would. But there was a little Rex-shaped spot in my heart that was growing stronger over time. We met on a wavelength that came easy to both of us.

Rex had decided to confront his past and move back to the area, and eventually bought a bungalow in the outskirts of Elyan Hollow. He was far enough from downtown to miss out on the bustle of the yearly Halloween festival but close enough to take a longish walk downtown to pick up coffee or drop by the bookshop. Rex had barely moved in—he hadn't even unpacked—when he'd gone on a trip abroad for a few months, although he'd texted me every few days regardless of where he was in the world. Since he'd returned last spring, he'd periodically left for conventions and to teach the occasional workshop. Whenever he was in town, we met up for dinner or coffee. Sometimes both over the course of a week.

But now Rex was back in town, supposedly until the end of the year. I was curious to see how his first year in the town with the Halloween festival in full swing would feel, even if he only caught the opening days and tail end of it. This wasn't the sleepy, former logging town he'd left when he graduated high school, vowing never to return, only coming back for his mother's funeral when he was in college. He still had ghosts here, mainly the memories of his parents, and regrets that he hadn't gotten his mother into a safer situation before she was diagnosed with an aggressive form of breast cancer. Not to mention the path not taken, which I was proof of whenever he saw me.

As I glanced around Elyan Spirits, I thought about how it feels like walking back into the 1940s, as it purposefully has a vintage speakeasy vibe with lots of art deco glam. Our regular table in an alcove off the bar was open, so we opted for it instead of a table in the main dining room.

Sometimes, I wished I could travel back in time, and change a few decisions. I wondered if Rex felt the same, even though we'd both ended up in a good spot.

After we settled in and both ordered a club soda, Rex spoke.

"I had a reason for asking you to dinner," he said.

"Other than my sparkling conversation?" I said. My eyes glanced back to the list of seasonal small plates. Past history told me we'd order the Caesar salad and one of the olive bowls, to start, along with a mix of the current offerings.

"That's always a given," Rex said. "This query is art related."

My eyes looked up from the menu. "Okay."

Rex made steady eye contact with me. "My publisher always commissions custom art for my covers, and they frequently, maybe always, hire freelance artists for it. I told my editor about you and shared some of your art. After my editor talked with the publisher's art department, we hatched an idea I hope you'll love as much as I do."

"Okay." I hadn't known Rex would share the artwork I'd sent.

Rex sounded a bit sales-ish, which wasn't like him. He took a breath like he was steeling himself for the ask.

"Would you like to illustrate my next book cover? It's not due until March, so you don't have to rush. Well, I assume you won't. I'm not actually sure how long it would take you to draw the cover."

"Umm..."

"If you say yes, I'm sure my publisher will insist on mentioning that my daughter illustrated the cover in the marketing."

"So people will assume I got the job on nepotism?" I'd always dreamed of selling a graphic novel, but I wanted to do it on merit. Not because my biological father was known in the book world. Although maybe I should take any hand up offered.

"No one will think that once they've seen your art," Rex said. "I know an artist rep you can talk with. I'm sure he'd be willing to negotiate the deal. If you two hit it off, it could open doors for you in the future if you're interested in more illustration work. I don't know much about the comics industry, and I know you can submit to some houses without any agent or rep, so you'd want to ask him about that. He might be able to get your career started. While I never tell people to do things for the exposure, this could be a good way for you to launch your career as an illustrator."

"You know I'd do it for free, right?" I said. A glow of happiness tried to invade the sadness I'd been wallowing in all day. I was touched that Rex had asked me. The idea of my art on book covers, on the sort of books I saw in trade magazines and book reviews, would be a dream come true.

Rex shook his head at me. "Don't undersell yourself. Your work is worth getting paid for."

"Isn't that Rex Abbot?" a voice behind me asked. I'm pretty sure the person was trying to whisper, but her voice still carried through the cocktail bar.

"Humph. Celebrities."

"I went to school with him. He's not exactly a celebrity, even if people here act like he's a big deal."

"That girl is practically young enough to be his daughter," one of her friends said.

"You don't say," Rex muttered. He shook his head slightly as he made eye contact with me. His eyes are a similar hazel to mine. He'd shown me photos of his mother, whom I resembled. Which had answered the long-simmering, unasked question about who I'd looked like since I didn't look anything like the Briggs half of my DNA, even if emotionally, I've always known I belonged with my grandparents.

"Scandalous," I muttered back. Rex had been a teenager when I was born, although legally an adult, in his first year of college.

One of their group made another scoffing noise, but I couldn't make out her words.

"About the cover design—" Rex said.

A man about Rex's age, so mid-forties, walked up. "Rex!"

"Hi, Wayne," Rex said. His voice was louder than normal when he said, "Have you met my daughter, Bailey?"

An "Ohh!" sounded from the group of women behind us.

"Yes, I think I have, although briefly," Wayne said. "I took my son to the craft hour at the lit festival, and you were there. And I saw you in Wine Ghouls yesterday. You were with those three loud witches and the girl whose friend purposely doused her friend's princess costume with wine."

"You thought the wine spill was on purpose?" I'd missed the lead-up to the spill.

"I saw all of it, including the smirk afterward. It wasn't an accident."

Wayne and Rex agreed to meet later, and I wondered if Harmony had attacked Ivy as revenge, with tragic consequences.

I pushed my thoughts back to the here and now. I'd worry about Ivy later.

Chapter 12

My alarm always rings too early on Monday mornings. Colby and I met for our usual run, and I wolfed down breakfast and left home fifteen minutes early and detoured by the Sleepy Hollow Inn on my way to work. Jack was annoyed when I chivvied him to hurry up.

To my surprise, I hadn't seen Nate since getting a glimpse of him at the wine bar. He'd been MIA on Sunday. Maybe he'd been exploring the local scene, finding unique things to photograph.

Supposedly, Nate was staying at Sleepy Hollow since Raven had complained that it had left one less room available for her to book.

As I walked inside, a man was about to walk out. I'd seen him last time I'd visited; he'd been mildly annoyed by the *Haunted Hounds* superfan.

"Marion said you're a business owner in town?" the man asked.

"Yes," I said cautiously, while trusting that Marion wouldn't have pointed me out to someone without a good reason.

"You seem young," he said. I could read the skepticism in his tone. He was probably in his early sixties, and I was willing to bet his wool Pendleton button-down was brand-new. Mainly because I'd seen it in this year's catalog and was debating buying it for my grandfather for Christmas. His face was tan, with lines suggesting he'd spent a lot of time in the sun.

Behind him, I glimpsed Nate walking with Emmett's dad into the breakfast room. They were talking intently.

I focused back on the guest talking to me now. "I took over the bookstore my grandparents founded," I said. "But it's mine."

"And that's doing well enough to survive?"

"We're thriving, thankfully. It's a challenge. But nothing in this world is a given, and thankfully, people love to read. I'm not the only 'young person' in town that owns a business. The yarn store, for example, has an owner about my age, and she's thriving. And there's more. The taproom. The new day spa. The jewelry store."

"Huh. Well, have a nice day," the man said. He left.

I shook my head. Weird.

Nate walked out of the dining room with a cup of coffee. His eyes widened when he saw me. "Are you looking for me? If you're looking for Emmett, he already left," he asked.

I nodded. "Can we talk for a moment?"

We moved over to the side of the entryway.

"I'd really appreciate it if you'd shared your footage from the Halloween festival," I said.

"That's my work product."

I wanted to snort, but held it in. "I'm not going to steal it. Is there a way you could, I don't know, upload it to a password-protected album, like wedding photographers do?"

"I'll think about it."

"So what'd you dress up as for the Halloween parade?" I asked.

"Who said I dressed up?" Nate took a sip of coffee.

"I didn't see you, so I assumed you were in a costume. It's logical."

"Maybe you just weren't looking closely enough," Nate said. He smiled and looked away. "Okay, I was a Templar Knight. I bummed the costume off a friend."

Nate turned and faced me again. "Okay, I'll create an album. But don't screenshot anything."

"I only use my own photos." I enjoyed photographing Elyan Hollow, the bookshop, new releases, and Jack. Luckily, our fans liked the photos I shared on social media. I didn't need to steal any of Nate's intellectual property.

"That's right. Your store's Insta account photos are decent. You have an okay eye, but I'm guessing you just use your phone." Nate sounded a tad dismissive.

Which, to use a phrase my grandmother had liked, got my dander up. "It works for my needs."

"I'll send you a link later this morning." Nate walked upstairs with his coffee without bothering to say goodbye, and Jack and I headed to the bookshop.

Not long after the shop opened, one of my favorite three-year-olds walked in with a bouquet of flowers for me and a bag of gourmet dog treats for Jack. Her mother gave me a hug.

"Thank you so much for taking care of Georgie during the parade," she said.

"Of course."

While her mother picked out a couple of new spicy romances, Georgie cuddled with Jack on his dog bed. Jack accepted the attention as if it was his due, and Georgie whispered secrets into his ear while petting him. The flowers were arranged in a mason jar with a diamond pattern, and I decided they'd look perfect on the front counter next to the register.

"Have you heard anything about the explosion?" I asked Georgie and her mother when they were ready to check out.

"Sadly, no, my husband is very tight-lipped about that. But it's intense—a bombing and a suspicious death in one weekend? Most crimes around here are easy to solve because, let's be honest, the town's not full of criminal masterminds. But no one caught the woman being attacked? Sure. Someone will come forward." She shook her head like she was disappointed in the people who hadn't automatically come forward and confessed their guilt.

They left after Georgie gave one final kiss to Jack's forehead.

Business was steady, with a handful of customers at any given time. I was slightly jealous of anyone who had time to read. My

Octobers are always my busiest months, and I don't make any inroads into my ever-growing TBR pile. But the first two weeks of November slows down enough so I can read a little bit before the Christmas season rush descends, which sates the urge enough to get me through to January through mid-March, which are always my peak reading months.

My eyes widened as the door opened again.

Emmett's mom walked into the shop, looking a bit shy. She headed toward the prominent display of Rex's books near the front of the shop.

"Welcome to the Lazy Bones Bookshop," I said.

"Hello." She picked up Rex's newest book. "These books are one of my guilty pleasures."

I hate it when people refer to books as a guilty pleasure or, worse, as a trash read. Discounting books because they're fun to read rankles me. It's even worse when parents try to steer their children away from the books the kid is enthusiastic about to a book the parent thinks is more worthy of the child's time. Taking the joy out of reading makes it a chore instead of a passion.

Some genre fiction deals with serious issues with nuance and care. Others are just fun or, in the case of some thrillers, heart-attack-inducing scary adventures, which is valuable. Research has shown that reading increases empathy, and I know I read because I want to experience other lives and the choices people who aren't me make. I'll never be on a spaceship floating in space as an engine blows up, so I might as welcome the chance to explore the experience within the pages of a novel.

Of course, I didn't say any of this to Emmett's mother.

I was just happy she'd come into the shop. I settled for saying, "Rex is a shop favorite. All of those are signed." I'd appreciated Rex's books before I knew we were related, and my grandfather had always featured his books in the store. Rex had been a customer here as a child and teen.

"All of these are signed?" She picked up several additional books and held them in a stack. "Is it okay if I leave these at the counter while I browse?"

"Of course."

As she put the books down, she looked at me. "Have we met?"

"We saw each other briefly at the Sleepy Hollow but didn't exchange names. I'll be at the wedding this weekend."

"You're the bridesmaid doing all the grunt work," she said. "I'm sorry, but I've forgotten your name."

"Bailey Briggs at your service."

"Bailey. I had that on my long list for my daughter, but my husband wasn't a fan. I'm Kathleen."

"I hope you enjoy your time in Elyan Hollow," I said.

"Do people really enjoy living in a Halloween-themed town?" Kathleen asked. Her eyes wandered to one of the books showcasing the filming sites in the town.

"I'm not going to claim the theme is right for everyone, but yes. The people who love it really embrace the spooky vibe. It's been a good choice for the town."

"Interesting." Kathleen sounded skeptical, but as she was polite, I didn't feel the need to argue as she browsed our mystery section. Some things in life are absolutes. For example, there are two types of people in the world, and this classification defies socioeconomic status and other background details: those who like stickers and those who don't. The camps of those who like Halloween and those who don't aren't as stringent, but there's definitely a group who absolutely does not understand why Halloween is the best holiday and an opposing group unwilling to accept that it's fine that Halloween isn't for everyone.

Kathleen brought up several more books. "I love it when bookstores feel unique," she said.

"I call that store curation. Customers should feel like they're in a unique space with hand-chosen books." At least, that's the goal.

"Well, you're curating your way to my attention." She put her books on her stack and resumed her hunt through the store.

The door jangled again, and Emmett walked in.

Emmett's gaze immediately returned to the drawing of three bears in a canoe above the children's section. "Your artwork in the store is perfect. Who do you hire to do it?"

"I don't hire anyone." My tone was awkward.

Emmett's eyes lit up as he looked at me. "You draw it?"

I nodded.

"That's right, Raven mentioned you were a talented illustrator, but I'd forgotten. She said you were way more talented than her but shyer," Emmett said. He looked at his mother, who'd stepped out away from a display of sexy romance. "Bailey and Raven were art students together. And now Bailey owns a bookstore."

Kathleen's eyebrows rose slightly as she looked at me, but she only handed over several additional books. Given the mix of titles she'd bought, I'd misjudged her when I'd overheard her conversation with Emmett. For whatever reason, Kathleen and her husband weren't happy with their son's wedding, but there had to be unique facets to her personality based on her reading material, even if she termed it guilty pleasures.

After Kathleen paid, she said, "As Bailey is one of Raven's bridesmaids, you should ask if she thinks it's a good idea for the wedding to go on after the maid of honor died during the bachelorette party. It's not seemly, but you call me old-fashioned."

As I bagged up her handful of romantasy and horror novels, with a few thrillers and mysteries to round it out, plus one sweet picture book about a girl whose house is on the back of a turtle, I doubted Kathleen was truly old-fashioned, at least deep in her secret self.

"What do you think, Bailey? My parents have been arguing that we should postpone the wedding," Emmett said. The tired note layered deep in his voice reminded me of the conversation I'd overheard. Maybe his parents were looking for any excuse to postpone the wedding, if not cancel it outright.

"Instead of a paper bag, I'll take one of these tote bags," Kathleen said. She handed over a store tote, complete with an illustration I'd drawn of a raven standing on a skull.

"As far as the wedding, I don't know what to say. Ivy was Raven's friend, so it should be her call." As far as the tote bag, I approved, but I was biased.

"You weren't friends with Ivy?" Kathleen asked me.

"Not really. We knew each other as undergraduates, but we'd lost touch. I hadn't seen her again until a few days ago," I said.

"I'm not sure anyone was really friends with Ivy except Raven. More importantly, did you draw the graphic on that tote?" Emmett's eyes studied the bag in my hands.

"Yep." I slid Kathleen's books into the bag, which only comfortably held about three-fourths of her purchase. "You know, I still have some of the promo tote bags that Rex's publisher sent. Hold."

I hustled to the workroom and grabbed one of the last totes that had come in last week from Rex's publicist. She'd been clearing space in her office and knew any extra swag would find a good home here. I'd been sad she'd sent them after the festival, but I was happy I had this.

As I returned, Kathleen said, "Weren't you listening? Even Raven's friends think postponing makes sense, even if they're too kind to say so. It's not fair to ask them."

"Ta-da!" I said as I stepped out the door. I held up the bag.

Kathleen's eyes gleamed. "My friend is going to be so jealous."

They left, and my bottom line for the day looked promising.

Another familiar face entered not long after Emmett and Kathleen left: Evelyn, the lawyer who rents the office space above the shop. Her law office is slightly smaller than the footprint of the store since there's a small interior staircase from the workroom that leads to my small but cozy office upstairs, with its own exit next to Evelyn's front door. She's a perfect tenant: quiet and pays her rent early.

"I heard about the death. Do you need me to represent you again?" Evelyn asked.

Another item on why Evelyn makes a good tenant list: while she doesn't do criminal law, she secretly loves it. She is willing to step in if I'm ever questioned by police.

Evelyn was dressed down compared to her usual work attire:

navy khakis in a casual cut, a matching striped button-down shirt, and pink running shoes. I nodded at her feet. "The shoes really make the outfit."

She looked down at her feet. "Darn it, I forgot to change shoes when I got to the office again. Well, I don't have any meetings today. Hence my casual attire."

Her casual is what I generally call my nice.

"I don't think I'm a suspect this time, but I'm afraid the police are looking at Colby," I said. Evelyn raised her eyebrows at me, so I added, "Ivy—the victim—wasn't an easy person to get along with. Colby took it on herself to reprimand Ivy when she was rude."

"Does that mean they argued publicly?"

"Multiple times. Quite loudly from what I've heard."

"As I mentioned, I have friends who specialize in criminal defense, and one in particular could be a good choice for Colby. Let me know if I should introduce them."

Evelyn purchased up a new mystery on my staff suggestions table and retreated back upstairs to her office.

Hopefully, Colby wouldn't need an attorney. And I really didn't want to call Hayes to let him know that his wife was in jail, although I was willing to bet the first joke he'd eventually make about it would involve smuggling a file to escape the pokey in a homemade cake.

If I could figure out a few promising suspects, even if I didn't solve the case, that'd help the cause.

I'd better get down to work.

As soon as my staff arrived and I could leave the business in their trusty hands.

Chapter 13

The Elyan Hollow Historical Society, one of the town's two competing historical societies, was a block off downtown in one of the town's few brick buildings. City Hall, also home to the Historical Society of Elyan Hollow in their third-floor attic, is about a block away. I didn't spend much time at the "other" historical society, which had been around longer, as their focus is further in the past, basically from when the Lewis & Clark Expedition first navigated the Columbia River in 1805, eventually wintering about seventy-three miles by modern highway from us at Fort Clatsop, to about 1912, when women received the right to vote in Oregon. I'd always assumed they stopped then because they didn't want to talk about the time the women of Elyan Hollow had been inspired by Umatilla, Oregon's "Petticoat Revolution" of 1916, when seven women led secret campaigns to take over the city council. Elyan Hollow's takeover in 1918 hadn't been quite as successful, but they did install the first female mayor and broke open a corruption scandal that had led to the former mayor ending up in jail.

Awkwardly, the corrupt mayor had been married to the first female mayor, and he went to jail before no-fault divorce was a thing. I've always been curious what happened to them, but their later lives seem to have faded from history. Maybe someday, I'll have time to dive into the historical archives of the town, and maybe hit up the state library.

At least the Historical Society of Elyan Hollow had a few exhibits about the area's pre-colonial history and artifacts from the local Native tribe, even if its vision was mainly focused on Lewis & Clark's Expedition through a very masculine lens.

The historical society I was heading to today was basically their sworn enemy. The Elyan Hollow Historical Society took a broader look at our local history and embraced our more modern events, including being the filming site of *The Haunted Hounds of Hamlet Bay*, which changed the fate of the town.

Part of me wished I'd brought Jack with me instead of leaving him in the bookshop. It'd be nice to photograph him against the backdrop of a movie display for the shop's social media feeds.

The ground level of their well-renovated building is the museum, while the upstairs holds an event space, a kitchen, and a couple of offices. As I entered, I skipped the museum, which was about halfway filled with displays paying tribute to our iconic film, including costumes and behind-the-scenes photos from the film. The other displays, mainly in the back, explored the region's history, including the female takeover of 1918, Elyan Hollow's efforts during both World Wars, and a few lighter displays, like the time the Elyan Hollow Explorers won the women's basketball state championship.

I unhooked the rope telling visitors to stay downstairs, rehooked it behind me, and started up the stairs.

"Excuse me, miss!" a strident voice said behind me.

I turned to look at one of the volunteers, who was also a regular at the bookstore.

"Oh, Bailey, I didn't recognize you without Jack. If you're on the way to see the director, keep going. I've had to chase multiple visitors out of the upstairs today."

We chatted for a moment, and I resumed my quest. For some reason, being a tourist in the spooky season made people metaphorically lose their heads. Signs that say "keep out"? Made tourists determined to see what the signs were shutting them out from, since it had to be something good.

Versus a handful of boring offices and an empty ballroom.

Fingers crossed, no one lost their heads for real since I already doubted the festival could survive a second year with a Halloween murder. We'd somehow avoided too much negative publicity last year, but Ivy's death, coupled with the explosion, could be the death knell for Elyan Hollow as a tourist destination.

As I approached the director's office of the historical society (also the only full-time employee alongside one part-time staff member, a very part-time archivist, and a group of dedicated volunteers), I could hear Jude's angry voice.

"You listen to me, Graham—"

It wasn't a leap in logic to guess Jude was arguing with Graham Clark, director of the Historical Society of Elyan Hollow. Graham refused to answer whether or not he was related to William Clark, which made me assume their sharing a name was simply a coincidence. He would have brought up their connection in every conversation if he was a direct descendent.

"—No, I will not—"

Jude sputtered another time and then added, "If you're in the mood to be reasonable later, we can discuss this like adults. Otherwise, goodbye!"

He hung up his landline with a clang. The sort of smashing noise you can't achieve with a mobile phone without ending up with a cracked screen.

"Is it a bad time?" I asked from the doorway.

Jude relaxed when he saw me. I could practically see the anger flow off his face.

Jude was older than me, but not by much, maybe about thirty-five. In addition to running the historical society, he sometimes taught history as an adjunct at a nearby Portland university and the local community college. His partner had a degree in architecture with a sideline in historical preservation but had taken a job with the county department that included building inspectors. During the last Chamber of Commerce meeting, I'd overheard Graham grumbling that Jude and his partner were somehow undermining the county. But Graham was vague on the details.

"Bailey, have I told you I might have a grant to finally map the tunnel system? You finding a branch of the tunnel that had been forgotten last year set all of this in motion." Jude's eyes lit up.

"That's amazing," I said. I sat down in the visitor's chair on the other side of Jude's desk. I'd found the tunnel at the Haunted House B&B by chance while exploring the closet under their main stairs. Jude wasn't the only person who'd insisted on clomping over to see the tunnel for himself. But as far as I knew, he was the only person to use it in a grant application.

"I'll know for sure soon, which, in my world, means anywhere from a week to six months. Maybe as long as a year," Jude said.

"Keep me posted." My eyes traveled to the framed historic maps of the town on Jude's wall. Someday I'd get a closer look.

"We'll have to have some sort of party to celebrate mapping the tunnels," Jude said. We chatted briefly about his plans until I finally changed the subject.

"I did have a reason for dropping by."

"Darn, I was hoping you'd just come up because you wanted to chat," Jude said. "Kidding, I knew you had a reason. Let's hear it."

"You were at the parade with a video camera. Any chance I can get a copy of your footage?"

"Why do you need it?" Jude asked.

"Well . . ."

"Is it because you were close to another death? Maybe a murder, although from what I've heard, it could've been an accident. The medical examiner hasn't weighed in yet, as far as I know."

I nodded. News, whether it's true or not, spreads faster than the Flash in small towns.

"I can send you the same footage I gave the police, as long as you promise not to use any of it in your social media outreach. Scratch that, as long as you don't use any of the footage without crediting us," Jude said.

"I'm not planning on using it for any public purpose." First Nate, now Jude.

"But you could use it because I trust you'd incorporate it into your social media accounts well," Jude said. "Your shop does such a great job."

A few minutes later, I escaped after promising to volunteer at a holiday fundraiser.

Something told me Jude thought he'd come out ahead in that negotiation. But I would've said yes even if Jude hadn't sent me the video footage.

As I climbed down the historical society's front steps, I paused, my eyes on an SUV with dealer plates. It had just parked crookedly, with the back end sticking too far away from the curb.

The man climbing out was familiar, but it'd been a while since I'd last seen him.

And he wasn't just any man.

I placed him.

Aaron.

He'd texted me about Ivy.

Aaron was one of the college crowd I would generally term a friend, although I'd never been close to him. I hadn't even realized he'd had my phone number.

Had he RSVP'd to the wedding? If not, was Aaron here because of Ivy's death?

"Aaron!" I trotted down the stairs.

Aaron's eyes were red. "Bailey. Fancy meeting you here."

"I live in Elyan Hollow."

"That's right. Do you know a good hotel or someplace I could stay?" Aaron looked around, like a hotel was going to pop up out of the sidewalk and say "come on in."

Hmm, I could use that idea in a kids' graphic novel concept that'd been floating around in the back of my brain over the past few months.

I made my voice soften. "That's a tricky question. Normally, I have some recs, but this is our busiest time of the year. I'll text you a few places, but you'll probably need to look for a hotel in Scappoose or Portland."

"Maybe I'll just sleep in my car." He flashed a sad smile my way. "Not that I'm going to get much sleep regardless of where I stay. But a shower would be welcome."

"While I don't recommend staying in your car, the library parking lot is safe for a night." The library's social worker would end up knocking on his door and offering help, probably escorted by a local police officer carrying bottled water and maybe a snack, but it wasn't the worst choice. Along with one of the local churches, it was supposed to be a temporary safe parking shelter.

"Do you know when Ivy's funeral will be?" Aaron asked. He ran his hand through his dark brown hair, making it even greasier.

"I'm sorry, I have no idea. Raven might know."

"Do you know where Raven is?" Aaron's tone was shifting into annoyed.

Raven was probably getting ready for bridal tea this afternoon or doing something else wedding-related. "Sorry."

"You don't know anything." Aaron looked away from me. His eyebrows crinkled when he looked at the historical society.

Whatever. I didn't have the time or energy for this. I turned and walked toward downtown.

Aaron took a few quick steps and started walking beside me. "Why so fast?"

"I have a mighty to-do list to tackle." And dealing with Aaron wasn't on the list.

"You need to tell what you know about Ivy," he said.

"No, actually, I don't."

Aaron grabbed my arm, and as I wheeled to face him, I jerked my arm out of his grasp. "Don't do that again. Ever."

He held his hands up. "Whoa, I'm sorry, I just wanted your attention, and you were walking away."

"That should've been a hint." Idiot.

"I'm sorry, okay? I wasn't thinking or trying to harm you. I don't even know which direction is up and which is down right now. I just want to know what happened." Aaron's eyes started to tear up.

"Listen, Ivy came to town and acted like a total pain. And honestly, maybe her death was an accident. Maybe she tripped and fell during the parade. No one knows," I said. "Plus, she seemed high all of the time. She could've crossed someone if she was dealing in town. Although I'm not sure if Elyan Hollow has much of a drug market."

"Every town has a drug market. You might be too goody-two-shoes to know about it, but trust me, it exists. And Ivy said she quit her side hustle, so I doubt that's it," Aaron said.

"What side hustle?"

Aaron's eyes scrunched as he looked at me. "You knew Ivy sold drugs when we were in college, right?"

Yes, but I wanted to hear Aaron's version of his and Ivy's shared history.

"Ivy could hook almost anyone up with Ritalin, Adderall, you name it. Plus pot or maybe Molly. She rarely dealt in anything harder. And she didn't take too much of her own merchandise if you know what I mean."

Rarely doesn't mean never.

"She struggled for a while out of college, but then she took a job in hospitality, I think. In Denver, since she wanted a fresh start. She said she was doing well, which didn't surprise me. She always knows where the best parties are, which bars are about to become huge, and which are on a downward trend and getting stodgy."

And Denver is known for its raves.

"Ivy had been a recreational drug user for years, but I doubt she was high all of the time while she was here. She might have just wanted to cut loose at the bachelorette party. Have some fun. I bet you just didn't understand."

I thought of how Ivy had looked when she arrived. She'd always been thin, but she'd been too stringy, and she had looked lank. Her hands had seemed shaky at times.

Could she have been sick? Versus, after a lifetime of casual drug use, having descended into a full-blown addiction?

Or had Ivy simply been deeply dedicated to the vibe of 1990s heroin chic fashion?

Was Aaron right about the town having a drug trade? Pot is legal, and even though I didn't want to admit it, I knew harder drugs had to have infiltrated the town. I'm not sure any place hasn't been touched by the opiate epidemic, even if the problem isn't as visible as nearby Portland's.

Had Ivy made the mistake of trying to sell drugs to the wrong person in Elyan Hollow? Or run into the wrong person at the parade? Could her death have been an accident crossed with a warning from a rival?

My silence seemed to have unnerved Aaron.

"I think Ivy has been taking Adderall occasionally," Aaron said. "But she wasn't addicted. She was too smart for that to happen. Too experienced."

"I wasn't being dramatic when I said Ivy seemed high." We were almost to my shop.

"Ivy's just naturally spacy. Her brain is in there, running faster that everyone else's, and everyone assumes her head is in the clouds."

"And were Ivy's pupils always naturally blown? I don't remember her eyes being mostly tiny rings of green around pupils so dilated they could be black holes." My tone was sharp, but Aaron ignored it.

"There were always so many BS rumors floating about Ivy. That she slept with a psych prof to get a passing grade, or she posed nude in a magazine, that she made a girl OD, or she secretly had a giant trust fund and that's why she was so connected and able to get into parties. It's just jealousy."

And Aaron's grasp of reality was lacking.

"Good luck finding a place to stay," I said, and bolted for the bookstore.

This time, Aaron didn't try to stop me.

Chapter 14

After walking away from Aaron, I kept trotting past Lazy Bones instead of heading back to work.

But at least I had a good excuse, and this would check one of two significant items off my to-do list.

I needed to stop by the new jewelry store in town, Uncanny Little Charms, for official Lazy Bones Books purposes, but I had a secondary reason. Jet, the owner, had run the other way when she saw Ivy leaving the taproom the other night. If I played my cards right, I'd ask Jet about Ivy. Something told me there was a story there.

Jet had gone with a Halloween-themed name for her shop, although her jewelry line had existed long before she'd opened her Elyan Hollow storefront and had been carried by a select number of small boutiques nationwide, and one medium-sized store with a handful of retail shops and a robust online-slash-catalog business. She added a whimsical Halloween-inspired line when she'd decided to settle in town. I'd carried some of her book-themed jewelry in the store for several years. One of her outdoorsy-inspired necklaces had been one of my go-tos for years.

In November, we were doing an extra-special pre-order box for a shop favorite, romantasy author Melanie Wilde, complete with a custom necklace produced by Jet. The design had a Celtic vibe, and so far, Melanie's fans were, to use a pun, wild for the pre-order. They'd also run with the idea the box would make the perfect holiday gift, and some readers had ordered multiple boxes. It was on track to be our biggest pre-order ever, and I was debating if I needed to cap it. I knew I could acquire the books, but needed to verify how many necklaces Jet's company could produce.

The window of the Spooky Little Charms was seasonally festive, with displays of their Halloween-inspired jewelry and a few non-themed pieces hinting there was a variety of styles to be found inside.

Jet had done a fantastic job renovating her shop to be light and airy, with an art deco flair, thanks to the overhead chandelier and bronze accents of the furniture. Long glass-covered counters took up both sides of the shop, forming a long U with several built-in pass-throughs. A door in the back presumably led to Jet's work area and office.

Up front, by the door, there was a small seating area with a shell love seat and two hardback chairs with sunburst patterns grouped around a round coffee table.

Jet was sitting on the love seat with a tablet and pen in her hands. A mug of tea sat on a coaster in front of her.

"Hiya, Bailey," Jet said.

"How are things?" The wooden chairs weren't comfortable enough to make me want to spend all day sitting here, but it was okay for now.

"Would you like some tea? I have a setup in the back." Jet waved over her shoulder.

"Not today, thanks." Although I wished I'd thought to bring my water bottle before running all over town. Rookie move on my part.

"Are you here about the pre-order boxes?"

I nodded. "Safe assumption."

"The numbers are unreal." Jet's smile warmed her whole face.

"Unreal like you can't fulfill them?" A few nerves sprung up inside. I couldn't bear the thought of having to cancel orders.

"Oh, no, that's not a problem. Unreal. It's way bigger than I expected, but that's fine. It's a nice boost to my margins."

"For sure. And hopefully, it'll lead to repeat customers," I said.

"For both of us." Jet smiled again. She was always a tad elusive, like she lived in a different reality and just visited mine.

"Did you check out the parade this year?" I asked.

Jet shook her head. "No, I had to pick up stock from my workshop after a run on pumpkin necklaces, and was sad to miss it at first. But when I heard about the explosion, I realized maybe I'd lucked out. I would've panicked. I hate loud noises."

"You wouldn't have been the only one who panicked." In retrospect, the crowd in Elyan Hollow hadn't covered itself in glory.

"I heard you were all stoic and saved a kid from the stampeding crowd." Jet propped her feet up on the lower rung of her coffee table.

"That's an exaggeration," I said. "You know, if you'd come into the taproom on Wednesday, I would've introduced you to my friend Raven."

"The one who is getting married?" Jet raised her eyes, making them look wide, almost like a Margaret Keane painting.

I nodded. "We would've invited you to the bachelorette party, although, as I'm sure you've heard, that was canceled afterward."

"Joining a party of people I don't know wouldn't have been my thing," Jet said. "But I would've enjoyed meeting someone who dreamed of holding a Halloween wedding."

"The movies, pizza, and board game portion of the night was essentially open to all. Lark and Ash were supposed to be there, plus a few other people you would have met in town. But it's moot at this point. We cut the evening short." I needed to redirect this conversation, but I couldn't get it on track.

"I'm sorry for your loss. Losing a friend must be hard," Jet said. She leaned over and patted my hand.

"I didn't know Ivy particularly well, but Raven is pretty cut up."

"You know, I never sent you my security footage," Jet said. She stood up. "I'm going to do that now while I'm thinking of it. Unless you need anything else?"

"I'm good." I forced a smile.

I'd have to find a new approach to find out why Jet had fled when she saw Ivy.

Olivia was outside the taproom, loading a handcart with bins and boxes to transfer food from the Boorito cargo van to her food cart. They did most of their pre-work in a commissary kitchen.

"Hey," I said as I walked up. "I wanted to say hi at the taproom on Sunday night, but you looked like you were slammed."

Olivia nodded. "We knew it'd be busy, but we didn't expect that. We can't complain, as it was one of our best nights of the festival."

"You heard about what happened at my friend's bachelorette party, right?" I leaned against the side of the van.

"It sounds tragic." Olivia flashed me a smile, but she felt evasive. Or maybe she was just busy.

"See you soon, Bailey." Olivia pulled her cart to the gate to the taproom's backyard.

Zero for two with Jet and Olivia. I'd have to decide on a new approach.

Or this wasn't my business, and they both deserved privacy.

Detective Whitlock flagged me down as I passed the taproom's main door. He was dressed in his Elyan Hollow Police polo and cargo pants, so he was on the job.

Given the crime spree, the entire force was probably on duty.

Detective Whitlock's tone was quiet when he asked me, "Did Ivy tell you where she'd traveled here from?"

"We barely talked. I thought Ivy flew here from Denver. That's where she lived, I think." Aaron had mentioned Ivy moving there to get a fresh start earlier today. I tried to remember if Raven had said something similar.

Detective Whitlock shook his head slightly. "She was evicted from her rental in Denver three months ago. Which was a few months after being fired from her job in event marketing, whatever that is. I'm struggling to find out where she ended up."

"I'd help you if I could, but we weren't close. We're not a bridal party of besties who lived in each other's pockets." Most of the group couldn't stand each other, with the squabbles to prove it.

The bridal party was not bringing out the best in anyone, and I realized this was something I needed to think about later.

"What does that mean? Live in each other's pockets?" Detective Whitlock sounded legitimately interested.

"I've seen it used in books before. It's an idiom that means people who are too close. Co-dependent, maybe, in some cases."

"Good to know. So, if I asked you about Ivy's next of kin, you wouldn't know? We're struggling to contact them."

"Raven said she called Ivy's dad, but as of yesterday afternoon, she hadn't heard back. I've heard that Ivy spent part of her childhood in foster care. This is all secondhand, but supposedly, Ivy's mother has been in jail since Ivy was a small child. Her dad lives somewhere abroad, and left behind Ivy with a now-deceased grandparent. She doesn't have any other family."

"Do you know which state she grew up in?"

"Let me think. Ivy wasn't from the Pacific Northwest 'cause I remember her complaining about the rain our freshman year of college. But I don't think she was from the East Coast 'cause she said she'd always wanted to visit New York City or Boston. She said she didn't go on her eighth-grade class trip to Washington, DC, because she didn't have the money to fly. So maybe Arizona? Or New Mexico? Or both?" I tried to remember back to those early days of my freshman year, when Raven was my new roommate, and I was just getting to know the women on my floor, including Ivy. "I think she mentioned both."

"You really remember all of that?" The detective sounded faintly skeptical.

"Yes, and I have no idea why, except we—Raven, Ivy, a few other girls, and me—were hanging out, and Ivy kept talking about it. I remember feeling like Ivy's family had struggled, which makes sense now that I know about her mother and grandmother. According to Raven, Ivy was in foster care for a while, so they'd have to have some sort of records, right?"

"You'd hope. It'd help if we knew where she'd lived these past few months and where she grew up."

"Would her social media give you clues?"

I opened Ivy's Instagram and noted that one of the most recent photos showed a desert background with part of a camper van. "Is there any chance she was on the road with a camper van? Although if Ivy acquired one, I don't know where she would've parked it."

"Hmm." Detective Whitlock wrote something down, then bit on the end of his pen.

"I assumed you pulled Ivy's phone data, which had to narrow down her movements," I said as I scanned through Ivy's photos. Her photos weren't linear, with a post of a winter view mixed in with summer festival photos.

"Do you know what a burner phone is?" the detective asked me.

"My extensive crime reading in the bookshop has taught me that's a cheap, pay-as-you-go phone," I said. I paused. "Ivy used a burner?"

"Looks like it."

"If Ivy was dealing drugs again, that's logical. And I bet that's a cash-only business, so she wouldn't leave a credit card trail. That'd make her difficult to track." I looked at a photo of Ivy with a brilliant sunset behind her. "Back at home in Arizona." The next photo showed red rocks that reminded me of pictures of Sedona.

"Wait, what's that about drugs?" His gaze sharpened.

"This is something I don't know about firsthand, but Ivy supposedly put herself through college by dealing." I gave the detective the rundown and added, "And Aaron, at least, thinks she was dealing again, while Raven would prefer to think Ivy was trying to go legit, but also told me that Ivy's social media has hints she was dealing again. And look at this photo, Ivy calls Arizona home."

"Aaron?"

"Aaron Blanton. Ivy's college boyfriend, and I think he was hoping to reignite their passion." I explained who he was and how he'd arrived in town earlier.

"Did you catch where he's staying?"

I shook my head. "He asked me about hotels, and said he might sleep in his car. I did notice his SUV had dealer plates like he just acquired it. And I suggested the library parking lot if he decides to stay in his car, so maybe check there tonight?"

Detective Whitlock studied my face for a moment. "What do you think about Ivy going legit?"

I shrugged. "I didn't know Ivy well, and I don't know if she was dealing or not, but from her behavior, it seems like she was doing drugs."

"What do you mean by that?"

"Her pupils were blown, she looked heroin-chic thin—although she's always been skinny—she was erratic. Textbook, really. Shaky hands a few times, mood swings."

"Is your friend Colby anti-drugs?"

The question made warning bells ring in my ears.

"You know that Colby didn't do this, right? She never would've harmed Ivy."

"When someone has multiple public arguments with someone, and that person ends up dead, they have to expect police attention," the detective said.

"Petty arguments are a long way from murder," I said.

"Who said they were petty?"

"You know, I need to get back to my bookshop. And Colby doesn't do drugs, by the way. Neither do I."

I marched off.

I really needed to clear Colby's name.

Given the choice, I don't spend much time in the Lazy Bones Bookshop's basement. We store seasonal decorations down there, but we never use the basement to store books, as the thought of lugging boxes of books down here just to carry them back upstairs again is exhausting. More importantly, I'm afraid the air is too damp. I could run a dehumidifier to make it safe for books, or simply pretend the store is positioned over a dragon's lair. And while the dragon is friendly, it doesn't enjoy visitors. So we rarely use it.

The basement runs under the entire block, but only the bookshop has stairs down to it. The underground space isn't as interesting as the tunnels in Pendleton, Oregon, dug out in the 1860s by Chinese workers who'd come to the USA to build the transcontinental railroad. Most of downtown Pendleton is connected by the tunnels, for good and bad. While Elyan Hollow's system is smaller.

And we just have a basement. Rather boring, really.

But when I'd returned to the shop, Tara had told me she thought she'd heard noises downstairs, so I'd grabbed the giant flashlight I kept with the emergency supplies and headed down into the bowels of the earth, with Jack at my heels, followed by Milo.

"So you're the muscle?" I joked.

"I'd prefer to think that we're a buddy system." Milo held a smaller Maglite that he'd grabbed from his car.

The air in the basement smelled different than usual. Not quite fresher, but different. Earthier, maybe.

I directed the light around the room, which was mostly empty except for the shelving units along the wall by the stairs, which were covered in a series of neatly arranged and labeled plastic bins. Milo stood in the doorway, his feet on the bottom stair, as if the basement floor were lava.

Jack had stiffened up in attention and took off at a trot for the far corner. I followed him.

"Slow down, buddy," I said, but Jack was on a mission.

The wall near the far corner of the basement had crumbled inward, resulting in a pile of bricks.

Part of me wondered if I should evacuate the building. But as I shone my light toward the hole, I saw the truth. At least, I thought I knew.

This part of the wall wasn't structural but, at some point, had connected to a tunnel.

I looped my arm around Jack's neck, careful not to pull on his collar. I should've put his leash and halter on him. "Don't go into the tunnel," I said.

He tried to worm forward, clearly thinking that putting his

snout, and probably more, through the entrance of the tunnel was the right move.

The tunnel had just extended the perimeter he needed to patrol. And if he went into the tunnel, who knows where he'd end up.

I dragged Jack back to Milo.

"What's over in the corner?" he asked.

"I think it's an entrance to a tunnel or, at the very least, another building. Let's get Jack upstairs, and I'll inspect it more."

Jack wasn't happy being shut into the workroom upstairs, but I really didn't want to lose him to the tunnel system.

Milo reluctantly followed me back down the stairs and across the brick floor of the basement. When I shone the flashlight into the hole, I suspected my initial assumption was correct: Lazy Bones' basement connected to the tunnel system.

My brain short-circuited. I owned a building on the tunnel system.

"I should tell Jude about this," I said. Hopefully, Jude wouldn't be too disappointed he hadn't been able to include this tunnel entrance in his grant proposal.

"This is way more exciting than I thought it'd be," Milo said.

"You want to go explore it?"

"I'm not that excited."

I laughed.

"We could start our own speakeasy," I said. "Do you know how to distill moonshine?"

"That's a no." Milo laughed.

We walked upstairs.

I glanced at Milo. "Let's keep this under wraps for now."

He nodded, and then a huge smile split his face. "We have a tunnel," he said. "That I am absolutely not going to tell anyone about until you give the okay."

Chapter 15

I'd just returned to work after exploring the basement when my phone dinged.

Ash.

Can you help me now?
On my way with Jack.

Ash offered me a drink of my choice even though the taproom wasn't open yet, but I declined.

"What do you need me to help with?"

"Packing up Ivy's room once we can get inside."

"Oh." This wasn't on my top ten list of fun activities.

"I didn't want to do it alone, and you seemed like a good choice." Ash's tone ventured on pleading.

"I understand." If I owned a hotel, I'd prefer to have a second person with me when forced to pack up someone's room.

A guy with a bushy beard, wearing a hoodie with DREAD LOCKS written over a skeleton key across the front, walked in.

"You called for a locksmith?" he said.

"I did." Ash introduced herself and then me. "As I mentioned on the phone, I'd like to rekey one of the rooms upstairs."

"You lost the key?"

Ash shook her head. "It's a long story. The first key disappeared, and I gave the backup key to a woman who reserved the rooms, who promised to guard it with her life."

"And now it's lost?" The locksmith cracked a smile.

"Yes." Ash sounded defeated.

"Those are the people who keep me in business. Show me where to go."

As Ash led the way upstairs, she said, "And then the police needed to get in, and I gave them the okay to pop the lock because I have to replace it, so it's boarded shut."

"Now, that is not a normal occurrence in my job."

Once we reached the landing, Ash looked at me. "I know I should go with a higher-tech route, but I like physical keys versus a keypad."

"Raven lost the keys?"

"I suspect Ivy lost both, but Raven is on the hook for the cost," Ash said.

Ash pointed out the room Ivy had stayed in. It was one of the smaller rooms facing the main street, next to the small communal living room.

It was also the room nailed shut with a two-by-four.

"It's nice up here. I like all of the brick," the locksmith said as he got to work.

Ash hadn't covered the original brick walls. Leaving them exposed gave the room a rustic feel. She'd found the microsuede couch at a resale shop, and it faced a TV on a stand made from recycled wood, made by a local carpenter.

"It's done," the locksmith said. He'd swapped out the broken lock for a new one and handed over two keys to Ash. "Looks like a tornado hit inside."

"What?" Ash reminded me of a prairie dog as she looked in the room.

I joined Ash in the doorway. The room was simple inside, with an iron bedframe, a squashy chair in the corner, and a shelving unit crafted from reclaimed wood.

Clothes covered the floor. Ivy's suitcase was upside down at the foot of the bed. The Pendleton blanket was half off the bed, with shoes strewn over the top. A black backpack gaped open from the top of the shelving unit, with toiletries spilled on the floor in front of it.

Discarded towels were bunched on the floor. I bet they were wet when they were tossed down.

Good job, Ivy.

"You've got to be kidding me." Ash clenched her fists.

"I bet it's usually real serene in here. I'm going to tell my sister for the next time she visits," the locksmith said. "She'd love to stay up here, 'cause she was always in love with the fire station and was glad someone cared enough to rehabilitate it."

His words calmed Ash. While they settled the bill, I hooked Jack's leash to the coffee table by the couch and stepped into Ivy's room.

Had Ivy always been this messy?

Or had someone broken in, looking for something? Had someone stolen Ivy's key, versus it being lost?

I doubted the police had trashed the room. If I asked Detective Whitlock, would he answer? I snapped a couple of photos with my phone and saved them in a folder. Just in case.

"Let's get to work." Ash's defeated tone was uncharacteristic, making me glad I'd come to help, even if the task felt intrusive.

This wasn't the first time I'd helped pack up after a murder victim had died in Elyan Hollow. I grabbed the toiletries and tossed them in the backpack.

Cheap sunscreen, a ratty toothbrush without a case, a couple of tubes of eyeliner, mascara, and a half-used value-sized bottle of baby shampoo that told me that Ivy hadn't flown here because it was way too big to carry on a flight. Although she could've checked her luggage. But her suitcase was carry-on size.

I shifted the shelving until I could get to a bottle of hairspray, which dislodged an Altoids tin that had slid under it. Something told me to check inside.

Instead of mints, there was a mix of white-and-orange pills, round all-white pills, and oval yellow pills.

"Check this out," I said.

Ash looked over my shoulder. "I know some people who carry ibuprofen in breath mint tins. My friend had a whole pharmacy in one."

"Yes, but this was Ivy. What do you think this could be?"

"Is there a serial number on the pills?" Ash pulled out her phone, and we searched.

"Exactly what I want in my hotel," she said once she saw the results.

I texted Detective Whitlock a photo of the tin and its contents. **Found this in Ivy's hotel room. We think it's Adderall, hydrocodone, and Ecstasy. Should we throw it away, or do you want it?**

I want it, he texted back.

Ask Ash at the tap room for it.

Ash and I shoved Ivy's clothing back into her suitcase. It was mainly black T-shirts, ratty underwear, two pairs of jeans, a short jean skirt, a worn-in leather jacket, a pair of black running shoes in surprisingly good condition, and the '90s-style baby doll dress she'd worn to the taproom last Wednesday.

Wait.

No dress for the rehearsal dinner, or anything nice for the pre-wedding events.

No club clothes, like the kind Ivy wore in her social media feed.

Most of her stuff was somewhere else, which made sense since she'd traveled here from somewhere.

Ash carried the suitcase (and drugs) downstairs while I shouldered the backpack and stopped to lock the door.

"What are you doing up here?" a snotty voice asked.

Harmony.

"Just helping Ash clear Ivy's room now that the police have released it."

"Isn't that hypocritical of you? I saw your face. You didn't like Ivy any more than I did."

"Maybe, but Ash is a friend, and she asked for my help."

"Whatever."

"So what happened to you on Saturday? You disappeared for a while. You had us worried for a while." The last part was stretching the truth, but I wanted to get Harmony to talk.

"Like anyone actually noticed I was gone. My sister ditched me after the explosion—she didn't even check to see if I was all right—and I ended up by myself. I knew we planned to go to that stupid dingy movie theater after the parade, so I headed there."

"It's not dingy. It's rather fabulous." It'd been painstakingly remodeled to maintain the existing vintage flair while incorporating the most current technology possible for the space.

Maybe Harmony had hung out on the sidewalk, hoping her sister would notice she wasn't with the group.

Hoping someone would notice she was missing.

Unknowingly putting her sister in the position to fail.

"Whatever. I need to get ready." Harmony walked into one of the rooms and shut the door.

Well, okay then.

I checked the time, unhooked Jack, and bolted downstairs.

If I didn't hurry, I'd be late. Although saying "I'm late, I'm late for a very important date" would be fitting for this situation.

Chapter 16

Last spring, when the Oldies but Ghoolies antique store closed, a Portland company moved in and opened the Mad Hatters tea shop. I missed wandering through the antique shop's sprawling mix of rooms, which had contained a mix of treasures and what Colby termed "wtf items."

The Mad Hatters also had a store in the St. Johns neighborhood in Portland, and when they'd announced they were coming to Elyan Hollow, Colby and I had snuck in to do reconnaissance. Their Portland store was purely Alice in Wonderland–themed. They'd gone with an Alice in Wonderland meets steampunk with Halloween flare for their Elyan Hollow location to match the town's vibe.

Their main tearoom is always first come, first serve, and so far, it'd been bustling with people dropping by for a to-go cup of tea or snacks. But they'd decked out one of the rooms in the back as a reservable space for events. When I sent the link to Raven, she quickly approved it for her pre-wedding festival of events. As a Monday isn't a highly sought-after day for events, even during the spooky season, the tea shop was happy to host our bridal tea party. We would've been out of luck if we'd tried to book it on a weekend.

The shop's display case reminded me I was hungry. Their frosted sugar cookies shaped like ghosts or pumpkins looked amazing, as did their scones and assorted pastries.

I smiled when I walked into the far back room. The shop offered a classic high tea or one that was Halloween-themed to the max, and Raven, true to form, had chosen the spooky route. The tables had different seasonal themes, and I wanted to inspect all of them.

Raven stood in the middle of the room, looking surprisingly demure in a sleek black dress. But when she turned, I realized her sleeves opened up to be lacy bat wings.

And I realized her silver shoes had a spiderweb pattern, with bats on the toes.

"Bailey," Raven said. She seemed relieved to see me. "If I beg, will you help run interference today?"

"Of course I'll help. Just let me know what you need."

"I just want today to go smoothly." Raven's eyes looked tired, which she'd tried to hide with slightly heavier than usual makeup, including a perfect cat's-eye eyeliner.

I tried again. "Is there anything specific you need me to do, or should I just be ready to jump in when I see something?"

"Both. Help me steer Emmett's mother and her friends to the cutesy table," Raven said. She motioned to a table with various orange teapots, cups, and saucers, several with pumpkin themes, although nothing matched. A handful of carved pumpkins with flickering tealights inside adorned the center of the table, leaving plenty of space for the towers of tea sandwiches, scones, and desserts on the way.

"I'm planning to sit there," Raven said, pointing to a table with decorations centered around a fake coffin with a skeleton hand reaching out. "I'm debating whether you should sit with me so I can relax, or stick you with Emmett's mother and entourage to make sure they're taken care of."

"Your call. I'll do whatever you need." Should I tell her I'd chatted with Kathleen earlier?

"You're the best." Danby's comments nudged at my brain, and I wondered if Raven said that because I was, seemingly, the least complicated of her bridesmaids.

"I'm going to see if I can get Colby to sit with my mother and aunts at the table with the ravens. My mother's obsessed with corvids, hence my name. They'll love Colby," Raven said. She looked at one of the tables, and I followed her gaze. A raven sat on top of a gothic candelabra with skulls. The porcelain cups and saucers on the table had a black theme, but like the other tables, none of the cups matched.

I needed to ask the tea shop where they found their Halloween decor because it was perfect. It felt like it'd been collected over time by someone passionate about the season.

"Is something going on with Emmett's mother? Is there anything I should watch out for?" I asked. I suspected I knew the answer, but I was curious what Raven would say.

"Kathleen—that's Emmett's mother—just seems unhappy to be here. Neither of Emmett's parents seems remotely enthusiastic, which is hard on him. Can't they at least pretend to be happy for their son?"

"What about his siblings?" He had at least one brother and a sister.

"They're living it up in Portland, and his sister declined to attend the tea. They'll come out for the wedding. They're having a grand time—they even booked their own private party bus to the wine country. They haven't said anything, but I'm positive the wedding was just an excuse for the trip and is their least interesting item to check off their itinerary. Versus wanting to support their brother."

Three women came in, and I realized they were the witches from the bachelorette party. They were all in vintage-inspired dresses with Halloween prints. I suspected they'd gone shopping together at HalloQueen, as I'd noticed these dresses in the shop. The fit and flare design of the dress was the same, but they all had different illustrations.

"Ladies!" Raven greeted the witches and ushered them to a table on the other side of the room, where she planned to stick Emmett's mom and family. Several of Raven's work friends came in, and she ushered them to the witches and made introductions.

The witches seemed delighted to meet new people and had

them chatting right away. The witches would, clearly, be exemplary bridesmaids.

Raven walked back up to me as Colby arrived.

"This is amazing," Colby said. She spun and took in the ambiance.

"The decorations are perfection," I added. "I love the different themes."

"It's my dream tea party," Raven said. "Did I tell you the Mad Hatters are also making my wedding cake?"

"They make wedding cakes? News to me," Colby asked.

"Not usually, but we only wanted a small tiered cake to cut, surrounded by a mix of cupcakes and cake pops. They agreed to work with us because our ideas sounded fun," Raven said. "It will be black-and-white-striped with purple accents, with a bride and groom on top. But my description doesn't do it justice."

"I can't wait to see it," I said.

"The cupcakes and cake pops will be a mix of simple purple or full-on Halloween-tastic. The dessert table is going to be gorgeous. We'll have themed sugar cookies and chocolates on either end, plus fresh fruit. So there should be something that appeals to everyone."

Harmony arrived, dressed in a wonderfully cut pink dress with a vintage vibe that flattered her hourglass build. She marched up to us. "I'm the maid of honor now, right? Since Ivy's . . . out of the picture."

A trio of emotions flashed across Raven's face. After flickers of annoyance and betrayal, Raven seemed to settle on simmering anger.

"Actually, I'm asking Bailey to step up. Considering all the help she's given me, I should have asked her from the get-go. She's been doing the work this whole time, and giving me emotional support." Raven turned to me. "I couldn't have planned this without you, and I'll be forever grateful."

"But I'm your sister." Harmony crossed her arms over her chest.

Raven turned and stared her sister down. "Then why don't you act like it for once." Raven mirrored her sister's stance, making their family resemblance clear.

"Let's take a moment and breathe," I said.

The instantaneous switch to a happy mask that crossed Raven's face chilled me as she turned to greet Emmett's mom. "You're on," she whispered, and I followed.

Although maybe it was Harmony that made me feel cold deep inside. Harmony wouldn't have harmed Ivy just to take over the lead role in a bridal party, right?

But maybe she hadn't intended to kill Ivy but simply injure her.

Maybe Ivy's murder had been an accident.

And maybe Raven had been the one who snapped, not Harmony. She could clearly mask her emotions and code switch on a split second's notice.

Raven motioned to me after she greeted Emmett's mom and entourage. "Have you met Bailey yet? She's my new maid of honor. I'm seating her with you to ensure you have everything you need," Raven said.

Kathleen smiled at me but didn't mention her visit to the bookshop, so I settled for simply smiling back.

As we settled at the pumpkin table, one of Emmett's aunts looked at me. "So you're a good friend of Raven's?"

"Yes, we met during freshman orientation at college, and she's been one of my best friends ever since."

"Where did you travel from? Did you have to come far?" the aunt asked.

A genuine smile crossed my face. "Not far at all. I grew up here in town. I run the local bookshop."

Her face lit up. "You do? I'm planning to drop by and pick up some books. I heard your shop is the easiest way to get signed copies of Rex Abbot books?"

"You've heard right. Drop by anytime. But if you want a personalized copy, I recommend ordering it online for local pickup. I should be able to get it signed before the wedding. Or you can order it for delivery, and we can ship it to you once Rex signs it so you don't have to sacrifice suitcase space when you carry it home."

She put her hand on her heart. "My bestie is going to be so happy. She's his biggest fan."

"I told you the shop had all of his books," Kathleen said. She looked around the room and pursed her lips. "We could have held this at the B&B. They offer a proper high tea service."

I half smiled. "Sleepy Hollow's tea service is gorgeous, but the food here is excellent, and they carry blends from several local tea companies." I decided not to mention that a murderous scandal had rocked one of the main tea companies they ordered from. Thankfully, it hadn't affected the quality of their tea.

"Relax, this will be fun." Emmett's grandmother looked my way. She had a twinkle in her eye. I noticed the spider-shaped brooch in her cardigan, complete with sparkling black diamond eyes. "These kids have their own sense of style, that's for sure."

The bridal tea went off with barely any hitches. Kathleen enjoyed the food, even if the tea sandwiches were shaped like coffins and the icing on the scones looked like spiderwebs.

Emmett's grandmother stole several uneaten chocolate "crone cake" cupcakes with chocolate ganache centers and witch hat tops, along with a couple of petit fours with candy corn or ghosts on the top.

"I can't let these go to waste," she said.

"I don't blame you," I said.

She handed me a cupcake. "Sneak this in your bag," she said. She also handed over a small bakery box, showing she'd come prepared.

Something told me Emmett was his grandmother's favorite.

I hung back after everyone left in case Raven needed me as she said goodbye to her guests.

"I might join you," she told the witches, who left for the wine-tasting room.

Raven looked at me once they were out of earshot. "I just want to nap. Or maybe go for a walk along the river."

The tea shop manager came in and pulled Raven aside as they had a quick discussion of how everything went.

Raven's mother, grandmother, and aunts left, and Harmony paused behind them. She glared at me. "You were playing the long game."

"I have no idea what you're talking about." Maybe someone had been aiming for Harmony and gotten Ivy by accident.

"She's my sister. Know your place."

Harmony swept out. Years of customer service have taught me how to hide feelings of annoyance, but I let myself roll my eyes for once.

"And then there were two," Raven said as the tea shop's manager walked away.

"Can I help with anything else?" I asked.

"No, thank you, you've been amazing. I'll see you tomorrow?"

We walked out together, passing by several groups chatting over tea and plates of sandwiches and cakes.

For Raven's sake, I was glad the tea had gone off without a hitch. Hopefully, the rest of the week would be as smooth.

After Raven walked away, toward the taproom, I stopped for a moment and sat on one of the benches in downtown. Something Harmony said had bugged me.

Well, almost everything she said annoyed me. But this hit deeper.

I didn't want to believe anyone would kill someone to take over a maid of honor role, but Harmony's comments continued to rankle me. Maybe I was just feeling overly sensitive because Harmony had been annoying me all weekend.

I'd first met Harmony when Raven and I were roommates our freshman year in college. She hadn't gone to school with us, but was enrolled in a fashion design program at a craft college near their hometown, which had since closed. Harmony had shown up a few weekends supposedly to spend time with her sister. But she'd complained about whatever Raven had planned for the two of them to do. I remembered I came close to snapping at Harmony and telling her to appreciate the time her sister had spent planning. That same trip, Harmony ditched her sister and the *Twin Peaks* marathon we were attending on campus and gotten completely trashed at a bar off campus with a group of seniors. One of the guys called us, and we left the marathon intending to haul Harmony back to Raven's dorm room but ended up taking her to the ER instead for alcohol poisoning. I still remember Raven ranting about how poorly that night out could have gone for her sister.

"You only drink with people you trust," Raven had said.

How much had Harmony grown up since then? Raven had tagged us both in several wedding social media posts in multiple apps, so I clicked on one of Harmony's profiles.

Harmony's bio called herself an influencer, which always makes me pause, feeling impressed. At almost twenty-five thousand followers, she fell into the micro-influencer realm. Which isn't as many followers as the top influencers, but it was an excellent following. From a few cross-posts, I learned she worked as a personal shopper for an upscale boutique, and I guessed her fashion design background helped. On the boutique's account, her short videos about new products and finding the right fit were surprisingly helpful. And some outfits she'd put together for clients willing to be profiled online were inspirational. She had a good eye for what flattered people. She seemed happier in the videos than I'd ever seen her, but she was on for the camera. Maybe if she filmed a reel here, she'd seem equally peppy.

Like most people's, the posts on her personal account were highly curated, showing a twenty-something-year-old on the go: wine tasting at an upscale vineyard, colorful macarons and a latte at a bakery, walks in a local park when roses were in bloom, covering the world in brief riots of color. The only glimpses of her unique personality came when she talked about choosing the right colors for your complexion.

I started to feel a little sympathy for Harmony, but I also wanted to quote Glinda the Good Witch the next time she annoyed me and said, "Oh-ho-ho-ho, rubbish! You have no power here! Now begone, before somebody drops a house on you!"

Chapter 17

I dropped by the bookshop after the bridal tea, and the shop was still standing. Tara had packaged a large stack of online orders, which always made my heart smile. Jack hopped up from his bed and gave me a thorough sniff.

"How was the tea?" Tara asked.

"Amazing. Hey, would you like one of the cupcakes?" I offered Tara the cupcake Emmett's grandmother had pilfered for me.

"Hand it over."

Jack looked disgruntled, as if he wondered why I hadn't brought a cupcake for him, too. Or brought him with me to the Mad Hatters so he could supervise my afternoon.

I headed to my office above the store with Jack on my heels. Despite everything going on, I had actual work to do, and a few hours in my office felt like the right call.

But before I opened the database we use for the shop, I looked up FinnRetroLLC. It led to a company that repaired and refurbished vintage arcade games and handled resales. They had a new-to-their-site Galaga machine for sale, along with a Donkey Kong and Ms. Pac-Man.

The sales price made my eyes widen.

I was clearly in the wrong business.

Did Finn have a sideline fixing arcade machines?

Something to look into once I'd finished today's book order for the store. During the spooky season, we submit a daily book order to our distributors. My booksellers add to it throughout their shifts, but I always give it a final review. Although Tara will review it on my day off.

Later, despite everything on my schedule that made me feel like I was behind and something was bound to go horribly wrong, Jack and I headed up the street to Stitch Craft. My usual knitting night with Lark and friends was a welcome moment of social normality. After everything, I needed a small moment of connection with people I liked without reservation.

Lark had bought the yarn store almost a year ago, and the changes inside were subtle. Before she took it over, she had been the only full-time employee, and knew exactly what made the store special and what would be improved.

On the way, I ducked into a doorway when I saw Aaron walking down the street, muttering to himself. He ignored us, and I suspected he hadn't clocked me, but Jack stared at him.

When we entered Stitch Craft, Peaches, the shop dog, trotted over to investigate us as we walked in, but after a quick nose with Jack, she quickly retreated to her bed by the couches, which was coincidentally near the traditional knit night snacks.

Almost half of the regulars were there, including Mrs. Sullivan, who'd taught math to my mother at the local high school before retiring nearly thirty years ago and had already claimed her favorite spot on the couch. She sometimes taught beginning knitting classes for Lark and frequently knit preemie hats for babies for one of Colby's library programs, with yarn Colby provided. Although today, she was working on something that was a cheerful yellow shade and most definitely bigger than a hat.

"New project?" I asked. I sat in my regular spot, and Jack settled by my feet like a fuzzy security guard.

"One of my granddaughters is having a baby, so I'm making a blanket," she said.

"Congratulations," I said. I pulled out the colorwork hand

warmer I was knitting. Lark had encouraged me to create my own colorwork designs, and this was a prototype with a ghostly dog and a moon in the background, inspired by the poster for *The Haunted Hounds of Hamlet Bay.*

"It's not my first time being a great-grandmother, but I still can't believe I'm old enough to have great-grandchildren," Mrs. Sullivan said. Her oversized plaid shirt made me wonder if she'd raided her granddaughter's closet.

"Which granddaughter? Not the one who lives with you?" I asked.

"Oh no, Maddy is too focused on school. It's my middle granddaughter, Clara. . . ." Mrs. Sullivan and I chatted for a moment.

Jonah, the lone male regular in the craft nights, chimed in with a few questions.

Marion came in next, followed by Colby, who looked slightly flustered. Ash arrived with a growler of nonalcoholic beer from her takeover the night before, along with a stack of glasses.

Lark put a pot of herbal tea and cups on the table, then sat down and picked up her project, which I suspected was a cardigan in variegated pumpkin orange. As usual, most of Lark's clothing looked handmade crossed with a manic pixie dream girl, from her knit short-sleeve sweater layered over a long-sleeved striped T-shirt, to a contrasting knit skirt. Plus handmade socks, beat-up canvas sneakers, and striped hand warmers.

"Now that we're all here, tell me about the murder," Mrs. Sullivan said.

"Umm . . ." was all I said.

Lark, Mila the co-owner and primary chef of the Boorito cart, and Marion all turned their heads my way. Even Peaches sat up straight and looked at me.

"Yes, please tell us," Mila said. "I have only heard rumors when I work in the burrito cart. But I'm cooking, so I only hear snippets. But Olivia and my sister are working the cart tonight, so I have time for all the gossip."

"I was so sad for Raven that her bachelorette party was canceled.

It looked like it was going to be a blast. But I'd imagine she'd rather have her friend back," Lark said.

"You'd hope," Colby muttered.

"Someone wasn't a fan," Lark said.

"Ivy was complicated," Colby said. "Putting her and Harmony, the bride's sister, in the same room is a recipe for a disaster."

"Were you friends with Ivy?" Lark looked at me.

"Sort of, but not really. We were in the same friend group in college but never really spent time together one-on-one. But she and Raven were tight." I paused to untangle the two balls of yarn I was using for the hand warmers pattern.

"Was she one of those people you had proximity to and are basically friends because of it?" Lark asked.

"More or less. I don't know if I would've even talked to Ivy without Raven. But she was fun in college—"

"If she thought she could use you for something," Colby said.

"—and I haven't really kept up with her since we graduated, except for snippets I heard from Raven." I resumed knitting, taking care to count my stitches so I'd know when to swap colors. After three stitches, I "carried" my second color behind the one I was actively using, metaphorically crossing my fingers that my tension was right.

Colby's tone was flat. "Ivy was always nicer to Bailey than me, probably because she didn't realize Bailey is granite under her easygoing exterior."

"I doubt it."

"I'm not even sure why I'm a bridesmaid, except I'm local," Colby said.

"The three of us spent a lot of time together in school, and we've gone on trips each March for the last five years," I said. Colby had been a lifelong friend and taken me under her wing when I was a freshman, and she was a junior in college, and Raven by extension, since we were roommates.

"Ivy was ridiculously jealous of Bailey. In some ways, it amused me," Colby said.

"I doubt that. Ivy was always more popular than me," I said.

"She was more social, but I don't think she had many true friends, which, I suspect, is why she clung so hard to Raven. She'd always try to prove that she was Raven's best friend." Colby put the shawl she was knitting down on her lap. "Ivy was always good at manipulating Raven. I remember once when Ivy started sulking because Raven was going to study instead of going out with her. Raven caved, of course, and fell in line. Because Raven always caved when Ivy pressured her. But it was a toxic sort of pressure."

"From what you've said, Ivy reminds me of a few students I had over the years," Mrs. Sullivan said.

"How so?" I asked the retired teacher.

Mrs. Sullivan's hands steadily knit as she spoke. "Occasionally, I'd have a student who'd use sulking to get what they wanted. It was a way they'd get power over their friends and keep their friends' attention directed on them. It's very manipulative and one of my least favorite personality traits. But it's subtle. Their friends would feel bad, and their attention would be focused on why their friend was sulking."

"And the friend is so focused on the reason why their friend is sulking that they don't advocate for themselves," Darla, a newish addition to the group, said.

"Exactly, it would make the friend feel rejected and isolated while keeping the sulker in the center of the drama."

"Main character energy," Lark said.

"If it's effective, it's one of the behaviors the offenders didn't grow out of," Mrs. Sullivan said. "The only way to combat a sulker is to ignore them, and if someone evaded their clutches, they'd latch on to someone new."

"My wasband was like that," Darla said.

"Your what?" Lark asked.

"My wasband. Was my husband," she said. "My ex and I divorced two years ago, and it was like a two-hundred-pound stole was lifted off my shoulders. No more sulking and silent treatment, with me trying to please him, followed by his explosions when he decided it was the right time to inflict emotional pain."

"It sounds like you're well rid of him," Colby said.

"I am. I took my half of the proceeds of our house sale and moved here, and I haven't regretted a single moment of it." Darla's hands matched the fierceness of her voice as she knitted a row of her sweater. "Oops, this row might be too tight."

"I can help you fix it," Lark offered.

"What about the explosion?" Ash asked. "Was that connected with Ivy's death?"

"I heard the explosion was a prank gone wrong," Jonah said. "It was just fireworks in a metal garbage can. Noisy as all get-out, but there wasn't any shrapnel or anything like that."

Everyone looked at him. He smiled. "The stay-at-home parent network is rarely wrong about matters like this. Especially when high school kids are involved."

"Do you know who?" Lark asked.

Jonah shook his head. "Just that a handful of seniors were called into the principal's office and taken to the police station. But one of the teens, maybe the ringleader, is on the run. His parents are worried. But I don't have names, but I'm sure I'll hear them soon."

I glanced at Colby, who had looked at me in unison.

"Someone has stolen Danby's crown as bonehead of the town," she muttered.

Her younger sister, Danby, had perpetrated a high school prank gone wrong that led to criminal charges. But Danby had kept her nose clean since and, after finishing her court-mandated community service, was on her way to having her record expunged.

"Danby didn't harm anyone or cause a stampede," I muttered back.

"What are you two muttering about?" Ash asked. "So Ivy's death and the explosion happening simultaneously was just a coincidence?"

"Or the explosion created an opportunity," I said.

As I said the words, they sounded right.

But I didn't know who decided to target Ivy. Or why.

The shop's door dinged, and the man I'd seen several times at the Sleepy Hollow Inn walked in. Jack straightened up, but lay back down.

The man wasn't a threat, at least not at this moment in time.

Lark stood up. "Dad? What are you doing here?"

"He's welcome to knit with us," Mrs. Sullivan said. She had a twinkle in her eyes when she looked at me.

Lark went over and talked with the man in a low voice. They walked outside. Lark's fluttery hands were clipped as she spoke.

"It's time for me to wrap this up for the night," Colby said.

"Do you have plans?" I asked.

She shook her head.

"I have something your help would be invaluable on."

"As long as we can do it at my house."

We packed up and said our goodbyes while everyone's knitting needles clicked on.

"So, what do you need help with?" Colby asked.

"I compiled a bunch of security and video footage from the parade and need to go through it." Jack walked in his usual spot alongside me.

"Oh, joy."

But my friend didn't tell me to go home, so she must be in.

We turned off Main Street and walked parallel to the river for a few blocks. "I heard more about your loud, very public fight with Ivy," I said.

"Who told you that?"

"Detective Whitlock."

"Oh. Well, it's true, but I can't believe people narced on me to the police. It was just words. I'm sure people have said worse in Morning Broo."

"What sort of words?"

"I did tell Ivy that if she acted like an adult, she'd have an easier time navigating through life without risking someone bashing her upside the head for being a brat."

Oh no.

"Wait, where did this happen?" This didn't match Danby's story.

"In Morning Broo. The afternoon after we put together favors with Raven, I was picking up the coffee and pastry order for the library staff meeting. October is always an intense month, and we like to do something special for the staff. Ivy rolled into the coffee shop, looking like she'd just woken up, even though it was two p.m."

"And that led to you two arguing?" The night air was chilling quickly.

"Ivy saw me pick up the carrying case of drinks and cookies and said she didn't know I was someone's assistant. I told her I'm the Youth Services Librarian, but was picking up the order since our admin is recovering from ACL surgery, and I enjoy the chance to get out of the library while on the clock."

"Didn't you also see Ivy in the Pumpkin Plaza?"

"Yeah, she was a right . . . jerk . . . when Danby and I saw her there."

"It doesn't look good, Colby. Multiple arguments?"

"Yeah, I know. And it really hit home when Detective Whitlock asked me to visit the police station again. I said no."

"Maybe the video footage will help clear your name." One could hope.

"It better because my mother will be heartbroken if I end up in prison orange. And those jumpsuits? Are rarely flattering. And I doubt they'd let me train for triathlons in the big house."

Chapter 18

Colby's apartment isn't too far from the library, in a garden-style apartment building, with parking, including a handful of garages. Colby's unit had one, which they used to store their bicycles and outdoors gear.

The sun was down, and I could trace the Big Dipper in the sky above us. It was a beautiful night, and I wished I was thinking about anything other than murder.

The apartment felt like Colby, with pale green walls I'd helped her paint and a row of bookcases along one wall. I knew she had more books inside Hayes' home office, with another bookcase in their bedroom. She'd bought the framed print over her couch from an artist enrolled in the same tribe as her family. She and Hayes were saving for a house, but prices kept rising.

But their apartment felt enough like home, at least when Hayes was in residence.

Colby snagged the couch, and I flopped on the matching lounge chair. Jack collapsed on his side next to me.

"I can't believe Detective Whitlock wants to interview me again. Can they seriously think I'd kill Ivy?" Colby said.

"How many times did you argue with her in public?"

"Someone had to. Ivy and Harmony give me headaches. But it's not like I would've harmed either of them. Even when Ivy came into the library and seemed high."

"Wait, what about the library?" I asked.

"Ivy was low on phone data and came in to use the computers in the library when I was working. But she couldn't walk in a straight line, and I knew she'd want to fight with me, so I had my coworker kick her out when she started making a fuss, upset that she needed a library card. It was glorious."

"This isn't good," I said. "Wait, do you need a library card to go online? I thought anyone could go online for fifteen minutes?"

"It's not my fault that Ivy misread the sign." Colby raised her hands in a "what can I do" gesture.

"Maybe we'll see something in the security or historical society footage," I said. I pulled out my laptop and opened the folder with the assorted video files I'd compiled.

"Or maybe it'll put us to sleep." Colby leaned back and put her feet up on a pillow. Her socks had cartoon bears on the ankles.

"Get your laptop, and I'll send you a link."

Colby leaned over, opened the drawer in the end table next to the couch, and pulled her laptop out. "Done."

Colby grabbed cans of lime sparkling water for us as we worked. Everything was feeling hopeless and my eyes were starting to burn. Were we wasting our time?

Then I realized something.

"Look at this," I said. I turned my laptop so Colby could see the screen, which I'd paused.

"What am I looking at?" she asked.

"This is a Grim Reaper that has green paint on the bottom of their robe," I said.

"You're right, but this matters, why?"

"Because at least four Grim Reapers were downtown during the festival, and one was hanging out near us during the parade. Oh, and one had a basset hound, and he only passed by once, at least with the dog."

"In retrospect, so many Grim Reapers was ominous," Colby

said. She leaned over my laptop and clicked play, and we watched the Grim Reaper move across the screen. "I can't tell anything about them."

"They're not short," I said.

"But they're not especially tall, either."

"Slightly taller than average," I said.

A different Grim Reaper, one without green paint, walked toward the camera. I paused the video again. "Now, this Grim Reaper seems tall."

This Grim Reaper's robe hit mid-shin and showed several inches of blue jeans and red sneakers.

"Let's find the next reaper."

Nothing was distinctive about the final two reapers, although one swung his arm weird.

I realized the costumes were basically protective coloration in birds. Everyone is in a costume, so no one stood out.

Colby yawned. "I need to call this a night."

"Good idea. I'll scroll through more footage tomorrow. Maybe there's a better shot of the Grim Reapers."

"You do know they could be innocent, right? It could be chance that one was hanging out near us. Maybe his friends chose the spot. Maybe it was five different reapers who just happened to show up near us."

"Yes, but they, or their friends, could have seen something they don't know is important."

Jack and I got ready for the walk home, meaning I pulled on my jacket and swung my bag over my shoulders while he stretched in a classic downward dog with his butt in the air.

I knew the video footage would help. I could feel it deep inside.

But there was so much of it to wade through.

It was later than we were usually out, but the streets of Elyan Hollow are generally quiet. Jack and I took a short detour and walked through Goblin Gate Park.

Jack stopped by a bush and refused to move.

"C'mon," I said.

He ignored me.

"Seriously, dude. I want to go home and go to sleep."

Jack nosed something on the underbrush beneath the bush.

"You better not be hunting for a snack."

A small meow sounded, and a tiny head popped up.

An all-white kitten, except for one black spot on its ear.

Jack leaned over to sniff the kitten, and it raised a tiny paw in warning, making Jack pause.

The cat meowed again, then walked forward and headbutted Jack's wrist.

"Do you two know each other?" I asked.

Only to be ignored by both the kitten and Jack. The kitten purred loudly and headbutted Jack a few more times.

I glanced around. No one was in view, and the kitten looked awfully small to be alone. I'm not an expert, but I guessed it was around eight weeks.

But no mama cat burst out of the bushes, ready to defend her wayward offspring from the giant dog. The nearest houses weren't particularly close, so the kitten probably hadn't wandered over from one of the homes.

A quick glance at the local social media neighborhood app didn't mention missing kittens. However, there were plenty of complaints about Halloween traffic.

Jack nosed the kitten, who purred and rubbed against Jack's nose, claiming him.

"I hope this isn't a mistake," I told Jack, and picked up the kitten. It promptly curled into my hands and started vibrating with a purr that should've come from a larger cat.

The three of us walked home.

Chapter 19

When I woke up, I saw Jack curled up like a donut on his bed, as expected.

"Where's the kitten?" I asked.

A tiny head popped up from Jack's hip, and I realized the look Jack was sending me said, "Help, please, help, now."

"She's your friend," I said. At least, I assumed the kitten was a girl based on a quick inspection last night.

I stood and rescued Jack by picking the kitten up. "Do you have a family we should find?" I asked her.

She purred, and I put her down on the counter when I visited the bathroom. She explored the sink, so I moved her when I washed my hands, then picked her up and took her and Jack outside. They patrolled the yard together.

My grandfather was starting the kettle when the three of us came inside.

"Who is this?" he asked. I handed him the kitten.

"Well hello, cat," he said. He gently put her down on the floor.

I put Jack's food down and looked around for kitten-friendly food in the house as I told my grandfather the story. "Now, what should we feed her as we figure out what to do?"

"Hmm."

I glanced over and saw Jack sitting sadly while the kitten carefully crunched on his food.

"I think we still have a litter box in the basement. I'll check, and pick up some litter and kitten food. I'll also check in with a few places and see if anyone is missing a kitten," my grandfather said. "I'll take her to the vet to be scanned for a microchip and see if they have any insight."

"I can also handle that."

"No, you have too much on your plate right now."

"Okay."

"Hmm, she'll need a name."

As I watched the kitten chow down on Jack's food, I said, "How about Moriarty?"

After I went for a solo run, I got ready for work and gave Jack a small second breakfast since Moriarty had stolen part of his usual morning meal. We left my grandfather reading in the living room, with Moriarty perched on his shoulder like she was equally invested in the story.

On my way to work, I saw my uncle Hunter's wife, Mandy, walking with another woman, both pushing strollers down Main Street. Mandy gave me an apologetic smile but didn't say anything. Jack pretended like he hadn't seen her.

Mandy used to come into the bookstore sometimes, barely missing the children's story hour with Ella, their toddler. But neither has spoken to me since Christmas. Something told me that was Hunter's decision, but Mandy was following along.

Jack brushed against me as we walked toward Lazy Bones.

Christmas last year. I can still see the day like a movie, although I'm sure I shaded in a few details. Made some colors a bit brighter, muted the sad, bittersweet moments.

And I can still feel the anger that had pulsated inside me when Hunter went on the attack.

My grandfather had invited Rex to join us for the holiday, and it was also the year my mother and uncle spent with us, as both alternate with their spouses' families. I'd never spent a holiday with both of my parents in one room before, and I wondered how my mother's husband would react. If it wasn't bittersweet enough, every Christmas without my grandmother gave me a new pang of sorrow. She'd only been gone a few years, but every accomplishment, every moment I couldn't share with her, made me feel her absence from my life.

I wish she'd been told that Rex was my father, mainly because I was curious how she would have reacted.

Rex and Marion joined us for breakfast and helped us prepare our usual Christmas dinner. Which wasn't particularly difficult, as years ago, my grandparents switched to a ham that simply needed to be heated up, along with a handful of easy sides, like mashed potatoes, roasted vegetables, and a salad. Marion brought her notoriously awesome mac and cheese, and Rex had brought a couple pies from a local woman, Elspie, whose bakery side hustle, Bake It Spooky Pie Company, had a waitlist for holiday pies.

"You managed to get on the list?" I said. "I've been trying, but I haven't made it to the big time."

"It turns out Elspie's a fan," Rex said. "I bribed her with a signed book, although she prefers audiobooks since she listens to them as she bakes."

"How reassuring to know these might have been baked while she listened to a horror novel," I said. Rex's books are rarely overly graphic, as he opts for the psychological horror that makes you afraid to sit at home alone. Shadows become scary versus gory. Usually.

"Seems like the perfect seasonal choice to me," Rex said.

Rex put his other reusable shopping bag from the Elyan Hollow Co-Op down on the side table, which Jack sniffed, so I knew more food was inside. Rex opened the front flap of his messenger bag and handed me two slim boxes wrapped in red paper, tied together with gold ribbon. "Merry Christmas."

"Thanks, I have something for you under the tree," I said. Rex once told me that when he's writing, he lives off snacks, including a lot of meat, cheese, and olives. As I got to know him, I noticed he appreciated artful charcuterie displays and a shared deep love of olive tapenade. So I'd bought him a handmade walnut platter from a local artist, perfect for charcuterie boards, with a quote from the book that'd launched his career discreetly adorning one corner. The artist's wife specialized in ceramics, and the platter had slight cups to hold two small bowls, perfect for dips. So, I bought two pine green bowls from their family store to finish the set.

"Open the smaller box first," Rex said, so I did.

I looked at the fountain pen. It had a shiny black resin body and cap with a white star at one end. When I twisted the cap off, I took in the gold nib, knowing it was either 14k or 18k, depending on the model.

A Montblanc pen. I wanted one for years but had balked at the expense.

"If that's not the right pen for you, let me know, and we can exchange it for a different model," Rex said.

"It's perfect."

"If the nib isn't right, we can swap it out."

"I bet I guess what the second box is," I said, and was proved right when I slid the wrapping paper off.

Black ink for my new pen.

It couldn't express how perfect the gift was.

"It's kind of expensive," I said.

"I'm making up for a lifetime of missed gifts," Rex said quietly.

"I'm surprised you knew I wanted one," I said. Although I wanted to tell him that he didn't owe me anything.

Rex smiled. "I ran into Colby in the library and asked her for advice."

It was weird to think of my father and friends having their own relationships. But now that he'd moved to town, it was inevitable.

I walked over and picked up the box for Rex.

"Merry Christmas," I said before handing it over.

Rex smiled when he opened it. "I love it. You'll have to come over for charcuterie," he said.

A while later, my uncle Hunter arrived with his wife and toddler, followed by my mother and her family. My younger half-siblings, Laurel and Ryan, aren't strangers, but our relationship is distant. Their life, which revolves around competitive soccer and events at their private school, has a different flavor than mine. Plus, when they were born, I was almost as old as my mother had been when she'd had me. My concerns and theirs didn't even meet in an overlapping circle of a Venn diagram. And my childhood was very different from theirs.

My mother's husband, Spencer, looked uncharacteristically stiff when he shook Rex's hand. Spencer is tall, about six foot three, and physically fit, usually with a calculated, easygoing air that borders on overly hale and hearty. There's a current underneath that I've never quite cracked the meaning of. He never felt authentic to me. I wasn't sure I'd ever seen the real Spencer versus the façade he wore around his father-in-law and stepdaughter.

Spencer and my mother met when they were in medical school. When they were done with their residencies, they moved to Portland together. I'd never lived in the same house as Spencer, and I always sensed notes of disinterest when it came to me. Is he upset that I mar the otherwise perfect façade of their life? If anything, my mother being a teen mother who beat the odds is inspirational, although he might prefer that she'd never taken that step. And it's not like she had abandoned me, as my grandparents had stepped up and taken over the role of parents in my life while also supporting her. Although without their help, I doubted either of us would be where we are today. They'd done their best to find the positives in a difficult situation.

"These are my younger two, Laurel and Ryan," my mother told Rex. If anything, my half-siblings looked bored. Laurel takes after her dad, who has dark brown hair, while Ryan resembles our mother, who has dark blond hair and a rather cute pert nose.

"You have a lovely family, Lizzie," Rex said.

"Her name is Elizabeth," Spencer said.

"I was Lizzie for years," my mother said. "Most people call me Liz now, some call me Elizabeth, but I love that my old high school friends still call me Lizzie. Those days were something else, although they feel like they were a whole different lifetime ago."

Spencer frowned, and Rex stiffened in response to my stepfather.

"Who'd like a drink? We have hot cider," Marion broke in, calming the situation down. Once my half-siblings had cider, they sat on the couch, glued to their phones.

Hunter's toddler, Ella, sat with Mandy on a blanket in the middle of the room and built a tower with red plastic party cups. Jack lay at my feet, but he kept eyeing the cups.

"Ella's going to want to build things like her daddy," Mandy crooned.

"This is for your family and for yours." Rex passed two identically wrapped gift boxes to Hunter and my mother.

My mother smiled widely when she opened the package. "Oh, I love peppermint bark." She showed me the fancy tin of candy.

"We're going sugar-free in January, remember?" Spencer said.

"I agreed to a mostly healthy January. The occasional piece of peppermint bark surely has a place in a balanced life," my mother said.

"We still have, like, six days to eat that peppermint bark. I can start now," Laurel said. Her tone was bored, but she was clearly paying attention, even if her eyes were mainly on her phone.

I smiled, enjoying the touch of sass that hinted at Laurel's real personality.

My half-sister looked up from her phone and glanced at Rex. "You're, like, a writer?"

Rex nodded. "More or less."

"Your books have been made into movies."

"A few have. One was absolutely terrible. But one did well."

"I told my English teacher my mother knew you, and my teacher was flabbergasted. I think she wants to write her own books. My teacher, not my mom."

Rex's smile was laid back, but I sensed he was enjoying this moment, although Spencer's eyes had narrowed.

"I've yet to meet an English teacher who doesn't love books," Rex said.

"My teacher last year hated books. We only read articles and essays. It was so boring," Laurel said. "Thankfully, we're reading some novels now."

"What do you like to read?" I asked.

"That book you gave me last year was awesome," Laurel said. "I read all of the books you give me, but I really loved *We Were Liars*. The twist was like, earth-shattering. I've read everything I can find by that author."

"I loved *We Were Liars*, too," I said. I enjoyed the proof that Laurel and I were related after all.

"I guessed that's why you gave it to me, since it would've sucked if you'd given me a book you hated," she said. Laurel's subtle snark was back, but it didn't feel targeted, just like it was part of her.

Hunter's voice cut through the room. "Dad, we really do need to talk about the bookstore."

"What about it?" My grandfather's voice was controlled. But it was the tone I instinctively knew not to push against.

"As I've told you, now is a great time to sell the building downtown. Investors are looking for commercial real estate in town. It'd ensure your retirement income is smooth." Hunter's tone bordered on smug self-assurance.

"The building could continue to gain in value," my mother pointed out.

"Or the market could crater," Hunter said. "Dad, you've retired. It's the perfect time to let the building and the store go."

Hunter might as well have told my grandfather, and told me, to tear our hearts out of our chests. Lazy Bones Books wasn't just a shop but a space for everyone in Elyan Hollow. A place where everyone was welcome and where we'd never judge what books they decided to read.

The store was also my grandparents' legacy—proof they believed in Elyan Hollow and books.

And it was a legacy I was dedicated to honoring.

"Just think," Hunter continued. "You could use the money to travel. Go explore the world. You could even sell this house and downsize, too. Maybe into a nice condo."

My eyes narrowed as I looked at my uncle.

"The bookshop is successful," I said.

Hunter briefly glanced at me, then locked eyes on my grandfather.

"Bailey will need to leave the nest someday; the sooner, the better. She's not a child anymore," Hunter said.

Hunter's wife said softly, "Bailey deserves the chance to stand on her own two feet."

"Bailey is sitting right here," I said.

"Bailey is standing on her own two feet," my grandfather said. "The bookshop sales numbers have grown since she took over the store. She's made smart changes."

"Are you sure that's not just a fluke?" Hunter nodded at Rex. "The drama around Rex's return to town won't prop up sales forever."

"While sales of Rex's books have been steady, we'd still be ahead without them," I said. "For example, my mystery subscription boxes have grown so much that I've had to start capping the total number each month, which has made them even more popular. And that's not the only area that's shown increased profitability. Foot traffic and in-store sales are up, and not just during the festival. Online orders are also up, with repeat customers from all over the country."

"So you're saying the business is in good shape to sell," Hunter said.

"That's absolutely not my point," I said.

Hunter turned to his father like I hadn't spoken. "All the signs point to now being the best time to divest."

"Why are you so worried about it?" my mother asked her brother. Her look was intense as if she were diagnosing him with a character flaw.

Although maybe I was reading into her expression.

But why was Hunter so focused on selling or closing the store? Was he obsessed with status? With money? With his future inheritance? Did he dislike me running the family business so much that he'd rather burn it to the ground than see it succeed?

"Because I want to ensure our father has a stable retirement. If the bookshop fails, it could drain his savings. I don't want to see him destitute," Hunter said. "I can't believe you don't see that."

"That's rather pessimistic. Our parents operated the shop for years, through economic downturns, and still managed to come through. I doubt Bailey taking over means the whole place will fall apart." My mother straightened her green sweater.

"But our mother also worked for the city. The bookstore alone didn't pay for this house." Hunter's tone was starting to take on an angry note.

"No, your mother's inheritance from her grandparents bought the house," my grandfather said. He rolled the sleeves of his flannel up with a controlled movement that, if I was Hunter, would make me realize it was time to shut up.

"Think of the return on investment if you'd invested that money properly instead of using it to start a bookstore." Hunter waved his hand in the air.

My grandfather rolled his sleeves back down. His face had flushed slightly. "We did invest the money, both in Elyan Hollow and in a business we believed in. I don't understand why you can't understand that. You grew up here. You know how much your mother loved the shop."

"Just because she loved it doesn't mean we shouldn't let it go."

My grandfather eyed his son. "I don't actually have a say, as I signed over the controlling interest of the bookshop to Bailey last year."

"What?" Hunter shouted.

"Lower your voice." My grandfather's low tone was the one I hated to hear as a kid since I knew I was doing something wrong.

Hunter quailed, then thrust out his chest. "You didn't consult with me."

"Wow, I thought a vein pulsing in someone's forehead was just something from cartoons," Laurel said. She eyed Hunter.

"Hush," our mother told her. But I saw the smile my mother suppressed. Spencer looked like he wanted to join the debate but wasn't sure which side to support.

My grandfather kept his eyes on his son. "I didn't need to consult you nor explain myself. As I told you several times, your mother and I planned how to handle our estate. You, Lizzie, and Bailey are currently willed equal shares of our retirement accounts, life insurance, and this house. But the bookshop was never part of that. Your mother and I always hoped one of you would take over the bookshop, and it was obvious to us when Bailey turned out to be the most likely candidate. We did our best to support her interests but were proud when she wanted to work in the shop, and we knew it'd be her business to run one day. You never wanted to be part of it, so I supported you in other ways."

"That's not fair." Hunter's tone was a mix of anger and petulance.

At this rate, dinner was going to be fun.

"Keep pushing me, and I could change my mind. I don't have to split the estate into thirds as planned."

My grandfather's level tone made Hunter look even angrier.

My mother's tone was calm like she was trying to lower the heat in the room. "It makes sense. Mom would be proud of how Bailey is running the bookshop. I'm glad to see she's continuing the legacy. I can't imagine Elyan Hollow without Lazy Bones Books."

"What about the building? It's a valuable asset." Hunter waved his hands in the air.

"That was passed along with the business," Grandfather said.

"It's worth more than this house!" Hunter yelped.

"What about your other grandchildren?" Spencer asked. "Aren't they a factor? They're also family and deserve consideration."

My mother sent him a sharp glare. He closed his mouth and turned his head away.

"Do you treat Bailey like family?" Rex asked Spencer. "When's

MAYHEM AT A HALLOWEEN WEDDING 163

the last time you invited her to join you and your family at Christmas?"

"Mind your own business," Spencer snapped back.

Rex held up his hands in a "let's not fight" gesture, but I could see his comment had hit home.

"Bailey, you're totally invited to my next birthday party," Laurel said. "Especially if I can send you a book wish list beforehand."

"You can always send me one, even when it's not your birthday. Remind me to tell you about the joy of ARCs," I said.

"Boats? Like Noah's?" Laurel said.

"Advanced copies of books, called ARCs for short," Rex told her quietly. "Booksellers like Bailey get earlier copies of books so they can read and review them, and hopefully stock them in their stores."

"I could read books before they're published?" Laurel asked. "Before everyone else?"

"If you'll review them," I said.

"I'm in." Laurel bounced in her seat.

She was definitely my sister.

And from the way my uncle was glaring at me, he was in the process of excising me from his family.

Hunter's nostrils flared as he turned his glare onto his father. "It's unfair that Lizzie having a kid in high school means my child gets less."

"I didn't raise your child as my own," my grandfather said.

"If anything, it should come out of Lizzie's part of the inheritance. You didn't consult my wishes when you bailed her out of a stupid teenage mistake." Hunter crossed his arms over his chest.

"Hey!" My mother's tone was furious. "You didn't need to be part of the decision. We could've gone with a different adoption route, but our parents adopting Bailey made the most sense at the time, and it worked out. And Bailey is not a mistake. She's a gift."

"I was adopted?" My voice was shrill enough that even I flinched.

Laurel looked at me and mouthed, "Dude!"

My mother turned to me. "Wait, you didn't know? It's not like we tried to hide it; everyone knew you were my kid. We realized it was easiest if my parents adopted you since I wasn't going to be around to raise you."

"No, I didn't know." The shape of my life had just gotten clearer.

My grandfather looked perplexed. "I could've sworn we talked about this several times."

"So how old were you, exactly, when Bailey was born?" Laurel asked our mother. Ryan looked up for the first time, clearly interested.

"We can have this conversation later, Laurel." My mother's tone was clipped.

"I'll start making my list of questions." Laurel started typing something on her phone. I wondered if it was a list or if she was Snapchatting her friends about today's drama.

My money was on Snapchatting.

"Your middle daughter is definitely yours; no DNA test needed," Rex said to my mother.

My mother chortled.

Hunter stood up. His hands were clenched by his sides. "This is ridiculous. And I can't let this disrespect go. C'mon, Mandy, we're leaving."

"But we haven't eaten dinner."

"We're going."

Hunter grabbed his down coat and flounced out, leaving Mandy to wrap Ella up in her jacket and fuzzy pink hat.

"Say Merry Christmas, Grandpa," Mandy said to Ella.

Ella waved.

"Close enough," Mandy said. "Merry Christmas, all of you. I'm sorry."

Mandy left, and I stepped over to the window, glad Hunter hadn't driven off and left his wife and daughter behind. But he looked angry as he paced next to his car.

"Who wants to have a cheese course as an appetizer?" Marion asked.

Laurel raised her hand.

Dinner was awkward, and my mother gave me a bigger hug than usual before she left. "Call me, and we can talk this through."

I nodded.

"Most exciting Christmas ever. Do you think we can top it next year?" Laurel told me before she followed her parents out the door.

"Thanks for the graphic novels," Ryan told me, then followed his sister.

And then there were four. Marion, Rex, my grandfather, and me.

No one noticed that Marion and my grandfather were now a low-key couple. They had slid into it slowly, and it had taken me ages to realize they had moved on from long-term friends to something more. So maybe that's why neither Hunter nor my mother noticed.

My grandfather and Marion carried the last serving dishes into the kitchen. Christmas songs started floating through the air, so one of them had turned on the radio.

Rex turned to me. "On a positive note, I have a fantastic guest space. It's basically an apartment with a small kitchenette. Not that anything is going to happen to your grandfather. But if worse comes to worse, you have someplace to go if needed while you figure things out."

"Thanks."

"You really didn't know that your grandparents adopted you?" Rex asked.

"No, but it makes sense. But they were always in the parental role. So I'm not surprised, even though I am, if that makes sense."

And Hunter hasn't spoken to me since that day.

Some people can hold grudges regardless of good times in their shared pasts.

Chapter 20

Downtown Elyan Hollow was gearing up for our big day: Halloween was tomorrow.

And Raven's rehearsal dinner was tonight.

Opening the shop went like clockwork, thankfully. Jack looked exhausted when he collapsed on his bed, making me wonder if Moriarty had kept him awake all night.

I'd barely flipped the shop sign to OPEN when Kristobel, the owner of the nearby pet boutique, Bad to the Bone, dropped by for her usual perusal of the Tuesday new releases. As always, she'd brought a biscuit along for Jack.

"Nice plaid bandana, even though you didn't get that from my shop," she told Jack, who stood still to, presumably, make it easier for Kristobel to scratch behind his ears. When I'd found the orange and black houndstooth bandana in a pet shop on the Oregon Coast next to my favorite bookstore (that I don't own), I'd had to buy it given the color combo and the fabric name, even though Jack generally uses his allowance to shop the accessories in Bad to the Bone.

"I need to pick up kitten toys from you," I said.

Kristobel looked at Jack. "Is there something you're not telling me?"

"Yes, Jack found a lost kitten last night. It's small, too—maybe eight weeks old? Tiny little thing, but feisty."

"You rescued a kitten? What a good boy," Kristobel said, and scratched Jack again. We talked about Jack's thoughtful rescue.

"Found kitten, explosion at the parade, murdered bridesmaid. It's been an odd couple of days," I said.

"Your friend Olivia in the Boorito cart might have insight into that woman who died. What was her name? Ivy?" Kristobel said. "I saw the two of them arguing a couple of times."

"What's that?" Did Olivia and Ivy even know each other? Then I remembered Olivia's face when she saw Ivy in the taproom.

There must be a story there.

"When I saw them, Olivia said that Ivy had almost wrecked her life once and to 'keep her bad mojo far away.' Ivy said she was sorry, and Olivia said to save it for someone who cared."

"Sounds dramatic."

"Olivia was so angry that I was surprised steam wasn't coming from her ears. While Ivy seemed sad, honestly apologetic. I actually felt bad for her."

Kristobel turned her attention back to my dog, who was still waiting patiently next to her in case she had more treats to share.

"I'll see you later today," she told Jack. She glanced at me. "I know he's on the g-r-o-o-m-i-n-g schedule. I'll assemble some kitten supplies for you to pick up then."

"Later."

Jack glanced at me, and I said, "I bet you wished you knew how to spell, huh?"

And I got back to work, even though I wanted to leave the shop and track down Olivia.

There was something small I could do. I texted Sam. **Can you also look up Olivia Rojas?**

As I was putting my phone away, he responded. **Is that the Olivia from Boorito?**

Yes.

On it. You can explain why later.

* * *

After working for a few hours, I took a quick water break. Since I had a moment, I looked up Nate's photography website. Partially to find his email address to remind him to send me a link to view his Halloween parade photos.

Nate had said he was a documentary-style photographer and mentioned bands.

But he hadn't said he'd photographed bands I would likely hear if I flipped on a radio station that played current hit tunes. At least half of his photos showed bands in action in concert, although he'd taken the sort of moody planned shots that adorn album covers.

Nate also had a sideline in photographing events, including a few corporate bashes. He'd freelanced for a few newspapers, covering community events. His work was professional, crisp and clean, and he had a good eye for composition.

Raven's firm wasn't the only agency who'd licensed his photos, and I recognized a few national ads that used his work.

The art side of his site was interesting, with a mix of urban shots and found photography that felt like a continuation of his senior project that had impressed younger me. Nate had done a few shows, with his shadowy photo of an abandoned doll on a bench being the main advertising for a swanky show at a gallery last winter. When I clicked on his Instagram, one of his pinned posts was a collection of photos from the show, including a picture of him and Raven holding champagne glasses at the opening reception.

But why did he choose to photograph Raven's wedding? It didn't really seem like his thing.

I returned to the photo of Nate and Raven at the gallery opening. Maybe it was just chance, a split second that was easy to misinterpret, but there was a glow of adoration in Nate's eyes as he gazed at my friend. The photo would make Nate my number one suspect if Emmett had been harmed.

But Nate had also seemed close to Ivy. He'd taken her out to dinner when she'd worn out her welcome in Ash's taproom. Had they been friends during our college days? I couldn't remember them together, but I'd done my best to avoid Ivy.

MAYHEM AT A HALLOWEEN WEDDING 169

Nate's Instagram was mostly professional, featuring photos he'd snapped, although there were a handful of pictures of him at work. One of him standing next to his camera, which rested on a tripod next to a stage, caught my eye. He was looking at whoever took the photo with a broad smile. He looked more relaxed than I'd seen him. But maybe he was in his element while doing a gig. Nate hadn't posted any photos of friends or anything from his non-work life, assuming he had one. Not even a food photo or a pet rock.

Instead of musing on Nate's enigma status, I opened Discord and checked. Nate wasn't a member of my college friends Discord group, or if he was, he lurked under a screen name that didn't hint at his real identity.

My friends had posted reminiscences from our college days, with people posting photos that included Ivy. I scrolled through a few, curious if I'd see Nate.

Aaron had posted an album of photos of Ivy, including multiple of them acting lovey-dovey.

"Don't make us puke, bro," someone had written.

"Leave Aaron alone. He's in mourning."

"And denial. Ivy wasn't good for you, bro. But I'm sorry for your loss."

"Remember the time Ivy got Aaron a MIP?"

"MIP? Don't you mean VIP of the fourth floor?"

"Minor in Possession. Ivy acquired a bunch of beer during our freshman year, and when the party was raided, Aaron took the fall."

"Oh yeah. Didn't he end up in Diversion and had drug and alcohol tests for a year? He had to be a good boy."

I didn't remember any of that. But I wasn't surprised that somehow, other people had taken the fall for Ivy.

I was in one of the photos. During our first semester as college students, we all had to take a first-year seminar, although the class content varied depending on who was teaching it. A trip to the Portland Opera was part of the class for all of the new students, and we'd all dressed up. Ivy had her elbow linked with Raven, and one of our dorm mates was striking a dramatic model pose next to them.

I was laughing over on the side of the photo, not quite lurking, but definitely not center stage.

I'd never sensed that Raven overly cared about being in the spotlight, although she found herself there often. Our professors had loved her. Our classmates, male and female, had adored her. She'd naturally been in the center. Maybe she'd just accepted we'd all be in her orbit, although Ivy had fought for space in the center with her.

Maybe Danby had a point when she said that Raven had been complicit in Ivy's bad behavior, for example, when it had been directed at me.

I sent Nate a reminder email about the photos, and started to go back to Discord.

The door of the shop jangled, and I put my phone down.

Time to get to work.

Atticus had come in for his shift, and I'd retreated to the workroom to pull stock for my sales associate to shelve. Then, as he shelved the books, I started packaging online orders. Jack had followed me to the back, concerned that treats might be involved. What would happen if I dropped dog treats without Jack around to clean them up for me?

Or he just liked keeping me in his line of sight. Unlike his Great Pyrenees ancestors, he doesn't have sheep to protect, so he's decided I'm his sheep.

I heard a thunk from the basement as I pasted a label on a flat rate box. I glanced over at the haunted dollhouse Rex had given me, which I'd shifted into the back corner of the counter as I waited for a chance to start refurbishing it. It was still, while I heard another faint thunk.

Definitely coming from downstairs, versus the dollhouse.

I stuck my head out of the back room. "Hey, Atticus? I'm going down to the basement. If I'm not back in five minutes, get help."

"Umm . . ."

With Jack at my heels, I grabbed a flashlight, opened the basement door, and descended into the darkness.

As I stepped onto the basement floor, I heard a flailing sound, followed by a thud. I shone my light toward the noise.

A teenager in an oversized royal hoodie finally freed his feet from a fleece blanket.

Make that her fleece blanket. She had a long, greasy ponytail and an elfin face. She was tiny, barely over five feet, and slight.

"It's okay. Please stop panicking."

The girl breathed heavily and clearly wanted to flee.

"What are you doing in the basement of my bookshop?"

Jack stood against the side of my thigh, quietly letting me know he was there.

"Hiding, obviously. Wait, I'm under the bookshop? I thought I was closer to the river." Her hand trembled as she pushed a few hair strands behind her ear.

"So what's your name?" I channeled my inner Colby and made my voice sound stern.

"What's it matter to you?" Her voice was hoarse.

She better not have caught pneumonia sleeping in my basement.

"I'm Bailey. I own the store above us."

"I know who you are. You've helped at some of the library events," the girl said. She sat down on her blanket. "I'm Kylie."

"Okay, Kylie. What's going on? Are you afraid of someone, and that's why you're hiding?"

"Yeah, I'm afraid of the police." She stared at her feet. "Can you point the flashlight somewhere else?"

I adjusted the flashlight so it didn't shine directly at Kylie but still lit her up enough for me to see her.

"Is there a reason why you're afraid of the police?"

"Duh, because they want to arrest me." She looked up briefly, then her gaze went to one of her battered running shoes. She fiddled with the laces. "I caused the explosion during the parade."

"I thought multiple teens were responsible? At least, that's what the rumor mill said."

"I was what adults call the ringleader. It was my plan. But we didn't mean to hurt anyone. But if that woman died because of us, we're responsible, right? I could go to jail for, like, forever."

"What's worse? Facing the consequences, or hiding out in dingy basements?"

"Actually, the tunnels are pretty cool."

"Are there rats down here?" I asked, and shivered.

I really hoped we didn't have rats.

"Not that I've seen, at least around here. It might be different, closer to the river, but I haven't explored those tunnels much. Those seem dangerous and damp. But the ones around here seem more stable."

"Then this clearly is a paradise." There's nothing like sitting in a dark basement, talking to a runaway-slash–teenage fugitive. She had to be hungry.

"It is a bit dark, and I miss running water. And heat." Kylie half smiled, then looked down again.

"Don't you think your parents are worried?"

Kylie scoffed. "I doubt my dad has even noticed I'm gone. He's not around much."

There were a lot of layers to unpack there, but it wasn't my immediate concern.

"You should know that the woman most likely didn't die because of your fireworks. Someone attacked her."

Kylie's gaze darted up. "She wasn't knocked over by the crowd and trampled?"

"I don't think so."

Kylie started to cry. "I'm sorry she's dead, but I hope you're right. I never wanted to kill anyone."

"Why'd you create the bomb?" I asked.

"It was just a prank. The homecoming court thinks they're such hot stuff, and I thought making them jump would be funny. Maybe pee their skimpy dresses. So I talked to some friends and we came up with a plan. It was just fireworks in a metal garbage can. We tested it. It's loud, but it's not dangerous."

In retrospect, the teens were lucky no one had fallen off a float and broken something, including their necks. But I kept that tidbit inside my brain where it belonged.

"C'mon, Kylie, let's go upstairs. You can use our bathroom, and I'll make you a cup of tea while I call my friend at the police department. Facing the police has to be better than sleeping down here." I also didn't want to call Detective Whitlock and tell him I'd had the missing teen in my basement, but she'd fled in a previously unknown tunnel, as I was waiting until after the holiday to tell Jude.

Kylie closed her eyes for a moment, then nodded. She stood up and picked up her blanket and a tattered backpack. I motioned for her to go up the stairs first, which let me notice her left sneaker had a hole. Jack followed along behind me.

Once we were upstairs, I pointed out the bathroom and set the kettle to boil while I called Detective Whitlock.

"Long story, but I found a teenage girl named Kylie hiding in my bookshop's basement," I said when he answered. I put teabags of my favorite Hot Cinnamon Spice black tea into two mugs.

"Kylie Andrews?"

"She said she's the mastermind behind the bombing at the parade."

"Keep her there, and I'll be right over."

When the kettle came to a boil, I poured the water over the tea bags and set the timer for five minutes. I pulled crackers out of the break room snack closet, along with peanut butter, honey, a plate, and a spoon.

Kylie came out of the bathroom. She'd washed her face, but her hoodie and baggy jeans were still dusty.

I motioned to the food, and her eyes lit up. She loaded up a cracker with peanut butter and shoved the whole thing in her mouth.

The timer chimed, so I pulled the tea bags out and handed a mug to Kylie.

"Why are you being so nice to me?" Kylie asked. Her voice was muffled since her mouth was full of her third cracker.

"I found you hiding under my store. What was I supposed to do, sit on you?"

She half smiled again. Her elfin face was probably adorable when she hadn't been hanging out in a dank basement for several days.

Hmm, Jonah had heard a teenage boy was missing. I'd need to tell him the rumor mill had only been partially right.

"Where did you get into the tunnels?" I asked. "I'd like to know to make sure people aren't sneaking into my store."

"The groundskeeper's hut in Goblin Gate Park is my usual entrance. It's supposed to be locked, but I don't think the park workers know the tunnel entrance is there 'cause they frequently leave it unlocked while they work. There's also an access point not too far from the river, but it's my least favorite."

"Bailey! Someone's—"

"Send him back!"

Detective Whitlock walked in, followed by a uniformed officer. Kylie turned pale. She put her cracker down, and her hands started to shake.

"Kylie, I'm glad you're safe. You had us worried," the detective said.

"So, I'm like, free to go?" From her tone, she knew the answer was no, but she had to try.

"No, I'm arresting you. But I'm glad you seem healthy and are in one piece." Detective Whitlock stood in the doorway like he was blocking Kylie's means of escape. Little did he know she could burrow underground. Which explained why no one had found her.

Kylie gulped down her tea, and ate another cracker before saying, "Okay, I'm ready for my perp walk."

Detective Whitlock shook his head. "You watch too much TV. Okay, hands behind your back, please."

The uniformed officer read Kylie her rights and escorted her out of the store.

"Thanks for calling," Detective Whitlock said.

"As I told Kylie, there was no way I was leaving her in my basement."

"How did she get inside? Did she break into your store? Sneak in?" the detective asked.

"No, and no. You know the tunnel system, right?"

"I've heard of it. It's mostly rumor, right?"

"No, it's real, and it turns out there's an entrance in my basement, which I just found out about several days ago. Kylie used it to access the basement, which is evidentially drier and less creepy than the tunnels by the river."

Detective Whitlock understood my point before I had to spell it out. "Some of the teens in town are exploring the tunnels?"

I nodded. "One of the entrances is in the groundskeeper's hunt in Goblin Gate Park. It's supposed to be locked shut, but that didn't stop Kylie."

"Let's talk more about this later. I need to go deal with our bomber now."

"She didn't mean to hurt anyone!" I called out as he left.

I sat down with my tea, as I clearly deserved a short break.

The explosion and Ivy's death weren't directly linked. Had the killer just seen their chance and taken it?

There had to be more to the story.

And I realized that if Kylie did her community service in town, as I assumed that would be her eventual juvenile sentence, I should connect her with Jude.

He'd love to hear about Kylie's tunnel explorations.

Chapter 21

Not long after Detective Whitlock escorted Kylie out of the shop, my phone calendar dinged with an appointment reminder. Sadly for Jack, he was scheduled to be groomed at Kristobel's pet shop, Bad to the Bone. I could've gone the DIY option at her shop or tried to give him a bath at home, but I hate the way Jack gives me sad eyes like I'm torturing him physically while saying bad things about his mother. The groomer would Dremel his nails, and he'd come home smelling faintly of perfume made for dogs and, most likely, wearing a new bandana.

Kristobel fawned over Jack when we entered like she always does. But when she tried to walk Jack to the far back of the shop, where the groomer worked, he dug in all four paws.

"C'mon, buddy," she said.

Jack turned and tried to walk to the front door. His tail was tucked between his legs, and I felt my resolve waver.

But Kristobel was made of sterner stuff. "You're a tough boy, Jack. You can handle a bath."

His eyes didn't waver from the front door.

Feeling like a traitor, I gently turned Jack, taking care to miss a rack of sunglasses made for dogs. I helped Kristobel escort him to the grooming studio. He begrudgingly jumped onto a table, and the groomer gently put the grooming loop over his head, then pushed a lever with her foot to raise the table to waist height.

Jack looked at me with big eyes, and I turned.

And I fled, leaving him to his fate. Kristobel followed me out into the store.

"Jack will be fine," Kristobel told me.

"I know. He just looks so sad." Like he couldn't believe we were torturing him like this.

"Yet as soon as he's done, he'll want the groomer to pet him."

"I know. I'll see you soon."

I paused on my journey back to the bookshop after leaving Jack behind, trying to forget the soulful look in his eyes.

I finally remembered where I'd met Finn.

But he hadn't been Finn then. He'd been Séraphin and pronounced the end of his name more like "fun" than "fin." I still remember how angry I felt when I heard him being teased and called Sarah by one of the boys on our swim team, who'd always been a bully. Séraphin had spent the summer with his grandparents in Elyan Hollow when his family was undergoing some sort of turmoil, and he'd trained and competed with our swim team while he was in town. He'd been small for his age, with a squeaky voice. But his eyes were the same.

We'd become friends after I'd told off one of the boys who kept calling him Sarah and threatened to put itching powder in his goggles, even though I wasn't sure what that was, although I'd read about it. Séraphin and I had shared graphic novels and books, and I'd cried when he left. We'd promised to stay in touch.

But we didn't.

In our defense, we'd been maybe nine years old.

And now he was back in town, and he clearly remembered me. Was he offended that I didn't recognize him?

I detoured and headed to the Museum of Peculiar Oddities. I bypassed the pie machine and smiled when I saw Finn behind the counter of his shop.

"Hello, Elyan Hollow's own Miss Marple."

"Hello, Séraphin Tremblay," I said.

He smiled. "Took you long enough, Bailey Briggs. Although that's no longer my name."

"You changed it?"

"I legally changed my first name to Finn when I was eighteen. When my mother remarried when I was ten, she changed our last name to Thomas. It's boring, but it's easy." He slowly smiled, and something in my stomach quivered.

"Knowing that I recognized you but not being able to figure out from where was rankling me."

"You know, you could have asked." Finn closed his notebook and put his pen down on top of it.

"True."

"And I had faith you'd get there eventually." Finn leaned forward and rested his arms against the counter. "You're still the same. I was afraid when I came back that Elyan Hollow wouldn't live up to what I remembered. But it's better in some ways."

"Do you also do something with retro arcade games?" I asked.

"Random change in subject, but yes. I started helping out a guy who refurbished machines when I was earning a degree in electrical engineering. He retired right after I graduated and sold me his business for one dollar plus a greasy spoon breakfast. Best value for crappy hash browns ever. It was a side hustle for a while, then my main gig, and now it's a side hustle again while I get my empire here set up."

"Empire?"

"Don't pretend you haven't been fascinated by the construction on the other side of the building."

"That's right. I'm curious."

"Here's a clue, and I heard this years ago, so I can't take credit for it. A man is in a room with no windows and no doors. He has a mirror and a table. How does he escape?"

A riddle emporium?

Wait.

"You're building an escape room," I said.

"How'd you guess?"

"The man escapes the room because he saw himself in the mirror, so he took the saw and cut the table in half. Two halves make a hole, so he escaped by jumping through the hole. Since your riddle was about escaping a room, the answer was a little obvious." It'd helped that I heard that riddle before, too.

The little voice in the back of my mind reminded me that Finn's grandfather had told it to us.

"Smart, Briggs. Smart."

"So you'll have two businesses and also refurbish arcade machines here?"

Finn shook his head. "I inherited my grandparents' house off of Birch, and they had a pretty sweet workshop that I've adapted. I considered adding arcade games or classic pinball to the Museum, but the idea doesn't quite fit my goals. And I will make more reselling them than I would if I let tourists use them. And you know some kid would break them. It's inevitable."

For some reason, I used my thumb to motion over my shoulder. "I have to get back to work, but maybe we could grab coffee soon? Or dinner?" I asked.

"I'd enjoy that." Finn raised his eyebrows slightly, and his smile felt a tad smug.

I realized why: I'd just asked him out. My stomach fluttered again.

"I don't think I said this before, but I really am sorry about your friend," Finn said. "I know I'm teasing you about being Miss Marple, but I can understand why you don't want to just sit and do nothing."

"It's a sad situation all around," I said. "Do you remember Colby? She was two years older than us but was on the swim team, too. She's one of my best friends, and she's a suspect, but I know there's no way she did it. So that's why I'm investigating."

"I see you're still loyal and fearless," Finn said. "Hey, give me your number, and we'll set up that dinner. And if I hear anything that could help Colby, I'll let you know."

After we exchanged numbers, I said, "I take it you're good with electronics?"

"Why do I feel like an ask is coming up?"

"Someday, if you feel up feel up for it, and you can say no, I'm rehabbing an old dollhouse, and the lights installed it in don't seem to work. It's for the children's section of the bookshop."

"You don't want your miniature house to burn down due to faulty wiring?"

"And I'd hate if it took out the store along with it. Bookshops are full of paper, which I'd guess burns well." The sprinkler system going off by accident was on the reverse side of that fear coin.

"Safe assumption. I guess it'll depend on how that dinner goes, but it sounds like helping you would be a public service."

A few minutes later, I was almost positive I was blushing as I left the Museum.

One thing Finn said made me realize something.

The way our friends see us is colored by past interactions. What we did five years ago can matter as much, if not more, than our current selves. Finn was inclined to like me because my younger self had been kind to him.

Raven had been tied to Ivy by their bond of friendship, and Ivy may have been a good friend to Raven over the years and vice versa. Although I doubted it.

But I strongly suspected I knew what had happened and why.

Now I just needed to prove it.

Chapter 22

While I could think of many things I should do, both wedding- and bookshop-related, I still headed to my usual Tuesday volunteering gig with my local library. Delivering books to shut-ins was always a highlight of my week, and thankfully, Colby had promised to make sure my route was lighter than usual. Added bonus: Jack should be ready to be picked up once I am done.

When I parked outside the library, my eyebrows rose.

Aaron was in the parking lot, skulking near the book return drop.

Which made this a fortuitous moment.

"Hey, Aaron!" I called out.

He started to walk away, but I did the same thing he'd done to me and practically ran to catch up with him.

"I have a question for you," I said.

"Umm, hi, Bailey," he said.

"Do you know where Ivy was living before she came to Elyan Hollow for the wedding?" I asked. Maybe, if I could figure out Ivy's recent history, it'd lead to evidence I could give to Detective Whitlock to prove Colby was innocent.

"Denver."

"Nah, I heard she left. She had some financial issues."

Aaron sighed. "Fine. We spent a few months traveling in a camper van, all right? But then I dropped her off in San Francisco a few weeks ago, and she was going to take a train to Seattle after the wedding, and we were going to meet up there. I'm going to start a job there in a few weeks, and Ivy was going to move in with me. We were finally going to be together. Obviously, that plan wasn't meant to be."

If Aaron was telling me the truth now, he had lied to me the other day.

Could I trust anything he said?

And if he had thought he was due to have a happy ever after with Ivy, maybe he'd also been lying to himself.

"Listen, I have a commitment, but we need to talk again later." I turned and marched into the library.

But this fit my theory: Aaron had done it. He must've come into town and been at the parade in costume. He'd snapped for some reason, hit Ivy, and fled. He must've left, then rented a car and returned so no one would see his camper van and put it all together. He kept changing his story as I caught him in lie after lie.

Maybe he'd seen Ivy with Nate and realized his happy ever after wasn't meant to be. That Ivy would never match up to the vision of her in his head.

It would've been wiser to leave and pretend he'd never been here in the first place.

Colby waved to me when I walked back to the volunteer zone. She wore a jaunty teal and white scarf over her Elyan Hollow Library long-sleeve polo shirt.

"I just have two deliveries for you. I tried to make it zero, but I just couldn't make it work."

"That's fine."

My deliveries were on the north side of town, and both were regulars on my route. One of my fellow volunteers arrived, and since she had agreed to take most of my deliveries, I helped her and Colby load up the cart she'd use to roll the books, all packaged in tote bags, out to her car.

As we pushed the cart out, the other volunteer suddenly said,

"I'm just going to visit the little girls' room, but you know what my car looks like!" and darted to the women's room.

"Bladder issues, I think," Colby muttered. "Not that it's any of my business. But she's talked about it loudly in the library before."

After a few steps, the head of the library said, "Bailey!" So I stopped, and Colby pushed the cart outside.

"Are you still willing to donate books to the Jolabokaflod children's book drive?" she asked. The library was starting its own version of a giving tree for children's books, based on Iceland's famed "book flood," where everyone gets a new book to read on Christmas Eve. They planned to have a party for the kids and give out their books and cups of hot chocolate.

"Of course. I've already sketched out a few plans to encourage donations, which I'll run past you after Halloween. Marion at the Sleepy Hollow Inn is joining forces with me."

"I'm relieved. Well, don't let me keep you. And thank you for being such a dedicated volunteer."

"Thanks," I said, feeling awkward. I walked outside and turned toward my car.

Only to see Colby kneeling on the sidewalk about ten feet past the book return, next to someone who'd fallen to the ground.

Her cart was abandoned in the middle of the parking lot, and it slowly rolled to rest against the bumper of a minivan.

I rushed over. "What can I do to help?" I said.

I realized the body was Aaron. Colby held a scarf to his throat, which was gushing blood. His eyes were wide open and blinked at me.

"Call nine-one-one," Colby ordered.

I did, and a crowd collected around us. Someone handed over a towel, which Colby layered over her scarf and pushed down on, knowing that removing the scarf would harm any clotting that had started.

A police car screamed into the parking lot, followed by a second one and a fire truck. The firefighters jumped into action, with one of them seamlessly taking over for Colby.

Then the ambulance arrived.

But from the way Aaron's body had turned limp, I knew it was too late.

Once the professionals had taken over, Colby and I retreated to the ledge between the planters and the sidewalk. "Did Aaron say anything?" I asked Colby.

She shook her head slowly. She stared at her hands, which were still streaked with blood. "No. I just came out, and he was on the ground. So I grabbed my scarf and did what I could to help. I liked that scarf."

I put my arm around her shoulders, and she leaned against me.

Detective Whitlock walked up.

"What happened?" he asked.

Colby stayed quiet and just stared at the pavement, so I said, "Colby found Aaron on the ground and started first aid. I came out of the library and called nine-one-one."

"Stay here." The detective walked off.

It felt like ages, but it was maybe an hour when Detective Whitlock returned.

"You weren't with Colby when she found Aaron?" he asked.

I shook my head. "No, I was waylaid as we were taking a book cart out, and Colby left the library first."

Detective Whitlock's eyes lasered in on Colby. "Aaron Blanton just happened to be stabbed in an area of the library parking lot without video coverage? Something all the librarians on staff know about, but especially the librarian applying for grants to get additional security cameras?"

"I can't help it if I'm the go-to grant writer, and clearly, we need more coverage to protect our patrons," Colby said.

"Colby Snow, you're under arrest for the murder of Aaron Blanton. You have the right to remain silent—"

I stood up. "This is ridiculous. Colby didn't do anything wrong. She just tried to save him!"

"Anything you say can and will be used against you in a court of law. You have the right to speak to an attorney and to have an attorney present during any questioning."

"Don't say anything, Colby. I'll call Evelyn and get an attorney for you."

Colby nodded at me and didn't say anything or resist as Detective Whitlock cuffed her and escorted her to a squad car. She looked defeated.

Or maybe she was just in shock. A man had just died as she tried to save him.

I called Evelyn and explained the situation.

"I'm going to call my friend. If she can't make it, I'll go to the police station and stall until she can be there."

Evelyn hung up, and I stared at my phone for a moment.

Who should I call next? I metaphorically put my feet in Colby's shoes and followed my heart. I scrolled through my address book and made a call.

"Hayes? We have an emergency here in town."

Chapter 23

I felt wrecked as I drove back to work. I parked at home and just wanted to go upstairs, fall into bed, and nap until this nightmare was over.

But that wouldn't help anything, so I walked back downtown.

At least Jack was ready to be picked up. He was sitting behind the pet boutique register, supervising Kristobel as she did something on her laptop. When Jack saw me, he trotted over. He was wearing his halter, and his leash dragged on the ground behind him.

He also wore a new orange Americana bandana and smelled slightly of dog cologne.

"Jack was an angel as usual," Kristobel said. I could hear the smile in her voice.

"Good." I paid for Jack's grooming appointment and added my usual tip.

"Are you okay? You seem down," Kristobel said.

"Just tired." I really didn't want to get into the story of what had happened. That I'd watched a man die.

Jack and I left and headed to the bookshop. As we approached Lazy Bones, Sam Maki walked up.

"You okay? You look off," he said.

"It's lovely to see you, too," I said. Sam followed me inside. "Come back and chat with me in the workroom?"

"Sure, book dealer," Sam said. "Hi, Atticus. And Tara, it's lovely to see you again."

Once the workroom door shut behind us, Sam said, "Seriously, what's wrong?"

I paced while Jack and Sam watched me. I explained what had happened. "There's no way that Colby did it."

"And we'll prove it," Sam said. "Want to go over what I've found out?"

"Might as well."

Sam pulled a tablet out of his satchel and opened a file.

"Your friends getting married seem like a good match," Sam said.

"What do you mean?" I turned to study Sam's expression.

"They seem to be similar, but in a good way. They also seem like they never resist the opportunity to dress up. From their socials, they had four different Halloween costumes last year. Their cosplay at comic cons is good enough that people ask to take pictures with them."

"Raven's always been a fan of costumes." At the moment, I wondered if her whole life was a costume and if I'd ever met the real person deep inside.

Maybe the key to this whole case was Raven, and I'd been distracted by Ivy. Maybe Harmony really was supposed to be the victim.

But then why had someone attacked Aaron?

"Raven and Emmett also seem matched in other ways. Granted, this is just what they show on social media, but they seem to have fun together, even when they're not dressing up. Like Emmett said, after a week and long hours, Raven made his favorite dinner from scratch, and they had a weekend in, even though Raven had other plans."

"Most people only post the good things," I said. "The people who focus on social media drama concern me. As bad as things turned with Hunter, I'm relieved he didn't take his grievances to social media."

"True, but Emmett's throwaway Reddit account talks about his plans, and keeping Raven happy is a huge factor. But it doesn't feel like she's demanding; he just sees the big picture and how decisions can affect their partnership. I'm a little jealous."

"You found Emmett's throwaway account?" The whole point of throwaways is to stay anonymous.

"Emmett has three, while Raven only has one throwaway. But Emmett regularly forgets which account he's logged into, and he has accidentally commented on his throwaways multiple times, answering people's questions. In one, he asked for ideas for a surprise for Raven for her birthday."

"What's the other one?"

"Emmett likes to give employment advice to people graduating with degrees in math, but he doesn't want it to link back to his main account. He seems genuinely nice. So nice, I'm almost suspicious."

"It's hard to believe I'm saying this, but I agree." Was Emmett too nice? He'd hoped Raven and Ivy would drift apart after he and Raven tied the knot. Had he gotten impatient and taken matters into his own hands? Supposedly, he was at his bachelor party, but people were in costume at the parade. He could've been one of the Grim Reapers skulking around town with his friends. Only to see an opportunity during the panic following the explosion.

He'd shown up at the Popcorn Palace awfully fast.

"Your friend Raven is quite the artist. Her old DeviantArt profile is fire."

"She's truly talented." My only complaint about her art, which our professors had also mentioned, is that Raven's work is technically perfect but somewhat derivative. She'd never quite figured out her unique style and copied other artists. But that same chameleon ability must've served her well when creating ad campaigns.

But it could be another hint that Raven didn't even know herself.

"Did she quit drawing?"

I paused. "That's a good question. The last time I asked, Raven said she was working a lot for her ad agency, and she's an art director these days, so she manages projects. She could be too tired to draw at the end of the day." Now that I thought about it, Raven had quit sending me clips of her artwork when she'd jumped wholeheartedly into cosplay. Now she was more likely to send me photos of costumes in progress and tidbits about the history of sewing.

"Next up. Raven's sister, Harmony, is nothing like her sister," Sam said.

"Tell me about it." I started pacing again.

"All right," Sam said, and started talking quickly, showing me we needed to discuss the meaning of sarcasm. "Raven, as you know, is artsy. Their mother is a potter with her own shop, and it looks like the shop's sales are steady. She's had the same studio and shop for decades, so I'd guess they own them both free and clear. Their father is a bit of a jack-of-all-trades and does a lot of handyman gigs. He seems to be a skilled carpenter. But he also makes sculptures with driftwood, which people actually buy. Based on the examples, I can see why people appreciate his work. But Harmony seems more, I don't know, conventional."

I nodded. "I've always thought she was jealous of her sister."

"Harmony's also in debt. A scary amount of debt."

"I thought you were only going to search public records?" I asked.

"I did. I found her bankruptcy filing."

My eyes widened. "Dang."

"She'll come out of this okay, but it's the worst type of debt. It's not like she had medical bills or something traumatic."

Did Raven know about this? Or their parents?

"How did Harmony get into trouble?"

"My guess is overconsumption, but this is just speculation. Harmony is trying to live the life of a glamorous social media influencer. But she's not making enough money from paid social media posts to fund her desired lifestyle. From what I can tell, some of the posts she claimed are sponsored aren't even paid."

I shook my head. "She lied? Please tell me she at least received free products."

"I'm fairly confident her pants were on fire. Which might be why she kept buying new pairs of designer jeans."

"Other than that, Harmony's life seems unremarkable, and I can't see any connections between her and Ivy. But speaking of connections, there is one between Olivia Rojas and Ivy Monroe, but it's tenuous. A few months ago, they were tagged in a post by a chef who had just opened a new café in Sellwood. She thanked the servers and kitchen staff she'd worked with over the years for giving her the knowledge and inspiration to follow her dream of bringing artisanal fried chicken and jojos to the masses."

"Did she honestly write that?"

"I made up the part about the masses, but her reviews primarily focus on her chicken and jojos. Some of the reviews praised that she got jojos right, and I hadn't realized that jojos were a local specialty that people take seriously until looking into this for you. She has a Hatch green chili meatloaf sandwich I might have to try the next time I'm in southeast Portland," Sam said. "Olivia seems respectable. You probably know that she's a first-generation American, and she did very well in high school. She's posted about higher education costs being ridiculous, so I'd extrapolate that's why she did a certificate program at a community college versus the traditional university route.

"Mila, her partner, also looks pretty good. She has a bachelor's degree in a food science program, and her record is squeaky clean. She doesn't even have a parking ticket. She's received the highest rating for cleanliness every time their cart and commissary kitchen have been inspected. And she volunteers with a group that assists Russian immigrants and even does some English-to-Russian interpretation.

"Now Ivy—that girl is trouble. She's lucky a narcotics detective never focused on her because her social media makes it clear she's dealing drugs. I'm shocked I didn't pull up a single arrest report."

"She must've been lucky." I quit pacing and leaned against the workroom table.

"Or she was an informant, but that's a wild guess with no proof."

Sam raised his eyebrows at me and smiled slowly. "Thoughts? Want me to look up anything else?"

Sam's phone dinged, and he frowned. "I've got to go. I'll text you later."

He practically ran out, and I collapsed into the bean bag chair in the corner of the workroom. Jack came over and lay down partially sprawled across my lap.

I thought the bachelorette party was horrible, but today was worse.

Mila and Olivia. Harmony.

And Jet.

Something told me I needed to talk to Jet again.

Plus Olivia.

Could Harmony be the villain in this charade? It struck me that Harmony and Emmett had one thing in common: Harmony was the black sheep of her family, while Emmett was the odd man out in his. But for flip-flopped reasons. Harmony was too conventional, and Emmett wasn't conventional enough.

And Emmett had plenty of reasons to wish Ivy was out of the picture.

But why would any of them hurt Aaron?

I straightened up. Unless Aaron had discovered the truth, and found out who'd killed Ivy. He'd been sniffing around town. Maybe he'd discovered the killer. But the killer had struck again to keep the truth from coming to light.

Or maybe Aaron conspired with someone else, and that person remembered the adage, "Two can keep a secret if one of them is dead."

"I want this all to end and to unmask the real murderer," I told Jack. "And that will never happen if I keep sitting here, feeling sorry for myself."

I pushed up with my arms and raised my hips, and Jack reluctantly moved off me, and the bean bag.

"You can stay here or go investigate with me."

Jack chose to come with.

* * *

I'd just stepped out of the bookstore when yet another person stopped me.

"You're Bailey, correct?" Lark's dad asked.

"Bailey Briggs, at your service." I pulled deep into my reserve of patience to stay civil for Lark's sake.

"Do you know the botanical garden off of Highway 30?"

"The Campbell Estate? It's lovely. Or at least it was. I've heard that it's gotten rundown since the owner died, and his heirs put it on the market." I'd been there before, but it'd been a few years since it'd been open. But it was beautiful and serene.

I could use some serenity right about now.

"I'm planning to buy it, and I need someone to talk to Lark and convince her to listen to me. So far, she's only told me to get lost. I want her to be okay with me moving to town. Otherwise I'm afraid she'd leave."

"Umm, I can talk to Lark, but I don't know how you'd expect that to help." My hands wanted to fidget so I shoved them in my jacket pockets.

"I wish I had a few ideas on how to show Lark that I have good intentions, and that we can re-establish a relationship. And I have good intentions with the estate. I want to reopen the gardens for the general public. I've spent many years working long hours, and now that I'm retiring, I want a fun project."

Most take up golf or a craft project, but I guess buying a multi-million-dollar estate could be a hobby for some people.

It also made me wonder how, or rather who, Lark had gotten a loan from to buy her shop. She'd talked about the payment plan a few times during knit night.

A few ideas crystalized in my brain. "Well, as far as ideas, you could turn the garden into the 'fright forest' during the next festival and fundraise for a worthy cause, like children's literacy or education, or an ecological nonprofit," I said. "You could hire local students to dress up in scary costumes and wander the grounds. Or see if the local community college has a drama club that'd like to participate. Or even the local community theater. You could look into building a few temporary displays in the gardens, as long as it won't harm the plants."

"People would enjoy that?" His tone was skeptical.

"They'd flock to it. You could even do an after-dark program for older teens, or maybe just adults, 'cause that way you could sell overpriced glasses of wine. All in the name of charity, of course."

"Hmm."

I could tell he wasn't sold but he was thinking about it.

"You know," he said, "there's an amphitheater in the garden, not too far from the house. It needs a little refurbishment, but once it's fixed, your literary festival might be interested in holding an event there. Or maybe a summer lit series, or maybe music. Something that goes well with overpriced wine and could fund, perhaps, music education."

"Now you're getting it. Listen, I need to go, but I can chat with you or Lark after Halloween."

Jack and I made our escape, and I really did need to talk to Lark about her dad.

But first, I had to catch a murderer and get my best friend out of jail.

Chapter 24

As I walked into Uncanny Little Charms, I knew I should finesse my conversation with Jet. Coax her into talking.

But I was running out of time.

"Listen, Jet," I said. "I don't mean to be indelicate, but I saw how you turned and fled when you saw Ivy in the taproom a few days before her death. I need to know why. I promise it's important and not just me being nosy."

Jet blinked for a moment.

"I never met Ivy," Jet said. "She wasn't who I was trying to avoid that night in the taproom. But you're right. I did flee. Because I'm a coward, but I can't handle another year of hiding."

My mind worked through the various wedding guests who'd been in the taproom. Harmony? Did they have an influencer-designer collaboration that had gone bad? "Who were you avoiding?" I asked.

"Nate." She walked over to her couch and sat down. She crossed her hands in her lap.

I sat down by her. "Why?"

"I don't know if stalking is quite the right term. I mean, Nate didn't do anything so extreme that I could've gone to the police." Jet rubbed the back of her neck, and her eyes were focused on the table in front of her.

"I'm making a muddle of this. Nate's sister was one of my childhood friends, and when she had an extended seizure, it broke something inside me. I miss her so much. And it broke something inside Nate. She was only a teenager, and she'd never had a seizure or anything like that before." Jet looked down at her hands. One of her rings was a design of two linked hearts.

"Did she die?" Jet would probably hate me after today.

Jet shook her head. "That might have been easier. She suffered massive brain damage. The girl we knew is gone, but her body is still here. It's hard, especially because there's just enough left so she's happy to see me, but she can't communicate. And I feel guilty that I'm out here following my dreams, and she's in a group home. She was the smartest person I knew. She graduated high school at sixteen. She was going to be a pediatrician. And she would've succeeded. She was brilliant."

"That's so rough." Compassion welled up inside me. She wasn't my little sister biologically, but I'd feel devasted if something like that happened to Danby. Or Colby, for that matter.

"I stayed in touch with Nate because of his sister. When I needed some photography work done a few years ago, I emailed him. I wasn't sure if he'd be interested, but I thought he might know someone. When he said he'd be happy to do it, I looked forward to reconnecting with him."

"But things changed?"

"Nate did a good job with the photos, but he seemed annoyed with me. I thought I was hovering, so I gave him space. But then I realized he was angry at me for living my life while his sister would never recover. That's when I learned that his family struggles to pay for his sister's care. She's in a great facility, and they don't want to move her to one where she won't get the same level of attention. And I guess Nate just couldn't control his resentment."

"You said he stalked you?"

"Yeah, sort of. Every few weeks, Nate kept showing up places I'd be, even though we didn't live in the same city. It was freaky, and it made me paranoid about going out. But he never did anything.

Sometimes, he didn't even talk to me; he'd just nurse a drink at the bar, and I'd sometimes just feel him staring at me. When I'd look over, he wouldn't look away, and just smirk at me. I ended up getting a new phone and a new laptop. I moved. And I didn't see Nate for a year."

"Until last Wednesday."

"Exactly. It made me feel nauseated."

"I'm sorry for being so rude and demanding." I'd poked my nose into something that really wasn't my business.

"It's okay. I'm glad someone here knows about it now. It was hard to tell my friends because no one took it seriously. But it just made me nervous."

"And now the nightmare has started up again for you. If there's anything I can do to help, let me know."

"But I'm not going to let Nate throw me off my game again," Jet said. Her gaze met mine. "You know who you should talk to?"

I raised my eyebrows.

"Olivia. I saw the blonde with Nate try to give Olivia something, and she threw it back in her face. Literally bounced it off her nose. As Olivia walked off, the blonde said she'd regret this. And then later that day, she was dead."

"I guess I need to go find her."

Chapter 25

Before I confronted Olivia, I paused to look up the Boorito's social media accounts. I'd been friends with Milana, Mila for short, and Olivia since they'd moved to town and opened the cart in the taproom's backyard. They both come to our knit nights, although rarely together because one usually needed to manage the cart. Sam's commentary earlier minded me how Mila spent her rare nights off volunteering in an outreach program for Russian immigrants. She'd immigrated as a child and told me once that Russian is the fourth-most-spoken language in nearby Multnomah County, which includes Portland, the biggest city in the state.

Olivia had been tagged in a collection of photos by a local chef. She was in one of the last photos, in the center with her arm around a woman in a chef's jacket, also the woman who'd posted the photo, with six other people around them.

"Have I mentioned I have the best staff?" the chef had written.

And in the back row, looking like she wanted to fade away, was Ivy.

Or maybe I was reading too much into the turned head and posture that looked like she was stepping backward.

This must be the photo Sam had mentioned.

My thoughts trailed back to Mila and Olivia.

Mila once told me about earning her degree in nutrition and

food services systems from Oregon State, but that her favorite class had been a hands-on French pastries class when she was earning her associate's before transferring to OSU.

I'd thought Olivia had gone to community college for a business certificate, although maybe I'd gotten it wrong. The cart recipes were based on Olivia's grandmother's recipes, but Mila ran the cooking side of the business while Olivia handled the customer interactions. When I'd ordered catering for the Spooky Season Lit Fest, Mila had been on top of ordering the various ingredients Boorito needed while Olivia worked with Mila's plans and came up with a price.

I reminded myself of something important:

Ivy's death might have been an accident.

But there's no way Aaron's death wasn't calculated.

And Olivia might know something, although I couldn't imagine her attacking Aaron.

Olivia was working as I walked up to Boorito.

"Bailey, how's it going?"

My voice was flat as I spoke. "Colby was arrested, and I need to know your history with Ivy."

"You don't think I killed her?" Olivia put her hand on her chest.

"Of course not. But I think you know something about Ivy that might help me find her killer." I wondered if Olivia could hear the frantic note layered under my voice. I felt it, all the way from my brain down to my toes.

Olivia stared at me for a moment, then sighed. She reached down, pulled two bottles of water out of their fridge, and handed me one.

"Let's sit in one of the shipping containers for a few minutes."

One of my favorite aspects of the taproom's backyard is the shipping containers converted into covered seating. Ash even sets up tabletop fireplaces in the winter, making the containers cozy.

But I never thought I'd use one of the containers to talk about murder.

Olivia sat down across from me with a thump. "Yes, I knew Ivy, no, I didn't kill her, and yes, if she'd died when we worked together, I would be the primary suspect. But I've let go of my anger. Mostly."

"What happened?"

"Ivy and I worked in the same restaurant and were almost always scheduled to work together. She started acting really erratic, and customers complained. We kept our water bottles in the hallway between the kitchen and dining room, and one day, I started feeling woozy. I didn't get it at first, but Ivy had drugged me. She was trying to say I was the erratic employee, not her. We were both fired. And I needed that job desperately. My uncle loaned me money for rent that month, or else I would've been homeless. Luckily, I found another job, although it was terrible. The patrons of the restaurant Ivy and I worked tipped very well."

"Yet the chef posted a photo of you full of praise."

Olivia shut her eyes and shook her head. "She's a brilliant chef, but a bit of a flake. She probably forgot we were fired and just posted every old photo she had."

"So that's why you despised Ivy and didn't want to interact with her?"

"That's not the only reason I wanted Ivy to stay as far away from me as possible," Olivia said. "The other night, I ran into Ivy in the bathroom at the taproom, and she was taking a pill. She claimed it was ibuprofen, but I didn't believe her. I debated telling Ash, but instead, I just warned Ivy to stay away. Maybe if I had, and if Ash had kicked her out, Ivy wouldn't have been at the parade. And she wouldn't have died."

Olivia took a long drink of water. "Anything else?"

"Ivy really drugged you?"

Olivia nodded. "And I was applying to a training program, and she made me fail the drug test."

"You must've been furious." She must've wanted revenge.

"I was, but everything turned out all right. Owning Boorito is one of the best choices I've made. Are we done here?"

"I guess. Thanks for talking to me. I really need to figure out what happened." I'd struck out with Jet and Olivia. But there had to be something I could research; someone I could talk to.

Something I could do, other than sit in a converted shipping container while my best friend was in jail.

"Let me know if I can do anything to help except, you know, take the fall for something I didn't do."

"Thanks, Olivia."

Everything looked hopeless.

But there was one thing I could do.

Jack and I walked back to Lazy Bones and headed to my office. I pulled out the parade compilation and watched Jude's footage. It started out like it should have been the perfect night: clear enough weather to see the stars in the sky, even with the streetlights in town lit. The volunteer band looked peppy in their banana costumes.

Maybe I'd been looking at this from the wrong angle the entire time. Maybe Ivy hadn't been the intended victim. She'd been attacked, but maybe her death had been accident.

Maybe the goal had been to ruin Raven's wedding.

Why? Unchecked jealousy? Hatred?

I resumed watching the footage. Costumed attendees walked by. Scooby-Doo, two people dressed as the Mystery Machine, Waldo, a Grim Reaper, a sexy toothpick, another Grim Reaper, a Corpse Bride, the Grim Reaper with the fat silver cane.

Except it wasn't a cane.

And I knew what it was.

And I knew who'd killed Ivy.

The final piece of the puzzle clicked into place when I realized what I didn't see. Sort of like the dog in the Sherlock Holmes story who didn't bark at midnight.

Now I just needed to prove it.

I texted Evelyn. **Can I get advice on unmasking a murderer? Come on up.**

Jack and I let ourselves out of the secondary office door to the second-floor landing. Even with taking care to lock the door, we were at Evelyn's main office door in seconds.

"Okay, talk me through this," Evelyn said.

And we made a plan.

Chapter 26

Thankfully, the plan for Raven and Emmett's rehearsal dinner was low-key. We weren't heading out to the wedding site on Bardsey Island. Instead, we were practicing at the pavilion in Goblin Gate Park, followed by a catered dinner at the Sleepy Hollow Inn.

Hopefully, I would have enough time to unmask a murderer, practice a wedding, and get my best friend sprung from jail.

But first, I needed to change, and Jack needed his special rehearsal dinner bandana.

When we arrived home, I found my grandfather lining up a series of cans on the edge of the counter.

"Umm . . ." I said.

"I'm making a barrier to keep Moriarty away from my tea."

"Moriarty likes tea?" She was purring and rubbing against Jack's front legs while he stood still. He gave me a look that said "help." I almost told him that he brought this on himself, but instead, I led him upstairs.

Raven's rehearsal dinner wasn't especially formal, but I wanted to give it the respect it deserved. My favorite green dress seemed like a good choice, while the bandana I'd found with a bear print seemed perfect for Jack in his role of ring bear.

Jack, of course, had a different bandana for the wedding, along with a small leather box that clipped to his collar to carry the rings.

Wait, had anyone told Raven about Colby's arrest? Or that Aaron had died? Despite obsessively checking my phone, I didn't have news about Colby. Although her parents were debating picketing the police station until they released her.

I'd worry about that later. I laced on a pair of leather sneakers and double-checked that Jack's bandana was secure.

As Jack and I got ready to leave, Moriarty jumped over my grandfather's barricade and started drinking his tea.

I couldn't laugh, stay, or tell Moriarty she was too clever.

We had a murderer to confront.

In public, of course.

When Jack and I arrived, Emmett and his parents were already in Goblin Gate Park.

"Hi, Bailey." Kathleen gave me a shy smile.

"Hi." I glanced around, trying to decide how to get the murderer to confess. I'd already set the voice app on my phone to record, since no one in Oregon has an expectation of privacy in public places, including parks, and that extended to private conversations. Although ideally, I'd provoke a confession in front of a group, so there'd be plenty of witnesses.

"I've already read two of the books I purchased in your bookshop. I hadn't heard of either, but I loved them," Kathleen said. "This makes me think I should ask about your subscription boxes."

If this recording was ever introduced as evidence in a criminal trial, the attorneys involved were going to love this part of the official record.

Raven's parents arrived next, looking like the free spirits they were. Kathleen turned rigid, but maybe that was because Harmony was following Raven's parents, whining at a pitch that made my shoulders tighten, too.

"Mom, Dad, it's so unfair, you need to make Raven—"

"Honey, please chill. You're ruining my buzz," Raven's dad said. "Can we please just have a nice evening?"

Harmony stomped away and plopped on a bench on the path a few hundred feet away.

Everyone ignored her.

Finally, Raven arrived, followed by Nate, with the usual camera slung around his neck.

"Colby's not here yet?" Raven asked.

It was time. Everyone was here, even Harmony, who still had her arms crossed over her chest and a pouty look like a four-year-old who was told "no ice cream."

"No," I said. "Because Colby is taking the fall for someone else's crimes."

"You'll need to be more specific," Raven said. She looked exhausted.

"Let me put it this way. The person who killed Ivy is here right now, in this very group, and that same person killed Aaron Blanton earlier today. The police are looking at this situation the wrong way, and arrested Colby. But we can make sure justice is done."

I closed my eyes, then turned and looked at the murderer. "Where's your tripod, Nate?"

"Umm, I don't use one."

"Yes, you do. I saw you downtown with one. And there's a photo of you using one in your Instagram account."

"You stalked my Insta?"

He wasn't going to bluff his way out of this.

"No, I glanced at your public profile," I said. "I assume you're not using the tripod tonight because it either dented when you hit Ivy over the head with it, or it has blood on it, so you threw it away. But it'd be a useful tool so I'm surprised you didn't pick up a new one."

"You're hallucinating, Bailey. You should get some sleep or something."

Beside me, Jack growled softly. It was just a whisper, but it sent a loud message.

"Why would Nate harm Ivy?"

I looked at Raven. "Because Ivy sold drugs to Nate's underage sister, which caused a seizure. She's never recovered." After talking with Evelyn, I'd called Jet, who'd confirmed that an overdose had triggered the seizure.

Raven blinked. "The girl at school? The freshman?"

I turned and faced my friend. "You knew her?"

"Yeah, it was tragic. She was at a party the first week of school and took something. She didn't feel well, so she left and collapsed. If she'd been with people, maybe someone would've called for help or known what to do."

"Doubtful," Nate said softly. "Do you even remember her name?"

"I never realized that was your sister." Raven stared at Nate, who gave back as good as he got.

"Half-sister. Different dads. Different last names," Nate said. "But I love her with my whole heart."

"It's tragic, but I don't see why that would lead you to harm Ivy."

"You don't get what it's like," Nate said. "Ivy shows up, flounces around, and no matter what she does, nothing bad sticks to her. Other people suffer the consequences. She should've OD'd, and my sister should be living life to the fullest. And my sister would've been a doctor, versus, to quote Harmony, a plague on society. All of this happened because of Ivy pushing drugs on kids, presumably building up a clientele."

"Ivy didn't make your sister take them," Raven said quietly.

"My sister was seventeen. Still a child. She grew up sheltered. Ivy was older and should have known better." Nate's nostrils flared.

"So you decided to kill Ivy at Raven's bachelorette party?" I asked.

"I didn't mean to," Nate said. "I just snapped. Ivy was being terrible, as usual. Everyone was panicking after the explosion, and she laughed. Because she had no compassion for other people. I just meant to bump her with my tripod as a correction, like the way an adult cat nips a kitten, and hopefully embarrass her. I didn't mean to hit her hard enough to kill her. I wanted to see her go to jail where she belongs. But I'm not going to shed any tears for her."

"If Ivy was an accident, what about Aaron?" I asked.

Nate couldn't maintain eye contact with me. "He knew, or suspected, and tried to blackmail me. And I didn't want Ivy2.0 dogging my steps. That guy was never stable."

"Did you want to photograph my wedding so you could attack Ivy?" Raven put her hands on her hips.

"When I heard you were getting married here, it was my lucky day. I already had a hotel reservation since I was already booked to take Halloween photos for a project I agreed to do. Get paid double to be here while being on hand to document Ivy's bad behavior? And get to check in on Jet and ensure she's doing okay? It was ideal."

"Documenting or stalking?" I asked. Wait, make sure Jet was doing okay? In some twisted way, had he been trying to look out for her?

"It's not like I was sitting outside Ivy's house, planning our future together. Not that Ivy had a house or a dinky studio. She was evicted from her last place because landlords expect their tenants to pay rent. Yes, I kept tabs on Ivy. She kept changing her phone, but when she complained about wanting a new purse, I sent her a bag with air tag hidden inside, and she never noticed. I've compiled quite a dossier on Ivy, with photos of many illegal acts. I was so looking forward to seeing her downfall."

"You could've gotten justice for your sister if you'd turned in Ivy. Instead, you've killed two people." And he'd said he'd been dressed as a Templar Knight, which should've been the first clue that he was guilty.

In all of the extensive video footage, I hadn't seen a single Templar Knight. Which was an oddly specific costume that should've been picked up by at one least camera. But he hadn't wanted to admit he was one of the Grim Reapers. I should've remembered Sherlock Holmes' dog who didn't bark at nighttime earlier. If I had, maybe Aaron would still be alive.

Nate stepped toward me. "And what are you going to do about it?"

Jack growled loudly and stepped between us. I motioned to the crowd around us. Both sets of parents were united for once, with matching horrified looks. Emmett stepped up behind me, showing Nate that he had my back.

Raven stepped forward and slapped Nate across the face.

"You're evil and deserve to rot in prison."

I called Detective Whitlock. "Can you come to Goblin Gate Park? Ivy and Aaron's murderer has just confessed."

Chapter 27

Thankfully, Halloween morning was dry, and the sun promised to come out and stay out. The crisp air was quintessential fall, a good omen for the Halloween festivities downtown. It's always sad when it rains on Halloween, although that doesn't stop kids from trick-or-treating downtown with raincoats over their costumes.

Last night, I sent emails to a few contacts and, through one of them, found a part-time photographer willing to cover the wedding at the last minute. Erin, the photographer, was on time and bounced on the balls of her feet as a group of kids in costumes walked past us on their way to the festivities downtown.

"It's amazing out here. I'll have to bring my niece next year." Erin pointed out an older kid, maybe twelve, dressed in all yellow with high brown boots and a yellow pointed hat, pulling a younger kid dressed as a monkey in a wagon. "Look at that!"

Jack nudged her other hand, and she responded by petting him.

"You've never attended our festival?" I was going to miss seeing all of the children in costumes this year.

Erin shook her head. "I grew up on a Christmas tree farm, so Halloween was never a big deal since we were already gearing up for the winter holidays. We didn't have any neighbors close enough to trick-or-treating. But I clearly need to widen my horizons."

Raven and Colby showed up.

"No Harmony?" Colby said.

"We decided it was best if she attended as a guest," Raven said. Her face and tone were blank.

I offered her a smile. Hopefully, her wedding would be as close to her dream as possible despite the hits it'd taken.

Matteo, the island manager and water shuttle owner, helped me load Jack into the boat for the short ride over to the island. Jack looked nervous, but maybe he was annoyed by the dog life vest Matteo insisted Jack wear for safety. Raven and Colby, thankfully, climbed on board without help.

Once we pulled away from the dock, Colby said, "We should've just paddleboarded over."

The water was calm; it would've been the perfect day to crack out our boards for one last trip of the year.

"Jack would've loved to join us," I said. Jack's not a water dog and dug all four paws into the shore the one time I'd tried to coax him onto my paddleboard. He doesn't even like to get his feet wet.

Erin had us pose together in the boat with Elyan Hollow's waterfront in the background.

"I'm sorry we didn't have a chance to ask about what sort of photos you'd like me to prioritize," Erin said. "I can take photos of you three getting ready, or I can scout around the island for a few good spots for the posed photos?"

Raven handed over a sheath of papers. "Here's what I'm thinking."

Erin looked through the papers. "Wow, you even have a map."

"I've marked the most promising spots, but we expect to be flexible."

"That's what I love to hear."

Matteo pulled up to the dock, tied up, and then carefully climbed out of the boat. Colby and I lifted Jack while Matteo guided him onto the dock.

"I checked earlier, and the boxes and bags you marked for the cabin are all there. Thank you for numbering them," Matteo said. "Everything else is in the storage room off the kitchen."

"Thank you, Matteo." Raven's tone was formal.

"It's so beautiful here. I love the trees." Erin looked around with a wide grin. I understood her enthusiasm.

The island has a camping ground on one end, and the side we were heading to had a cabin and barn with a commercial-quality kitchen next to a large yard with a gazebo with a view of the Columbia River behind it. The barn was set up with long tables on one wall that I was positive would be the buffet, along with round tables with black tablecloths and chairs that spilled out of the barn door onto the yard. Pumpkin fairy lights were strung up next to the stage in the back of the barn and around the perimeter of the makeshift dance floor.

The far side of the yard held giant Jenga, a croquet course, and a few other games, while the other side led to a sandy beach that looked out over the Columbia and Washington State on the far side of the river. A few ships passed by, including a tugboat with a pilot house on top, freshly painted white with blue accents, that reminded me of the lifeguard towers I'd seen when visiting Raven in California. Those have always been my favorite.

Both the makeup artist and hairdresser were sitting together in the cabin's living room, holding cups of tea, with their gear already set up. I followed Jack as he took a sniff around the living room and bedroom, which was furnished simply with a bed with a plaid comforter and a wooden desk, and then returned to the living room. He lay down on the plaid area rug with a huff-slash-sigh. In addition to the plaid, the decor was simple, with a nautical wheel hung on one wall, a buoy hung facing it.

"Are there more bridesmaids coming?" the makeup artist asked.

"Nope, it's just the three of us today," Raven said.

Erin took a couple photos of us once Colby and I were adorned in our bridesmaid dresses. The hairdresser had crimped my hair and teased my bangs to sky-high level. Colby, whose hair was much longer than mine, ended up rocking a side ponytail with flowing crimped hair. The makeup artist had done her zombie best and had been heavy-handed with bright eye shadow and electric blue mascara. We pretended like we were helping Raven into her dress, and she photographed us zipping up the final inch of Raven's red gown, too. Jack sat in his bandana, solemnly watching the goings-on.

The makeup artist packed her gear away. "Now, something I haven't said before: I'm off to do the groom's makeup!" But she only took one box with her, leaving the rest behind, neatly packed in the numbered bins Raven had provided (and I'd picked up and numbered for her, then left in Marion's garage).

Raven had done so much to prepare for her big day, and I'd run so many small errands for her, which hadn't been a hassle as picking up extra bins on a shopping trip was something I was happy to do, especially since Raven had reimbursed me as soon as I'd sent her a copy of the receipts. Her expectations had been high. She'd done an excellent job planning her big day.

As we drank club soda—the prosecco Raven had brought sat unopened in the cabin fridge by group consent—I debated if she should've rescheduled. Said too much had happened, casting too big of a shadow over the day.

Casting too big of a shadow over the start of their lives together, even if they hadn't been responsible for anything that happened. Maybe they should've postponed and started fresh.

When the processional started, Colby walked down the aisle first, followed by Jack and me; I saw Emmett waiting for Raven at the end of the aisle next to the justice of the peace handling the ceremony.

Emmett beamed as Raven swept down the aisle on the arm of a court jester.

Maybe things would be okay after all.

Chapter 28

November first. The day after Halloween. Samhain.

When I tallied the books for the shop, I was sure I'd find that this year's festival had been a financial boon for Lazy Bones Books. Our revenues were up.

But I'd worry about that tomorrow.

Today, after sleeping in late and being lazy all day, Jack and I finally roused ourselves in the afternoon. We headed to our November first tradition, started by my grandparents but now passed along to a younger generation: the bonfire with friends along the Columbia River.

Some people think that fire can purify, even consecrate, the world around them. It can be the symbol of dispelling ignorance and gaining knowledge. Although when I think of the annual bonfire, I get more of the image of friends sitting around a campfire, drawn together by the warmth and brightness of the flames. Forging friendships. Connecting after a long month and preparing for the winter ahead.

As Jack and I walked to the waterfront, I thought about how love is also compared to fire. Either burning emotions illuminating someone's path, or burning so hot it consumes all reason.

The relationship between Harmony and Raven also seemed to

burn, but for the wrong reasons. Would they find middle ground eventually? Or would Harmony continue to burn with jealousy?

And deep inside, I was still reevaluating my friendship with Raven, although I thoroughly liked Emmett. I'd have to see if Raven found herself now that she didn't have Ivy manipulating her. Maybe I'd like her next evolution.

A man walked toward me, and I raised my hand in greeting.

Rex paused and waited for me. He had a reusable shopping bag slung over one shoulder.

"How was the wedding?" he asked. Jack immediately pushed his head into Rex's hand.

"Perfect. Want to see photos?"

I showed Rex a photo of Raven in the middle with Colby and me to either side in our zombie '80s prom kids' bridesmaids' dresses. I let him scan through my folder of wedding photos. There were a couple of Jack as ring bear as we walked up the aisle together, Jack faithfully by my side like always. Several group shots of people from college. It'd been nice to see everyone, although there'd been a sad air whenever Ivy and Aaron came up. The grim reaper had hit too close to all of us.

"It looks like a fun time," Rex said.

We continued the walk to the bonfire. "It went off flawlessly." Maybe because Harmony had sulked from her demoted position from bridesmaid to guest, and she'd stayed quiet in her princess costume, which Marion had managed to save. Maybe seeing how her fellow guests had embraced dressing in costumes shocked Harmony into silence; even Emmett's mother had come dressed in a gorgeous flapper dress with extensive beading, while his father had dressed as a prohibition gangster, complete with a violin case. While Emmett's grandmother was Little Red Riding Hood. I'd noticed her snag a few cake pops and hide them under her cloak.

Rex and I weren't the only people just arriving to the bonfire, which was still being built. Usually I help with this part, but everyone had been understanding when I'd bowed out.

Hayes and Colby walked up, wearing matching Fair Isle sweaters.

"I owe you," Hayes said. He lifted me off the ground in a bear hug.

Once he dropped me back on the ground, I said, "I didn't know you were back."

"I left for the airport as soon as we talked, but it took me three flights, and I finally got home yesterday. But it was worth it, even if I'm flying back first thing tomorrow."

"You sure all of that flying was worth it?" Colby asked.

"For finding out I married a bad girl? Oh yeah."

Colby laughed, but she sobered up as she looked at me. "Thanks again for finding the real killer. If you hadn't, and I'd avoided jail, people would've looked at me with suspicion for my entire life. Now they know I was innocent the whole time."

Colby introduced Rex to Hayes, and they started to talk about long flights. But Olivia and Mila joined us and gave Colby and me hugs.

"Good job solving the case," Mila said.

"If I'm arrested for murder, I want Bailey on my investigation team," Olivia said.

She must've forgiven me.

They left to set up a few carafes of hot chocolate, while Colby joined Rex and Hayes' conversation. I liked the quietness, with the murmur of voices around me. I appreciated Jack's warmth against the side of my leg. My loyal companion, and I suspected he'd be even more eager to leave the house these days as it looked like Moriarty was the newest permanent addition to our house. No one had claimed her, and when our vet's office scanned her, she didn't have a microchip.

Although Moriarty had one now, along with all of her vaccines and an appointment to be spayed.

"Miss Marple has saved the day," a voice said behind me.

Finn. "Or did you decide you're Daphne? I can't remember," he said.

"I think I'm just Bailey."

"That sounds just about right," Finn said.

Jack walked up and nudged Finn, who responded by scratching behind Jack's ears. "Someone had a bath recently," Finn said. "Unless you always feel this clean."

As I sat by the bonfire with Jack at my feet, I realized how lucky I was.

And I couldn't wait for next year's Halloween festival, which should be murder free. I mean, there's no way we could have a murder three years in a row, right?

Acknowledgments

Like Bailey, I went to college with a bunch of wonderful people. For this novel, I need to thank Brian Springberg, a former classmate and current lieutenant firefighter, for answering my questions about creating a believable (yet fictional) explosion that wouldn't harm anyone.

As always, thanks to everyone at Kensington and JABberwocky for helping bring this mystery to life!

Thank you to everyone who picked up the first book in this series, *Chaos at the Lazy Bones Bookshop*. Halloween is one of my favorite holidays, and I'm so happy my attempt to embrace the spirit of the season with creativity and enthusiasm in Bailey's world has appealed to readers. I hope you love *Mayhem at a Halloween Wedding*.

Visit our website at
KensingtonBooks.com
to sign up for our newsletters, read more from your favorite authors, see books by series, view reading group guides, and more!

Become a Part of Our
Between the Chapters Book Club
Community and Join the Conversation

Submit your book review for a chance to win exclusive Between the Chapters swag you can't get anywhere else!
https://www.kensingtonbooks.com/pages/review/